ANNIE McCARTNEY grew u
Dominic's High School and
She has acted since the age
appeared frequently in BB(
During the seventies and eig......., ...p.... .... j...... .. ..
working on radio as a rock 'n roll DJ. She returned to Belfast for
good in 1987, and for the past four years has turned her attention
to writing. A number of her short stories and plays have been
broadcast on BBC Radio 4 and her first play to be broadcast on RTÉ
won the P.J. O'Connor Award. Annie is currently working on her
next novel which is set in the USA.

For Sophie
— a chorus to be
reckoned with!

desire lines

Annie McCartney

Love & Best wishes

Anne

THE
BLACKSTAFF
PRESS

BELFAST

To Maura, who has been there since the beginning of my writing efforts, and for my all my friends and family who have been so supportive and encouraging.

First published in 2001 by
The Blackstaff Press Limited
Wildflower Way, Apollo Road
Belfast BT12 6TA, Northern Ireland
with the assistance of
The Arts Council of Northern Ireland

© Annie McCartney, 2001

Annie McCartney has asserted her right under the Copyright, Designs and Patents Act 1988 to be identified as the author of this work.

Typeset by Techniset Typesetters, Newton-le-Willows, Merseyside

Printed in Ireland by Betaprint

A CIP catalogue record for this book
is available from the British Library

ISBN 0-85640-702-X

www.blackstaffpress.com

For Joe McCartney

FEBRUARY 2000

The flight across the Atlantic had seemed endless. Clare was tense, apprehensive, her mood not helped by two hours of turbulence towards the end, when she had sat grasping the edge of her seat and imagining death. It struck her what a grim irony there would be if the plane were to crash and she was to die now, but she chased the morbid thoughts away. What she had to face, she couldn't escape by dying. And she had made up her mind that she was doing the right thing. The months in California had allowed her space to think. Freed from the pressures and familiarities of home her mind had felt sharper, made her surer of what she needed to say and do; she was still uncertain how it would all pan out, of course, but she was following her desire line.

She had decided she would simply arrive at the church and ask to see him. That was best. She had written to him of course, but words on paper never seemed real until she had sounded them, heard them out loud, made them flesh. And then she didn't know how they would be received. Would he forgive her? Or was she beyond absolution?

The plane landed in London and disgorged its weary load. She collected her baggage and made her way through Passport Control. The harshness of the airport lighting made everyone look washed out and unreal. Somehow, tired and tense, she managed to change terminals and board the plane for the last leg of her journey. She was allocated a window seat near the front of the plane. Then she must have dozed off.

The announcement caught her in the midst of tumbling dreams. She shook herself awake, shifting in her seat. The plane was beginning the descent into Aldergrove. It bumped its way down through the clouds, and there was a clunk as the wheels were lowered for landing. Clare pushed her dark hair back from her face and watched as the rivulets of rain raced across the pane, like angry tears. Suddenly the clouds cleared, making way for the fields, bright green as always. She could hear the woman beside her exclaiming to her husband in an American accent, 'Isn't it green. Oh look, a rainbow.'

Clare fixed her gaze down on the landscape, picking out Lough Neagh wide and blue in the distance. The fields of Antrim, sprinkled with white specks of sheep, a grey ribbon of road carving through them. Her brother Tony should be driving along it right now to pick her up. Her mouth felt dry and her breath thick.

The specks got bigger, then there was a thump, and then the screech of the brakes. She was home.

Tony was waiting for her when she came down the stairs to the baggage reclaim. He hugged her tightly. 'It's great to see you.' Tony shifted uneasily. 'You're back for good then?'

'Yes. How's Daddy?'

'The same. He was surprised to hear you were coming – he thought you would stay there. But he's looking forward to seeing you. Said he'd have your breakfast ready.'

'I want to stop by the church first.'

Tony raised an eyebrow. 'Oh, I see.'

'It's hardly out of the way.' She spoke sharply.

Her brother patted her arm. 'Take it easy, kid, I'll take you there, it's no bother. The church sticks out like a sore thumb now, there's hardly a house left standing, only the last four at the bottom, me da's and the three others.'

'Oh. When did they knock them down?'

'About a month ago. His is next. It'll be some job getting him to move. The new one'll be ready in a couple of weeks.'

'He'll be fine when he moves in.'

'I know, you're probably right.'

They drove in companionable silence into Belfast. They could catch up on all the news later. He was tired too – she could tell he'd had to get up before he was ready. She could smell the stale smoke and beer off him; no doubt he'd been out for his Friday night's fun.

There was little traffic, and they made good time. Although he had told her about the houses being cleared, she was shocked by the devastation, the brutality of it all. Nothing at all left: years of history, years of memories had been bulldozed into oblivion. The church had always dominated the streets, the older houses hugging in against its ornate iron railings. They had seemed to flow from it and complement it, making the church a nucleus. Distanced now from the rows of shiny new houses, it loomed larger somehow, anachronistic, and at odds with the new buildings.

Tony pulled the car into the church grounds and stopped. 'Do you want me to wait?'

'No, thanks, I'll be grand. I won't be long. I'll walk down to the house.'

'What about your bags?'

'Could you bring them round later on? In about a half an hour.'

'Why don't I come back and get you then – we can tell Tommy the plane was delayed. You know what he's like.'

'Yes you're right. That would be easier. OK, see you. Thanks, Tony, I appreciate it.' She hugged him.

'You'll be OK, kid, don't worry. You're doing the right thing.'

'Yes.'

He waved. She waited until he had driven off, then she walked up to the door of the presbytery and rang the bell. A sour-faced woman she didn't recognise answered it. What had happened to Minnie?

'Yes?' A thin line of disapproval hung about the woman's mouth.

'Father Lorcan O'Carroll, I'd like to speak to him please.'

'He's on the early Mass. Would one of the other fathers do?'

'No.'

'You'd best call back then – in about fifteen minutes.'

The older woman made to close the door. Clare pushed gently against it with her foot.

'I'll wait.'

'You'd better come in then.'

The room was sparsely furnished, with a polished wooden floor. It had the usual trappings of religious icons, and some reproductions of Renaissance art. She sat down, acutely aware of her tiredness. The chair was hard and her back hurt from the long plane flight. She moved her neck slowly, rotating it, feeling the bones crack. Then she stood up and stretched. She walked across the room, measuring her steps, and studied one of the pictures on the wall. It was a good print of Bronzino's *The Martyrdom of Saint Lawrence.*

Lorcan, Lawrence, she mused. She stared at the contorted shapes. Years ago, on a visit to Florence, she had seen the original fresco in the church of San Lorenzo. It was a huge fresco, and she had been deeply moved by it. The art was one of the better legacies of Catholicism. She checked her watch: almost fifteen minutes. She felt nervous, but determined. She had replayed this scene in her head a million times.

The door opened suddenly and there he was. She froze, tonguetied.

'Clare! Tommy didn't tell me you were coming.'

'He didn't know until last night. I came straight here. Where's Minnie?'

'She's retired, gone to live with a niece.' He raised an eyebrow. 'Was it Minnie you wanted to see?'

'No, I've come to see you.'

Clare pushed her tiredness to the back of her mind, and drove steadily. The last six miles of the motorway were downhill, through the green fields, the gleam of the lough lifting the eye from the urban sprawl. Almost automatically she followed the traffic round the town and headed out again, keeping her eye firmly on the mountains. The early-morning mist had lifted. Through the car window before her was the Hatchet Field, etched in the middle of Divis Mountain. Its familiar outline was fringed with hawthorn; a straggle of trees grew black against the sky at the far end. She was soothed, as on every visit, by the sight. It triggered memories of childhood summers, when the nearby hills were the sole relief from the confinement of the small streets. A few hours of scrambling up the mountain loney for bluebells in spring – or later in the year for blackberries – was as close to nature as the gang of kids from Kinsale Street were likely to get.

The unexpectedly bright green hills, luminous in the morning sun, pointed up the drabness of the surrounding town. Every day of her childhood she had walked this road, rushing up and down it on her way to school. She knew every shopkeeper in every shop. She was in and out of them daily: for sweeties, for her mammy's messages and on errands for neighbours.

The road had changed dramatically over the years and lost its personality in the process. Shops with metal shutters like grim unsmiling mouths, lining the road, had replaced the meandering rows of wee poky huxter shops, which were once dark and deeply filled with boxes of treasures. Alongside, like sentinels armoured for survival, a row of saplings, their spindly trunks enveloped in wire mesh, strained pathetically towards the winter sun. The little streets with their rows of redbrick houses were being replaced with shiny new boxes, each attempting to achieve a personality of its own by means of the extras favoured by the residents; anything from a full-size Roman statue to a trellis of bright blue plastic roses.

Two massive fortresses of police stations, about half a mile apart, dominated the urban landscape. Their high walls, solid brick now, replacing the corrugated iron, were crowned with barbed wire. There were plans to tone them down now that the Assembly was up and limping along, but they had become embedded. It was hard to imagine the road before they 'grew' there. The ramps outside each, although lower and easier to navigate these days, slowed her down, and the ever-watchful eye of the cameras focused on her small car, and registered her entry into the heart of west Belfast.

She turned right into one of the narrow streets. The houses were small and mean, out of proportion to the grandeur of the tall, twin-spired church at the top. The church dwarfed them physically now as ever.

Kinsale Street was deserted except for the few devout souls making their way to nine o'clock Mass. They watched with undisguised interest as the small car with its English registration plates pulled up outside one of the doors. The late-February sun had a thin lemony feel to it, and there was a distinct early morning chill in the air. The bright green fields on the way from Larne had sparkled in the frost. The trees, looking as though dipped in glass, had glistened in the sun. There were no trees in this street. Her father's street was one of the last in the district still standing. Several of the houses were boarded up with breeze blocks, accentuating the greyness of the district.

Clare switched off the engine. A wave of bleakness washed over her. She got out of the car, stretching her body, stiff from the long drive, allowing the invisible watchers, as well as the stragglers, the chance to get a good look at her. She walked to one of the doors and rapped. It echoed in the street, and she knew at once that her father wasn't in. She could always tell from the sound of the knocker if the house was empty or not.

Within minutes Mrs McDonnell from across the road was at her side. Her sharp face regarded Clare with false bonhomie. 'Ach, Clare is it? He's not in. Your daddy'd be down at the post office, love. It's pension day.'

'But it's not nine yet.'

'I know, love, but he likes to be first in the queue.' She paused, eyeing Clare up and down, inviting her to explain herself.

Clare said nothing, her smile fixed.

'Home on a wee holiday? He wasn't expecting you until Saturday. Anyway, love, he picks Winnie's pension up for her. He'll be leaving hers in about half nine if you don't feel like walkin' down to meet him.' She nodded towards the house next door. 'Winnie there has a key.'

Clare managed a smile, though she felt irritated. 'Thanks very much, Mrs McDonnell. I'll go and get it.'

She walked over to the neighbour's door, noticing how scrubbed and shiny the paintwork was. It seemed to point up the tawdriness of the houses either side, and failed somehow to prevent the small street from having an overall appearance of drabness.

Tommy Murphy, Clare's father, had been born and raised in these streets, and had moved into another of the small kitch-en houses when first married. Then, it had been possible to walk all the way to the mountain through fields. Now the urban sprawl had claimed all the lower slopes of the hills, as the heart of west Belfast was gradually choked, laid waste not by the bombing campaign, but by urban renewal. The whole soul of the town was going, finally consigned to everlasting concrete by another kind of terrorist – the developers. Tommy disapproved of the so-called improvements. Nothing would induce him to move.

'They'll not get me into one of those wee plastic boxes, no character at all, and all the dirt of the day getting into them too. I'll be here till I die.'

He would too. All his four children had moved out of the area at the first opportunity, though his son Tony had gone only as far as another ghetto further up the road. Why was she here? Clare wondered briefly. Would she fit in at all? All those years living in London had meant she had lost touch with this part of her life. She had changed. She was no longer the child who had been brought up in this small street, full of dreams and imagination, longing to be someone, to do something.

Kitty McDonnell lingered at her front door watching Clare, on the pretext of making sure she got the key from Winnie. Kitty's smile was fixed grimly as her eyes followed Clare to the next-door house. 'We don't see as much of you on the TV these days – are you still at the acting? Right enough you were great,' she called to Clare's retreating back. Her use of the past tense hit home. Clare ignored the remark and rapped on the door of the other neighbour, nodding her thanks.

Winnie appeared as if by magic with the key. She had obviously followed the entire scene through the curtains. 'Here you are love,' she said. 'Would you like to come in for a wee cup of tea?' Winnie's careworn face clocked her from head to toe.

Clare returned her smile. She had a soft spot for Winnie. God love the woman, she hadn't had much of a life. She had long ago forsworn a husband and children to care for her parents until their deaths. It was a fate she accepted with equanimity. She had perfected her homemaking skills – her apple tarts were a legend in the district. Her sewing ensured that she was much in demand to run up wee outfits for the 'harder to fit' members of the community and she made all her own clothes too, essential given her size. She was virtually square (doubtless the famous apple tarts had been a contributory factor), and her body swelled under a sea of vivid pink and green polyester. She sported a bright purple cardigan in an Aran stitch.

As they stood outside her father's door, she followed Clare's gaze towards the window. 'Aren't the curtains smashing? I got a wee remnant in the Spinning Mill. Tommy says it's like perpetual sunshine sitting in the room nigh.'

It was an effort not to wince at the garish yellow curtains. 'You're very good to him, Winnie,' Clare responded dutifully. 'Where would he be without you?' She meant it. It was humbling watching Winnie's anxiety to please.

She was rewarded for this remark by a maniacal smile revealing pumpkin teeth. It looked like they'd got a job lot on these teeth. They were a distinguishing feature of all the older residents of the street.

The ground in front of her was starting to sway. Clare reached for the key, suddenly needing to get inside and lie down. 'Thanks Winnie, I've just come off the Stranraer boat. I'm exhausted.'

'Well, I hope he has the bed aired. You're early. He wasn't expecting you till Saturday.'

She'd forgotten what bloody busybodies these people were. It suited her father, a retired widower, to have them about him. Her mother wouldn't have given most of them the time of day. But there was no point in feeling like this. She would have to bite her tongue. They were, after all, good neighbours, and her father depended on them for company and support.

She thanked Winnie again for the key and went to open her father's door.

She thought of leaving her luggage in the car, but years of living in London had made her cautious. So, tired as she was, she carried the whole lot in. It took her two journeys, watched by the two old crones.

'God, ye have a quare lot of stuff all the same. You're not moving back for good, are ye?'

Mrs McDonnell's sharp Belfast vowels cut into her thoughts. Pretending not to hear her, Clare closed the front door with relief. She sat down on the settee, and burst into tears. God! What had she done? Was she out of her mind coming back?

She would do her best here until she found her feet. She needed space and time to recover from the heartbreak she had left behind her in London.

She dried her eyes and looked around, her tension subsiding. A beam of sunlight shone through the glass door, specks of dust whirling silently in it. The room was small and poky, and smelled of cigarettes and socks. She wrinkled her nose with distaste, yet the smell was oddly comforting and familiar, indelibly part of the house.

She could conjure instantly the different odours of her childhood. Her father's tobacco, her mother's face powder, and various food smells. The kitchen and yard heavy with the acrid overlay of bleach, or Jeyes fluid. A clean tarry smell superimposed upon the heavy sourness of cramped conditions. She equated clean smells with space.

She looked ruefully at Winnie's curtains. From the inside they were even worse. Frightful really – clashing in a truly spectacular way with everything in the room. The place had been decorated in a hurry by her brother Tony, in honour of her previous trip home. She hadn't given it much attention then. She had stayed with Frances, her closest friend in Belfast, and had only been over here to visit Tommy. Tony was a painter and decorator, having arrived at this occupation by

way of several different trades. His choice of colour scheme –
pale violet walls with a lime green ceiling – was alarming, the
paint no doubt left over from one of his 'wee homers', as he
referred to them.

The picture of the Sacred Heart, red light throbbing, dominated the wall above the fireplace. A few block-mounted Turner
prints, and Renoir's *Les Parapluies* – sad remnants of her early
forays into art – still hung on the other walls. She was touched
that her father had kept them up all these years after she had
moved out. The suite was mock black leather with brown
moquette cushions. The carpet was a simply appalling sunburst
pattern. Tones in well with Winnie's curtains, she thought. A
shaggy rug bearing the US presidential seal – a present from her
father's sister Rosie on her annual trip home from Brooklyn –
covered the hearth in front of the coal-effect electric fire. The
overall effect was a telling example of what Clare's friend Paula
called the Ah Fuck It! school of decor.

Clare went into the kitchen, filled the kettle, and washed a
few cups while she waited for it to boil. There were three
downstairs rooms, the kitchen, the living room and a bathroom at the back. The last had been built on about fourteen
years ago. The bathroom suite was avocado with gold taps.
Tony again. No doubt he'd got a deal on it. She would just
have to sort the place out as best she could. There was nothing
a good spring-cleaning wouldn't sort out.

She scoured the brown rim off the bottom of the cups with
a Brillo pad, poured herself some tea, and sat at the kitchen
table to drink it. There was a copy of the day's *Irish News* open
at the obituaries, and she glanced idly through it. She was just
finishing her tea when her father came in.

'Well, you're back then. What's wrong? Did he leave you?'
Her father had a way of coming straight to the point, a gruff
manner of speech which was the nearest he got to showing
affection, except when he'd had a couple of drinks.

It had been a couple of months since she had seen him and he looked both strange and familiar, comforting. She felt a surge of love for him. He looked well for his seventy-five years. He had an intelligent face, bright blue eyes (which unfortunately none of his children had inherited), well-defined eyebrows, and a large, rounded forehead. He was small and dapper, about five foot six or seven, with a fresh complexion and a head of thick white hair brushed into a side parting. He rarely washed it, claiming that too much washing loosened the roots. He obviously had a point. He wore, as always, regardless of the weather, a shirt and tie with a grey jacket, and trousers with a sheen that told her they had seen better days.

He'd had his last five teeth removed a couple of years ago, which gave him a sort of slackness round the mouth, a sardonic look. They'd been 'playing him up something shockin',' he said. For a while he had sported a fine set of dentures, but he had finally given up wearing those, which was a relief frankly: the teeth had been overpowering. He was looking at her, waiting. 'Well, am I right? He's left hasn't he?'

'No, I left *him,* and I don't want to talk about it just yet.'

'Suit yourself, after all I'm only your father. Sure why would you tell me anything?'

'Daddy, please, I'm just feeling a bit tired. I've been driving all night; I came over by Stranraer. Is it all right if I stay here for a while?'

'Sure you know you can stay here as long as you like. Isn't this your home? . . . Mind you, it'll hardly be what you're used to now, but you can fix that wee back room up. You'll hardly be entertaining any of your fancy friends here anyway, will you? Not that I mind,' he added hastily, realising for once that he sounded too gruff. 'Your friends are all welcome here, sure you know that.'

Clare carried her suitcase up the narrow stairs. There was plenty of room in the house now for both of them. More, ironically, than when she was growing up, various improvement grants having extended the size of the house and added the bathroom and – luxury of luxuries – an upstairs loo. She thought of all the cold nights creeping down to the back yard.

She switched on the immersion heater, and went into the back bedroom. The room would do for a while. It was clean, and the bed was comfortable. She lay down on top of it, pulling the old eiderdown on top of her, and forced herself to sleep.

When she awoke an hour later she felt better. Her father had gone out on one of his wee jaunts – the place was beautifully quiet. She carried her soap bag downstairs and ran a long bath, then submerged herself gratefully in the hot water, which was blissfully free from the scum on the top that always gathered in London.

She ducked under the water to wash her hair. The blood pulsed in her ears. She liked the feeling of being submerged. She wished she could wash away the dull, persistent pain which had taken over her entire being. But it wouldn't budge. It permeated her, stealing her natural gaiety and love of life.

Clare had moved to London shortly after graduation. Her announcement that she was going to pursue a career in acting was greeted with the same incredulity that a career in prostitution would have been. Perhaps, she thought grimly, there had been some similarities, after all. Everyone had taken for granted that her love for acting would be satisfied by her finding a job teaching it, and teaching it in Belfast. To consider going on the stage was downright foolhardy, not to mention selfish. At the time, her mother had been her one supporter. 'Go,' she had said, 'You'll not settle if you don't, and if it doesn't work out, sure you can always come back.'

Leaving had been good for her. She had been able to reinvent a new Clare, with few or no points of reference to the old Clare. Seen through the eyes of her new friends, her working-class Catholic background had become almost appealing; the humiliations and deprivations of her childhood had come to seem romantic. Any shame about the foibles of her parents was blurred by distance. Their shortcomings were romanticised, and told in affectionate anecdotes to new friends. She had almost begun to believe in this new model Clare, and enjoyed the mileage gained from it, especially at a time when being from Northern Ireland was a double-edged sword.

She let the water out, cleaned the bath, and went upstairs to dress. When she came back down, her father was back in from his jaunt, sitting in front of the television. The gas heater, a Super Ser, was on low.

'I'll make some lunch, Daddy, Would cheese on toast do?'

'Never mind about me, I've eaten.' He indicated two tinfoil dishes and his plate. 'The meals-on-wheels weemen came today.'

She realised with a pang how little she actually knew about his life. She phoned him regularly from London, but he didn't care much for the phone, rushing her off it with admonitions about the size of her bill. She set about making the snack, noticing how sparse his supply of food was. 'Maybe I'll go to the supermarket and get a few things in,' she said.

'Well don't be getting anything for me, love. Winnie does my shopping today, and I get myself a wee bit of fish or a piece of cooked ham for the weekend. Twenty pounds I spend on messages. I'm a good manager. I get the electric stamps, the phone stamps, and a bottle of gas today too. That fellow McNulty brings it round to me in his van. Mind you,' he continued, 'if you want anything like coffee or curries you may buy them yourself. I don't think the pension would stretch to fancy food.'

Clare sat down beside him to eat, resting her plate on a tray on her knee. He looked her up and down.

'Well I'd say you're failed away to nothing. You could do with a bit of beef on you. You haven't turned into an anorexic have you? I saw a programme about them last week. You'd a seen fatter in Belsen – desperate-looking craturs.'

Clare smiled, amused in spite of herself. 'No, Daddy, I haven't lost any weight. I exercise to stay thin. Anyway I'm eight stone.'

'Well, don't listen to me, but I think you're scraggy-looking.'

He had been watching the racing on TV, marking up the winners. She guessed he had had his 50p each way bet on his way back from the post office this morning. When he was feeling lucky he would risk a double or a forecast.

She finished her lunch and rang her friend Frances. Clare had told her father that she was coming over for a long visit, but Frances was the only person over here she had told she was actually planning on moving back. She had made the decision only last week.

She agreed to have dinner with Frances the following evening. In the meantime a visit to the local supermarket was in order. The cupboards certainly were bare, and she would tell Tommy she was off to stock up on coffee and curry. She wouldn't bother to cook tonight. There was quite a good chip shop nearby. Comfort food, that was what she needed.

Clare had known Frances since primary school days. They had met and fallen in love with each other over their lukewarm bottles of school milk, and had remained firm friends since. An attractive woman, pretty and fair-haired with skin to match, Frances had never moved from Belfast. Her freckles, the bane of her existence as a teenager, had faded now. Her easy stretch of a smile was lopsided, engaging and frequent, and her wide green eyes were her most striking feature. She had retained a girlish figure – helped no doubt by running around after the children. It made her look younger than her thirty-eight years.

They had always complemented each other as friends: Clare's dark good looks and Frances's fair looks. 'You're like them two wee Scotties on the whisky bottle,' Tommy used to say.

The children in bed, for the past two hours Clare and Frances had been sitting at the table in Frances's kitchen, talking and drinking. Frances poured the remains of the bottle of wine into Clare's glass, waving away Clare's feeble protestations.

'Sure, you can get a taxi home and pick the car up tomorrow. Or you could always stay the night.'

'No, I can't stay out the second night I'm here. Daddy'll be accusing me of treating the place like a lodging house.'

They laughed. This had been her father's war cry when she had lived at home during her first year at university. She had moved into a flat with Frances during her second year. Normally, both girls would have been expected to live at home while students, it was common enough in Belfast. But the continuing Troubles had meant that many young people went to Scotland or England to study, and those that stayed were thought to be safer on the south side of the city, beside the university.

Clare sipped her wine. 'OK then, you've convinced me. I'll get a taxi. What about you? Gerry won't mind you sitting up will he?'

'No, he will not, he'll go straight to bed when he gets in. He always goes to bed before me. He likes to get into work early. I'm still a bit of a night owl. It's the only time I have to myself.'

Clare had been there since early evening. She had watched as Frances effortlessly cooked and served dinner, cleaned up the kitchen afterwards, supervised two homeworks, bathed and put the baby – aged one – to bed, and made two school lunches. Clare enjoyed being part of the cosiness, though she felt *she* would find all this domesticity confining. Frances took it all in her stride.

Gerry had gone out to his computer class. He was always improving himself. Not with a lot of success, she thought unkindly. She had never understood Frances's attraction to him. She could have had her pick of any of the men in their year at Queen's, but she and Gerry had started going out during final year and they had been together since. They seemed happy enough.

'He suits me, Clare,' Frances often said, aware of Clare's reservations. 'He's a kind man, not too exciting, but I don't mind that. I don't have your restless soul.'

Clare knew that Gerry had been glad to see her leave for

London. On the surface he was friendly enough. He probably thought that with her flighty ways, she was a bad influence on Frances. Anyhow she was happy to have Frances to herself tonight.

The two or three glasses of wine had loosened Frances up. 'Clare love, I'm glad for my sake you're here, but will you be able to stand it? You might find Belfast very dull.'

'Oh God, Frances, I couldn't give a shit at this point. I'm sick to death of all the bitching and petty jealousies. And I honestly don't want to be around to watch Tim nuzzling his young bride.'

'They aren't married yet, Clare.'

'I know, but I expect that'll be the next step.'

'Clare, don't torture yourself with this love. It's a waste of time and energy. Maybe it is for the best that you stay here for a few months, and then when you're feeling stronger you can think of going back. But I really wouldn't rush into selling the flat in London. Your feelings could change. It mightn't suit you being here. Seventeen years away is a long time – a lifetime. Maybe you could even meet someone else to distract you for a while.'

'I couldn't look at another person. I can't get him out of my head night or day.'

'Ah come on, Clare. You said yourself a few months ago that the relationship was almost over. There was no buzz left between you, you felt like moving out. Don't you remember?'

Clare paused to sip her wine. 'I can't explain it. I feel desolate without him, empty. We were together over ten years. It's nothing compared to you and Gerry. But it was a hell of a long time for me. I think I'm going insane. I should have listened to him. He wanted to get married five years ago. Have kids. Do all the ordinary things. I kept waiting until the big part turned up. Waiting to be someone. I should just face the fact that I'm a failure. And I'm old. I probably haven't a single egg left.'

Frances leaned over and patted her hand. 'Clare, that's the

drink talking. We're repeating ourselves here. If you *had* felt he was the right person for you deep down, you would have at least had a child, but you didn't. Surely that tells you something?'

Clare said nothing. Even if Frances was right, it was too soon to acknowledge the fact.

Frances waited, then continued. 'Look, give it time. Either you'll be back together, or someone better will show up. And if not, sure who needs a man.' She laughed. 'What does Paula think about it all?' Paula, a writer who lived in London, was another close friend of Clare. She and Frances had met on Paula's first visit to Belfast and had liked each other instantly.

'She thinks I'm running away. She thinks Belfast is a great place to visit, but not a great place to live *if* you want to make a career in the theatre – and of course she's right – on the second count anyway.'

'Maybe this is where you need to be right now. Away from it all, at least until you gather yourself.'

Clare pondered Frances's words on the way home in the taxi. It was such sensible advice. She knew Frances was right. But she wasn't ready yet to admit it. She knew, too, that the blow to her pride would take some getting over. Why had she not realised sooner and done something to stop it? Why could she not see the signs? It was such a bloody cliché really. Tim falling for his leading lady, but then that was exactly what had happened years before between Tim and herself.

Tim was English, from a working-class background not unlike her own, though this was not at all evident. Tim had thrown off his origins with a vehemence that Clare often found disconcerting. During his time at RADA he had rounded all his northern vowels into an upper-class accent, and he now specialised in playing effete Englishmen. They had been together almost four years before he had introduced her to his parents. Many actors chose to exploit their humble origins, but not Tim. He was an only child. His parents were a homely couple from Doncaster. His father, now retired, had worked as a bus conductor. Since Tim had left school, his mother had had a part-time job as a receptionist in the local health centre. They had welcomed Clare into their home, treated her like 'the daughter we'd always wanted, lass'.

In fact she used to think that she was more at ease with them than Tim was. He seemed to her at times like a cuckoo in the nest. The image was strengthened by the fact that he was tall and handsome and had a sort of glow about him, while his parents were small, neat, and quiet. When he and Clare went up to see his mother and father, he preferred that they do the round trip in one day, and stay only long enough to rest a little, evidently reluctant to stay a moment longer than necessary. Underneath, she knew that he did love them both fiercely. They were inordinately proud of him, and basked in the glory of his TV appearances. On visits to Belfast, he had frequently wondered at Clare's ease with her equally humble origins. 'You're lucky, really. You can move effortlessly between the social divisions,' he said on a number of occasions. 'You have the common touch, or is it an Irish thing?'

It hadn't always been so. Clare had worked hard at acquiring this so-called ease. She still had shameful recollections of lying, while still at Queen's, about where she lived. It was the leaving and the distance that had given her a solid perspective, a sense of the value of her stock. However, their similar social backgrounds were one of the main reasons Clare had always felt that she and Tim were a good match.

Lately, in her more lucid moments, she had wondered if in fact she had ever been in love with him, if she had simply fallen in love with the idea of him. During their time together they had each had one or two brief affairs. It happened a lot in their profession. Yet, despite these interludes, they had stayed together. She had needed him. They had needed each other. After five years on the loose in London, with all the sordid awfulness of fruitless relationships, offers of one-night stands, and dashed expectations, she enjoyed having a steady man. It was a weakness of hers to feel she could not make it alone. Despite her feistiness, her independence, she somehow needed a foil, a man to define her. Perhaps being alone would be the making of her.

The taxi driver broke into her thoughts.

'This it, love?' The taxi driver sounded dubious. They had just pulled up outside her father's house.

'Yes, lovely, thanks.' She got out and paid him.

As she put the key in the lock, the door opened in, causing her to lose her balance.

Her father was in the small hall. He eyed her up and down. 'I couldn't sleep. I don't need much at my age. Was that a taxi? Did something happen your car?'

She swallowed her exasperation. 'No, Daddy, not at all. I just had a couple of glasses of wine with dinner and decided to leave it.'

'Will I make you a cup of tea? Or is it coffee you take?'

'I'm fine thanks, I'll just get ready for bed.'

Tommy was on his way up the stairs when he stopped and shouted down at her. 'Tim phoned. I told him you were out on a date. That all right?'

Her heart jumped. She tried to sound offhand. 'What did he want?'

'Sure I never asked him. He asked me how I was. *And how are you keeping, Tommy?*' Her father's mimicking of Tim's voice was wickedly accurate.

She smiled.

'I must say I never liked him,' he continued. 'Your mother, God rest her, wasn't that fond of him either.'

'Well, it's a bit late in the day to tell me that, Daddy. You were always very friendly to him.'

'Sure, I didn't want to let you down. If he suited *you*, why would we interfere? Bit of a cold fish though, ach, they're all the same those types of Englishmen. They still feel we're just fresh out of the bog, but sure we were educated when they were still in caves.'

Clare said nothing: this was one of his rants, pure bluster, not really meaning a word. It was his clumsy attempt to show her that her pain was his too.

His voice softened. 'Don't you worry yourself about him, love, you're well rid of him. Maybe you could meet a nice fella here and settle down, one of your own kind. Have you ever thought of using your degree and getting yourself a wee teaching job? The holidays are great.' He didn't give her time to argue. 'Anyway I'm off up to my bed. I'm not used to these late nights.'

After he had gone up and the house was quiet, Clare picked up the phone and, trembling, dialled Tim's number – *their* number, really. It rang twice, and then a woman's voice came on the line, heavy with sleep, a theatrical voice.

'Is that you, darling? Where are you? Aren't you coming home soon? It's late . . .'

Clare hung up, and, her gut churning, climbed the stairs to bed.

Diana was holding forth down the telephone. Her rasping voice was punctuated by loud inhalations as she sucked on her cigarette. She had been Clare's agent for seven years, and was also Tim's, so they had developed a friendship of sorts. This friendship was always cosier and warmer when either of her clients had a good part going or, as in Tim's case recently, a run of big commercials. Still, she had been loyal to Clare, who was by no means one of her top earners. She was talking now about Clare's move back to Belfast, not a good one as far as she was concerned.

'Yes, darling, I *know* it's only an hour away, but you do see that they'll view you *here* as a provincial actress. *And* we all know they'd rather fly you over there – to Belfast from here – than cast you from there.'

Clare sighed, exasperated. It sounded like a line from *Alice in Wonderland*, but unfortunately it was true. She had always heard this complaint from friends of hers – actors who for one reason or another had stayed in Northern Ireland. It hadn't affected her up until now, of course, so she hadn't given it much thought.

'Well,' Diana went on, 'if you are serious about Lagan Theatre. I'll give them a call. But honestly, darling, you should just have a little break. And don't dwell on the Tim and Kezia thing. He'll tire of her soon enough. It's only a little flingette – a sort of mid-life crisis. He's mourning the fact that he can't play juve leads anymore. C'mon, darling, you know what this is all about. His hair is starting to thin. Imagine his gorgeous halo of blond curls! The horror! *And* he's getting a teeny bit thick round the middle.'

Her tone had changed to low confidential. Clare could hear her take a long drag on her cigarette. She exhaled again. 'Clare, darling, I know it's a bit naughty of me telling you this. But they thought he was a bit too tubby for the part in the last Screen One. That's why he was pipped at the post. I told him he needed to work out some more. They *all* go through it, darling. Kezia's just a baby really, and she's had *everyone*.' Diana sounded almost envious for a moment. 'Trust me, he'll get bored with her.'

Clare said nothing.

There was a pause as Diana checked with herself if she had overdone it this time and then she said hurriedly. 'Oh, darling, you can't go on tormenting yourself over him. It's pointless. No man's worth it. I love him to bits, but we both know he's rather weak. Take my word for it, he'll not settle for her. This is a passing fancy. He's flattered she wants him. Look, I must go, call me at home if you need to talk. OK? Byee.'

Clare hung up, glad that her father was out of the house. Underneath all the fluff, Diana had actually hit the mark a few times. Clare knew people were sick of the Tim/Clare story. It had been running too long, with no change of plot. She needed to find some work here quickly. She had too much time on her hands, to think, to go crazy.

She had been out of work loads of times before. But London was different. She could always get the odd waitressing job without too much loss of face. Then she had her classes: dancing, voice lessons, and, when she was in work and she could afford it, Pilates, her favourite exercise class. You could always tell if an actor was in work if you met them at Pilates. It just wasn't affordable on the dole. Then, too, there was the theatre, either half-price seats or the odd comp or two from friends. Christ, what *would* she do here? What was there to do?

Frances was the only person she was really close to, she thought. Then she remembered the bloody car – she'd better go and get it. She phoned a taxi. She knew she could easily have got the bus, but taxis in Belfast still seemed cheap to her. Within minutes a loud honk sounded in the street. She reached for her coat and left.

At Frances's, Clare paid off the taxi, and walked round to the back door and into the kitchen. Frances looked up as she entered, smiled hello, finished off some complicated-looking pastry thing, and put it in the oven. She took a bottle of Sauvignon Blanc, already opened, from the fridge and poured two glasses. 'Stay for dinner, go on, there's plenty, and you know I get fed up cooking just for this lot. Besides it's an excuse for me to have a glass of wine.'

'Thanks, Frannie. I'll have one drink, but I won't stay. I can't – that would be two days in a row. Gerry'll think I've moved in! Anyway, I should go home and make something for Daddy. He's already making veiled hints that I'm out and about too much, and I've only been back a couple of days.'

Drink finished, Clare left with a promise to join Frances, Gerry and some mutual friends for dinner on Saturday.

She drove home in thoughtful mood, observing the changes in Belfast since last she had lived here. There was a different feel to it somehow, hard to pinpoint exactly. The face of the town was changing rapidly, and not always improving. Large swathes of the inner city had been turned into urban motorways or car parks. Everywhere she looked, new buildings seemed to be going up virtually overnight. The whole city seemed like a continuous building site. It was a developers' paradise. There was an optimistic feel to the place as well.

More people in the streets, and lots more restaurants.

Clare had left Belfast in 1982 during one of its darkest hours. The hunger strike had brought the place to its knees. Margaret Thatcher had won. The nationalist population, both extremist and moderate, had been alienated beyond belief. The war of attrition would rage for years. It was a long time before Clare fully understood how traumatised and damaged they had all been by the hunger strike. Bobby Sands had died in May 1981, just before Clare began her exams, and the other hunger strikers were to follow him one by one throughout the summer. She recalled her feelings of rage and frustration. Firstly at Thatcher for allowing them to die, at the IRA for not stopping them. All the conflicting emotions of a girl from a working-class background – now moving up and out – had taken a larger emotional toll than she realised. Her way of coping was to leave, not to face it. She had gone to Bobby Sands's funeral, to watch rather than participate, though she had never been to a political demonstration in her life, having been only a school-girl during the civil rights marches. She felt like an extra in a film, reality slipping past her that day. Her feelings fluctuating, and the emotions the event had triggered overwhelmed her. She had gone with some people from her year, including the lad she was going out with at the time. He felt it was a momentous occasion in Irish history, and shouldn't be missed. It was one of the few times she and Frances had disagreed. Frances thought Sands had been stupid. Clare felt he was a victim, and going to his funeral was possibly the only political statement she had allowed herself to make throughout the Troubles. She had a fear of coming to terms with the darker side of her nature, the buried part of her that wanted an eye for an eye. The piece of her subconscious that didn't really mind *quite* so much a loss dealt to the other tribe. Or to those (despite her education or perhaps because of it) she continued to view in some way as the forces of oppression: the army, the RUC, unionist politicians, and, in turn, the PIRA.

She remembered the confusion of emotion. Feeling that the situation would drip on. Knowing it wouldn't end. This endless bloodletting allowed her no healing. All it left was a lapping of small corrosive incidents and, every now and then when something awful happened, a sudden wash of shock and pain. It seemed irretrievable then, and so long ago and far away now. Admittedly the current situation wasn't perfect, but, despite some in-fighting among the paramilitaries, and the atrocious punishment beatings, things were relatively quiet, though of course there was no way anyone with an inkling about how things worked here would have bet a penny on things remaining that way. It was hard to have a clear picture really, and Clare, with the advantage of viewing things from a distance, had developed a protective cynicism about the political situation.

She had found it best to avoid the topic of Northern Ireland like the plague while in London. She restricted her political rants to diatribes against the Tories. At least she was on safe ground there, since most of her friends felt the same. Half her life under Tory rule, until 1997 she hadn't even known what it was like to vote for the winner. Her feelings about the situation at home had been suspended while she was away from Northern Ireland. It was a defence not to focus too clearly on how she felt, in case those feelings overwhelmed her or in some way failed to match her new self. There was a button in her head she pushed to 'off'. She needed to, to stay free of it all. Of course, from time to time something would impinge, some particular atrocity would hit home with a vengeance, filling her with anguish, smothering her in a heavy black cloud of sorrow, confusing her. And then a surge of anger would rekindle her rage at the awfulness of it all. Instantly she would be politically alert again, until realism, or a feeling of powerlessness, would cause her to push these feelings back into herself, and the feelings would recede again to remain something she didn't want to examine: too dangerous, too threatening.

Over the tops of the houses, the evening sky was streaked with red, the city outlined starkly against it. There was a ridge of purplish blue-black cloud suspended like a blind against the horizon. The last slice of red disc slid out of sight. At the top of the street the twin spires of the church burned against the dying sun. The beauty of it touched her, and made her feel unexpectedly buoyant. She pulled up outside her father's door feeling in better form.

Her father was watching the news when she got in. He had a real bee in his bonnet about one of the local newscasters. He started to give out about him now to Clare, glad to have someone on whom to vent his spleen.

'That fella's a disgrace,' he said. 'All he talks about are priests who've run away with weemen or abused children, terrible state of affairs altogether. In the name o' God have they nothing else to report on?'

Clare was about to retort and managed to bite her tongue. There was no point in arguing with him when he was in this mood. 'Well, Daddy, turn over to the other side then,' she managed.

'Sure they're as bad. That other fellow reads the news to me as if it was my fault. Anyway when they get sick talking about the Assembly, and where they're going to hang the flags, they're all on about priests *this*, priests *that*. Have they nothing else to talk about?'

'Daddy, if it hadn't happened, there wouldn't be anything on the news about it.'

'What are ye talkin' about? D'ye believe everything ye hear on the news now. Do you? I thought you had more sense than that.' He looked at her scornfully. 'Oh aye, I suppose it's fashionable in London now to knock the Church, a pack of heathens over there. Well, yis'll all get a quare gunk when it comes to meeting your maker, mark my words.'

She took off her coat, hung it up, and went into the small

kitchen to start cooking. She was making a quick chicken curry. She knew he liked curries, despite his protests about all that
fancy muck. She noticed that the meals-on-wheels women
hadn't come today. It was every second day, she realised.

She had shopped this morning and felt touched when he
proudly opened the cupboard and showed her the curry spices
she had bought the last time she was over.

'There,' he said. 'I kept these. I hope they haven't gone off.'

An hour later he was clearing his plate, wiping his mouth
with obvious pleasure. 'I enjoyed that now. There's plenty of
iron in curries – good for you. I was reading in an article about
that in the *Irish News*, or was it a programme? Anyhow.' He
broke off. Jimmy McCabe from across the street had just put
his head round the door.

That was another thing she'd have to get used to. The intru-
sions every couple of hours. People lived on top of each other
in these wee streets, thought nothing of walking in and interrupting. It was good for her father, of course, when he was
alone, but she found it irritating.

Jimmy beamed at her. 'Well, Clare, you're lookin' well. I'm
sure you're glad to have her back, Tommy, eh? Ah, this
'peacefire' will be bringing all the young ones home.'

Clare smiled tightly.

Jimmy blathered on. 'Not married yet, the last to go, oh
aye, the last to go. Best-looking of the bunch too. Must be
hard to get, eh Tommy? We'll have to find you a man, eh?'
He grinned at her again. His regulation false teeth gleamed
alarmingly in his bright red face. He looked like a Halloween
pumpkin. He was a big man, and his bulk filled the small
room.

Jimmy's a harmless fella, her mother used to say. 'A wee bit
simple, but likeable all the same.'

In small doses though, Clare thought.

He sat himself down heavily on the settee, rubbing the
cheeks of his arse, lifting them as if to spread them evenly.

'I heard from Winnie you were home, Clare. You're lookin' well, need a bit of beefin' up, what Tommy?'

He and her father then began a long conversation about false teeth. The ins and outs of wearing them or not. She suspected that this was a regular topic of conversation between them. It sounded scripted. Apparently Jimmy had only recently collected his current set.

She excused herself as soon as she could and went into the kitchen to clear up. There was really no sense in letting the likes of Jimmy annoy her. He was just another reason she had to get a flat. Unless she was prepared to close her ears to all this oul chat, her staying here would not work out. Maybe she should think of renting until she got somewhere to buy. It would have to be furnished though; she couldn't face the idea of separating the years of belongings she had accumulated with Tim. The division of the spoils could wait, she thought grimly.

Later on that evening, in the pub at the bottom of the street, she recounted to her brother Tony the story of Jimmy's visit. Tony had called to take her out for a drink, no doubt to escape his own domestic mayhem. He was six years younger than Clare and had always been her favourite. He was a good-looking but feckless type, with an endearing manner, and he was always in good humour. He was the most openly affectionate of the Murphy family. Clare remembered her mother used to call him an 'oul plaster'. The old expression fitted him perfectly, because as a child he was always hugging and kissing her, sticking to her. He had been a beautiful baby, after two straight dark-haired girls, a smiling boy with blond curls. Whenever they wheeled him in his pram, Clare and Brid had got manys the sixpence from doting women for those blond curls. His hair was darker now, but he hadn't changed much over the years – the oul ones still doted on him. It had taken brother and sister twenty minutes to walk the hundred yards to the pub, so many people had stopped to chat.

She noticed that the outer steel gates were unlocked tonight as they came in, that was another new development. There was a lot less tension about the place. It was relaxed even. There were times she'd been home on visits with Tim when she'd sat on edge the entire evening, looking to see who was listening to Tim's English accent and worrying that some lunatic would take exception to it, or think he was a soldier.

Her father had always assured her that her fears were all nonsense. 'Sure haven't they seen him play the wee doctor on the TV. They think he's a doctor – they don't target doctors.'

Well, she would hardly have to worry about Tim now. She concentrated on finishing her rant about Tommy. Tony listened sympathetically.

'I suppose I should know better than to let it annoy me, he's doing his best. It can't be easy having me back when he's been so set in his ways.'

Tony drained his pint. 'Clare, love, you know what he's like, didn't we all tell you you were daft to even think of staying with him. You know all the oul ones that drop in to see him are all mad in the head. Sure they'd hardly have changed since Christmas, or whenever you were here last. You'd have been far better staying with Brid.'

'Tony, you know Peter gets on my nerves, and she's so uptight.'

'Well, I'm not dying about him either. He's slow to buy a drink. Me da's sure he still has his communion money, but he suits *her*.' He took a long gulp from his pint. 'Anyway I'm telling ye, livin' with me da'll do yer head in. Though he's talked about nothing else but your visit since you told him you'd been thinking of it last week. Sure he was all for me redoing the wee room even though I just papered it for you the last time.' He looked at her apologetically, as if reading her mind about the colour scheme. 'Ah know, it's shite isn't it? I got a good deal on the paint.'

Clare sighed. Tony's good deals were the bane of her

father's existence.

'So, kid, on your own head be it. I couldn't stick it. I was glad to move away from the street. He was round every morning near putting the door in, making sure I was up for work. It drove Sally bats.'

He broke off, and nodded up at a man of about Clare's age. The man was dark-haired, with an open face, his skin lightly freckled. His hair was straight with a middle parting – floppy, just shampooed by the look of it. He was wearing a navy blue woollen sweater. The man's eyes caught hers, and she smiled.

Tony spoke to him. 'All right, Lorcan?'

'Grand, Tony, grand. And you must be Clare?' He extended his hand. He had a soft southern lilt to his voice, and his eyes were so green it was almost a cliché. Probably contact lenses, she thought. She tried not to stare.

He was addressing her. 'I hear you're an actor,' he said. 'Your father's been telling me all about you. I'm glad to meet you finally. Tommy was saying you might come to the drama group and give us a bit of a talk some night? We meet again this day week, next Thursday. Would you be able to make that?'

'Well, isn't Tommy a great one for organising my free time. I'm sure the drama group are getting along fine without me.'

'They are, of course, but it would be an added treat if you were to find the time to talk to them. It's not always we have a celebrity living in our midst.'

'Hardly celebrity,' Clare said.

Lorcan raised his eyebrow. 'Well now, there's not many round here have been on the television. So in a manner of speaking you are. Anyhow, could I not persuade you to pop round just the once even? You'd be very welcome.'

Clare found herself agreeing, even though the very idea of a night with the group made her feel like screaming. Lorcan nodded his thanks and moved over to rejoin his group.

'Jaysus, Tony, is *that* Father O'Carroll? Why did no one tell me he looked like a movie star? Typical, I haven't looked twice at a man in months, and the first good-looking man I've seen since I arrived is a priest.'

Tony was smiling broadly. 'They say the attendance at Mass has rocketed since he got here. Tommy loves him. He calls in to me da twice a week, brings him communion if he's a bit under the weather. And he mixes with the people too, not like the last one at all. You'll usually see him here on Thursdays. He comes for a drink with the drama group. Has a Kaliber though – not a drinker.'

'Oh well,' said Clare ruefully. 'I expect I'll have to keep my word and go round next week. I suppose once won't hurt.'

She finished her pint, said goodbye to Tony, and left the bar. Maybe she'd get a job in the meantime, she thought, and wouldn't be able to go.

The days were longer but empty; the weather was sad, dull and blustery – April showers, shot through with bursts of sunshine. She felt hemmed in by the weather, and that was often reflected in her mood. She needed a marker, a sense that time was passing – an activity, albeit a useless one. Had she been in her own place, she might have stayed in bed longer, but Tommy was up at the crack of dawn, and had the dreaded cup of tea up to her about half eight. He would leave the house at about five to nine for Mass, and then she lay, listening to words on the radio; Jeremy Paxman on *Start the Week*, Libby Purves *Midweek*, Melvyn on a Thursday now. They were all confident people with too many opinions. She felt miles away from them all now, but the local stations sounded too unfamiliar, and she had formed the habit of listening to Radio Four and hadn't found a replacement.

She had this extra hour carefully timed, so she could leap out of bed just before Tommy came back in at ten, and have a cup of tea ready for him, trying to look like she'd been up a while. Maybe, she thought hopefully, the drama crowd would be interesting. Anyway, there was no way she could have got out of going. Tommy had been like a dog with a bone about it.

'Sure would you not just go round and pass yourself just the once?' he nagged.

She had been back in Belfast almost three weeks now. It had been hard enough to find things to do − only in one's own home, she thought, was it possible to truly relax doing nothing. She had visited by rote virtually everyone she was still in touch with, and had a few other invites lined up. Most of the parties or gatherings were ark parties − the animals coming in two by two. Single men in their thirties, to quote Paula, were as rare as rocking-horse turds.

She needed to be out of the house more − there was no privacy. The house simply wasn't big enough, with one small living room opening on to the street and Tommy sitting in as much as he did.

Tommy didn't have a radio, just the telly, but she felt uncomfortable going up to her bedroom to listen to the afternoon play, or to read. Not that he minded: they had always had a tendency to rub each other up the wrong way, and to stay sane they needed to get a break from each other.

The nights she did stay in underscored the fact that she didn't fit in any more. She had changed too much. Either her father felt he had to talk to her, or they sat in awkward silence, the gap between them looming unspoken. The TV was rarely off, not that she could blame him: as he said himself, it passed the time. But naturally enough, their tastes differed. Tommy wasn't behind the door in giving her his opinions on most of what they watched. It was predictable, she supposed, that she and Tommy wouldn't agree on everything, but oddly, despite this, there was a bond between them. He made her feel secure, providing her with a much-needed base, a centre, emotional as well as physical.

St Brendan's Amateur Drama Group − known as The Players − met in the parish hall. The hall was five minutes walk from Kinsale Street. Clare went round feeling a bit self-conscious. She met Father O'Carroll on the way in. She felt an unexpected surge of pleasure.

'Well, Clare,' he said with a broad grin. 'So, you've decided to give us a chance. I'm delighted. I wasn't sure if you'd be coming, although Tommy assured me you'd be along.'

'I'm glad I've given you both so much to talk about,' she said with mock indignation. 'Anyway, here I am.'

'Sure it'll pass the evening,' he said pleasantly. She ignored the quip. It was unfortunately too near the mark. He held the door for her and she went in, feeling cheered by the encounter.

Tonight the group members were discussing their choice of production for the annual round of drama festivals. It was between two Brian Friel plays, *Dancing at Lughnasa* and *Philadelphia, Here I Come!* This week they were starting to cast. She expected this to be tedious. Always, accompanying the certainty that these people would be exactly as predicted, was a vague hope that someone – anyone – would be special . . . someone other than the priest, that is. Someone to make a difference, to compensate for her need to come here in the first place. But the drama group had matched her expectations of them almost exactly, leaving her hopes of excitement unfulfilled.

Like many others in her profession, Clare lived for the future. She was always straining over the horizon for the next big event. It made for an unsettled frame of mind most of the time, but actors have little control over this state of affairs.

Clare had been a member of an Am Dram group in her teens. It had been full of men in corduroy trousers with bright pink faces and very brown shoes, and women who dressed in Laura Ashley clothes and always had a new white cardigan in the summer. An hour at St Brendan's convinced her that not much had changed in the Am Dram world in the intervening years. They were a typical group, with a hard core of about a dozen members plus a few floating 'thesps', as they were annoyingly called by Seamus, one of the leading lights of St Brendan's.

Seamus was an excruciating man in his early thirties: tall,

stooped and alarmingly skinny, a well-dressed scarecrow. He had large, irregular facial features and severe acne scarring. Perhaps his awareness of his physical deficits had made him work on his 'personality'. Although an extrovert, he obviously thought himself a New Man and had attempted to develop the sensitive, perceptive side of his nature. He had failed miserably.

Seamus introduced himself to Clare within a heartbeat of her arrival, and had obviously decided they were firm friends. He greeted her at the door with an air-kiss technique that wouldn't have been out of place in Hollywood. He found her a chair beside him, and treated her in a loud whisper to his 'résumé'. He had played many of the lead roles, and was now going to play the part of Gerry Evans in this production of *Dancing at Lughnasa*. That had been the consensus choice for next production, popular because there were five big parts for women. As ever in Am Dram, there were roughly three women in the group for every man, a statistic that was a constant irritation, since most plays had few good parts for women and always more parts for men. Seamus had been pre-cast, he confided to her, because the part called for a Welsh accent and he was *astoundingly confident* of his ability with accents. Despite this talent, his Welsh accent on this first read-through sounded to Clare more like that of a Pakistani from west Cork. They had also obviously overlooked the fact that Gerry Evans was supposed to be good-looking too, she thought unkindly.

There were some newer members joining the group tonight, attracted by the play. The regulars had conceded that they could not always cast from the core of keenies. The new arrivals were an uninspiring bunch, most of whom would comprise the technical side. One of them, a florid, over-madeup woman – Joan – offered to do the makeup, but tactfully one of the others convinced her she would be great at small props. Everyone did their own makeup these days anyway, Clare pointed out. There were two pensioners. The first was a sprightly little man, Billy McComb, a bosom buddy of

Tommy's who raced pigeons. He stood about five feet tall. Apparently he'd been a sensation as the cat in the Christmas production of *Dick Whittington*.

And there was Cassie, one of the regulars, a rotund woman with a startlingly high colour, hyperthyroid eyes, and a rather exotic fashion sense, who wore nothing but purple. Clare had already noticed her a few mornings walking down the street from church. Cassie had obviously spent years at elocution lessons. Every word she uttered was enunciated, her mouth contorting round each syllable for emphasis. The trouble was, she had a habit of placing the stress on the wrong word, making every statement sound as if she was about to start a row. It took Clare a few conversations to learn to disregard this.

She was cornered during the tea break by two of the other women in the group. The taller of the two introduced herself as R-O-S-H-E-E-N, spelling it out to Clare. '*Not* the common way, my mother was a real romantic,' she explained. Then she went on to tell Clare that in the last play they had done, *Juno and the Paycock*, people had compared her performance to that of Judi Dench in the same play. Allegedly, a member of the audience who'd seen the Old Vic production told her that for the first half of the performance she thought Judi Dench was making a guest appearance at St Brendan's.

Clare tried to keep a straight face as she looked up at Rosheen, who must have been easily five foot eleven in height and not far behind that in girth.

'Judi Dench is smaller than you are, though,' Clare managed to say finally, pleased with her self-control.

Undaunted, Rosheen grabbed her arm and told her with no hint of irony, 'I know, I know! That's where I have the advantage over her.'

Rosheen's buddy Eleanor was equally irritating. She preferred tragedy to comedy, she told Clare. 'More *content* normally, more of a challenge. Now take this play, it's the human tragedy elements that give it its force, don't you think? Of course,' she added, nodding sagely, 'Friel was writing from the heart: his old Aunts. *Oh*, a terrible life, heartbreaking, simply heartbreaking.'

Clare tried to move off, but Eleanor hadn't finished. Sighing dramatically she continued, 'I wish we could do Shakespeare. She gesticulated wildly. '*Lear, Macbeth, Othello*. Yes! And of course the play of all plays – *Hamlet*.' At least she'd got that right. Encouraged by Clare's nod of agreement she rabbited on.

Clare wished Paula were with her to hear all this. She would have hanged herself laughing. But it would make a good phone call. It was priceless, really, how utterly deluded some people could be; though if she was honest, they were no worse than large sections of the acting community, and they were probably kinder.

There was also a clique of younger ones, who were deferential to Clare on account of her being a real actress and having an Equity card.

The group was not strictly drawn from the surrounding area; several of the members were schoolteachers. Its reputation in the past had been excellent, but there had been a run of bad luck the last few years. The location didn't help of course, but now that the political situation was sort of settled they were on their way back to the top. Their aim was to make it to the finals of the Ulster Amateur Dramatic Festival.

As in the majority of the local Am Dram groups, this was their entire *raison d'être*. Past productions that hadn't made the final were referred to in hushed whispers as 'off years'. The choice of play was the reason for the lack of success in those years of course, never the production or the performances. The constant battle with the sourness and partiality of the adjudicators was a particular gripe of Cassie. 'They all have their favourite groups. Year in and year out, you see the same ones walk away with the prizes, regardless of what they put on. Honestly, it would make you sick.'

Being underrated was the least of their problems, Clare thought sourly. All this information was delivered to her in stereo: into her right ear by the ghastly Seamus and into her left ear by Cassie. Still, as Seamus pointed out quickly, in case Clare got the wrong idea about them, success shone on them from time to time. They had a big following, got huge audiences, and unlike a lot of professional groups, hadn't to worry about breaking even or making a profit. The last few years hadn't been typical, and now that Father Lorcan was giving a bit of credence to their efforts they'd be away on a hack in no time.

Father Lorcan was ostensibly the organiser/artistic director. He patently had a love of the theatre, Clare saw. The prime mover in the group for the last decade had been the indomitable but rather opinionated Breda, who was directing this production. Breda taught in one of the more progressive secondary schools – drama, of course – and this made her an expert in all things theatrical.

There appeared to be nothing from Greek tragedy to Steven Berkoff that she hadn't studied. Clare found her most unattractive to look at. She had a crown of wispy reddish hair, through which her skull could be glimpsed when the light shone behind. She had little piggy eyes, and thin lips which looked wet without lip gloss. Clare had taken an instant dislike to Breda, and this was compounded because she refused to accept that Clare could not play any of the parts.

'Now, Clare, I'm sure you're just being modest when you say you can't take part. You'd be ideal for the part of Aggie.' Her voice squeaked with emphasis.

Clare suppressed the inclination to punch her in the mouth. 'Breda, I'm a professional actor,' she said patiently. 'I have an Equity card. I can't take part in amateur productions.'

'Well, far be it for me to boast, but I'm sure there's very little to choose between us and some of the productions I've seen.'

'I'm sure you're right, Breda, but it's a rule none the less.'

Clare shrugged. 'But, I do know the play well. I played Chrissie in one of the London productions, and I would be happy to assist-direct or help stage-manage for the time being – that is, while I am not working.'

'You mean while you're resting, Clare,' Father Lorcan interjected.

She looked at him across the room and he smiled at her, his green eyes level. She normally found the term 'resting' irritating, preferring the blunter 'unemployed', but she guessed he had merely used it to tease her. Anyway, his intervention was timely. Suppressing her irritation at Breda, Clare allowed him to push the conversation on to a discussion about who would play Aggie. Finally they were able to agree who would read for the part, and arrange an audition night when Clare's 'valuable opinion would be sought as to the casting'. They had someone in mind. A woman who was normally one of their leading lights had recently had her first child. She could maybe be coaxed back from retirement. In the meantime, they read through the play. Clare read the part of Agnes, glad it was one of the smaller parts. She tried not to sound too polished, but they read with obvious enthusiasm and enjoyment, so by the end of the evening she was enjoying it too, her cynicism evaporated in the swell of good will.

Throughout the evening Clare was acutely aware of the priest. He was reading in the stage directions. He had a beautiful voice, she thought, and her eyes were continually drawn towards him. She had noticed when he pushed his hair back that he had big ears, but this hidden flaw only made him seem more attractive. At the tea break, she forced herself to join in conversations with the others, but he was her chosen audience. Everything she uttered was for his benefit; she was playing to him.

They broke up about ten, and one of the girls persuaded her to join them in the bar afterwards. The group didn't all stay for a drink. Clare agreed – she couldn't tear herself away from

Lorcan O'Carroll. Whether she had subconsciously engineered it or he had she wasn't sure, but in the pub afterwards she found herself beside him. He was easy to talk to, and very hard to reconcile with her notion of what a priest should be like – though she was aware that this was a stupid thought in itself.

From chatting to him, it was obvious that he had patiently listened to all her father's tales of her successes, God love him, and had formed some opinion of her already. For her part, she had really no notion of him other than as 'wee Father Lorcan'. But as the chat around the table became livelier, she found herself warming to him as well. It took a while to realise that he had definite opinions on everything, so skilled was he in allowing others to talk.

The talk was mainly about drama: plays they liked, productions they had seen, and different playwrights. Clare was surprised to find that many of these amateurs were regular theatregoers. They thought nothing of visiting the Abbey in Dublin, or going off to a weekend of theatre-packed days in London. And despite Breda being pushily obvious about her 'expertise' in all things theatrical, Clare had to acknowledge that she put a lot of time and effort into her hobby.

'And you, Father? Do you get to the theatre much?' Clare asked.

'Well, mostly in Belfast, and occasionally to Dublin, but not as much as I'd like. My pastoral work is fairly demanding. But I'm enjoying this work with the drama crowd. I look on it as my day off. They're a great bunch.' He indicated the present group of about six. 'This lot is involved in every production, but we widen the circle too. We do our best to involve the young people in a Christmas show, with some success. Although I don't know if they find it cool to admit to a liking for it.' He grinned at her endearingly when he used the word 'cool'. 'It keeps them off the streets, you might say.'

He turned towards her, focusing on her in such a way that

the others couldn't overhear. 'So what really brings you back, Clare?'

She wasn't expecting such a direct question and she was thrown. She took a sip of her drink, giving herself time to reply.

'I needed a change and I thought Daddy could use a bit of company.'

'I see, and are things working out? I believe you're looking at flats?'

'Yes, but I haven't found anything suitable just yet. I'm in no rush.'

'Is your boyfriend thinking of moving?'

'Why do you ask?'

'Because I'm nosy.' He laughed. 'And because your father had indicated that you might be a bit upset about things.'

'Well he's wrong, I'm not, but then it's my business if I am.' To her embarrassment, she was suddenly engulfed by a wave of sorrow. Her eyes filled with tears.

She hastily excused herself and went to the loo. She fixed her makeup in the mirror and took a deep breath. The thought that her father had been talking about her to the priest annoyed her, yet what did she expect? It was unusual for someone of her age to move back to the family home. It was regarded widely as some sort of failure, especially since to all intents and purposes she had bettered herself by leaving. The traffic from this part of town was all one-way. She needed to step up her efforts at house hunting, but she was out of work, and acting wasn't the sort of profession to help one build a nest egg.

When she came back out, the group had dispersed and Lorcan was sitting on his own.

'They've left.' He indicated the door. 'Not very many serious drinkers among tonight's lot. C'mon, I'll walk up with you.' It was a statement.

They were buzzed out of the steel gates of the bar, which had been locked when last orders were called. The coldness of the night air stabbed at her, making her pull her coat around her.

They walked the first few yards in silence, then, he said, 'I didn't mean to upset you, are you okay?'

'Yes I'm fine,' Clare answered brusquely, uncomfortable with his concern.

'Do you want to come and see me, to talk about anything?'

'What?' she said startled. 'Do you mean confession?'

'No.' He laughed. 'I'm sure you gave that up years ago. Not at all. I meant simply if you need a sympathetic ear, someone reasonably uninvolved, someone who's used to listening . . .'

'No, I'm fine thanks,' she repeated.

'Well, if you do, you know where to find me.'

'Yes, thank you, Father.'

'Lorcan, please. We're more relaxed these days.'

'OK, Lorcan.'

They reached her front door. She paused. 'I'll see you next Thursday,' she said.

'Or maybe during the week,' he added. 'Give my best to Tommy.'

'Goodnight, then.'

She probably should have asked him in. She wasn't sure of the etiquette of it all – did one ask priests in? Well, she didn't feel in the mood to entertain.

She went into the kitchen as quietly as possible and waited for the kettle to boil. She felt a rush of self-loathing. What in God's name was she doing here? She should be coming off the stage at the National, rushing round to the greenroom for a drink, and finding Sam Mendes waiting for her, with his arms outstretched, saying, 'Clare, please, reconsider my offer, the Donmar needs you. We'll change all the rehearsal times to suit you.'

Dream on, she thought sourly. How in hell's name was she going to stand this? She poured the camomile tea she had made down the sink. Tommy had a bottle of Bushmills under the sink beside the Domestos. She poured a large measure into the Minton cup and carried it upstairs. She sipped it while she listened to the soothing rhythm of the shipping forecast.

Next morning Clare got out a pen and made one of her lists. It was time she began to play a part in her own destiny. Paula, her closest friend in London, did. She believed in going out and making things happen. Clare envied her stamina and her positive approach.

'We all make our choices my love,' Paula was fond of telling her. 'And your doing nothing is a choice on its own.'

Clare got out a blank page, and, concentrating fiercely, wrote out a game plan.

Call Tim about flat sale.

Find a place to rent.

Get property brochure from estate agents – Belfast was full of them now.

Pester Diana to get her appointments with the BBC here in Belfast. They had a good drama department.

Set up auditions with the local theatres, or with one of the smaller companies.

That was another thing that had changed about Belfast. There seemed to be a profusion of new, young groups doing some quite innovative stuff. She had been to a few plays and was reasonably impressed. Besides, she needed to get working soon. Her savings, as they were small, wouldn't last too long.

She dialled Diana's number. Diana was busy with a client, but assured her she would call her back. Taking a deep breath, Clare dialled the number of the flat she had shared with Tim. She knew from Diana that he was between jobs at the moment, so it was likely he would be there. The line was busy. It felt odd dialling her old home number, painful. Tim had called her a few times when she had first left, but she had avoided calling him, fearful that Kezia would answer.

When Tim began his affair with Kezia, Clare had been in Southampton doing a play. She came up on weekends, and with a woman's sixth sense knew someone else had been there. It was as though their joint smell had been overlaid with something else. The sense of home had been disturbed. This feeling made her insecure, and rather than confront Tim, she tried to trip him up with seemingly innocent questions. But he parried them all expertly. Still sure something was going on, she searched the place for evidence. For the classic signs of another presence that her intuition told her was edging hers out. She looked in his drawers for letters, receipts, and found nothing. She reeled back the answerphone cassette for incriminating old messages, but the tape had been erased. The house was like a stage set with the telltale props tidied away. She spent hours with friends talking about her increasing alienation from Tim, hoping the feeling that they were growing apart wasn't real. If any of her friends were aware of something going on they weren't going to be the bearer of bad tidings. Finally she told him she knew he was seeing someone else. She made it sound as if someone had told her something, and she demanded that he tell her the truth.

They were in bed at the time. They had just finished making love. She could remember, even now, that heartbeat between the question and the answer. The searing pain when the knowledge was hers too.

Clare had returned from Southampton as usual late on Sunday morning. It was always too much of an effort to face the drive after the Saturday show. She had been feeling apprehensive, unsettled for no particular reason.

Tim was in the garden when she got back, having a late breakfast with the Sunday papers. He kissed her briefly. 'Well, how was last night?'

'Great, good audience, made up for yesterday's matinée, which was shite. Full of pensioners with buzzing hearing aids picking up the local taxi service.'

He laughed – a bit falsely, Clare thought. Or was she just going mad?

'What did *you* do?' she asked. 'Did you go out?' She had rung: there was no answer, and she hadn't waited for the beep on the machine.

'No, I watched TV. Nothing much on really, but I'd been up at six all week doing that bloody commercial, so I was absolutely knackered.'

'Did you have a visitor?'

'No. What makes you think that?' he said, as he went about the business of making a fresh pot of coffee, but Clare had noticed the sideways glance into the bedroom as if to check all was okay.

She changed the subject and they talked about work, friends, and their next moves. Anything but the issue, which hung between them like a fog, obscuring everything. Some friends called over in the late afternoon and Tim was Mr Charm, telling jokes, repeating Clare's story about the hearing aids. Trying too hard.

They were in the habit of going to bed early on these nights, and of getting straight down to the business of lovemaking, the weekly separation having provided most of the foreplay. They had both had a fair amount to drink. When they finished, Clare felt an unbearable urge to cry.

'What is it, Clare? What's wrong?'

'Tell me her name, Tim. Please. I know, you see. I know. Please don't insult me by continuing to lie. It's not worthy of you. Who is she?'

He almost whispered the name. 'Kezia Sheldon.'

He had done a radio play with her ages ago, maybe six months back. Clare knew the name Sheldon: her mother was a very famous actress. Easy for her, then, Clare thought – a leg-up. Kezia was young, in her twenties, doing rather well at present. Tim had mentioned her before, fleetingly, as a chum – there were lots of 'chums' in the business. Obviously the chumminess had become something deeper.

'How long have you been seeing her?'

'Not long, a few weeks at most.'

'But the play was ages ago.'

'I know. We've kept in touch a bit by phone. I met her by accident at the Court recently.'

'Are you sleeping with her?'

'Yes, I have once or twice,' he said quietly. Chillingly, Clare thought.

'Christ, you can't remember! Was it once or twice?'

Tim put his head down. He couldn't look her in the face. 'A few times. It's not important. Things between *us* haven't been great, Clare. Even you would agree with that.' He looked balefully at Clare and continued. 'Look, this has just been recently, no one knows. It happened by accident. We were at a play. We shared a taxi home. She asked me in for coffee. It sort of happened. I didn't think it would go any further, then she rang me again.' He shrugged. 'You know how it goes. Anyway, she's just a baby. She'll move on soon enough, when she gets the next big part. I think she just likes my friendship. We get on very well – the sex is incidental.'

'What about us?'

'I'm not sure right now,' he mumbled, not looking Clare in the face. 'Maybe we should both see other people for a while. Look, this won't amount to anything, but I'd like to continue my friendship with her at least.'

'Then I'm moving out.'

'Clare, please, you're overreacting. Things like this have happened before.'

'Not for years, and this feels different. I can tell. Are you in love with her?'

'No, of course not. I like her. She makes me laugh. She's bouncy, full of stories.'

'Like I was.'

'You still are, some of the time. Clare, this is not important. You're making a big deal out of it.'

Clare sat stony-faced, her heart breaking. Tim seemed not to notice.

'Look, I really would like to keep seeing her – as a friend at any rate. If I stop now I'll feel it wasn't my decision. I'd feel I'd been pressurised.'

'Don't you love me any more?'

'Of course I love you, how could I stop? Like I said, it's been a strain recently, but I know I love you. I'll never love anyone as much as I love you.'

'Are you still *in love* with me?'

'What does that mean, *in love*?' he said.

They had talked the night away. Clare couldn't stop quizzing him. She wanted to know every sordid detail – even though the pain was unbearable. When she pressed him, he said he wasn't sure of his true feelings for Kezia. He had been flattered by her interest in him. They had met doing the Radio Four Classic Serial, so they had more than a week together in a studio recording. He assured Clare that nothing had happened then, even though they had played lovers. Kezia had heard he lived with Clare. But despite this she had befriended him, and, he said, must have impinged somehow, because they had formed the habit over the week of having a drink together afterwards in the BBC club – with the others.

'So that's when it began, then – over six months ago!'

'No,' he maintained. 'I didn't go home with her then. It was months later, when we met at the play.'

Clare wanted desperately to believe that was the case, but her soul was crying out that he was lying. 'When did it start? Why? Wasn't I enough?'

He repeated his claim. It had started almost by accident. They had shared a taxi home from the theatre, both having had a bit too much to drink. She had invited him in, and they had ended up in bed. It had been confusing for him, but he thought that would be the end of it. He might have told Clare some night in a confessional way, but it hadn't worked out like that. Kezia had been distraught when he refused to see her again.

'Honestly Clare, I've tried, really tried, to stop seeing her, but she was so abject I couldn't do it. I told her I couldn't consider leaving you, and she said fine, she could live with that. Ten per cent of me was better than a hundred per cent of anyone else.'

'Oh please, don't make me sick.' Clare snorted. 'Ten per cent of you!'

He had the grace to look embarrassed. 'I know, I know it sounds pathetic doesn't it, but she needs someone at the moment. The last man she was with virtually left her on the altar steps . . . you've been so distant recently. Be patient with me, I don't think it will last. Like I said, she'll probably drift off when she gets her next big part.'

'What's the sex like?' she asked when she had stopped crying, wanting him to say, as of course he did, 'OK, nothing special, ordinary.'

But what had she expected? That he would suddenly tell the truth? She pursued the questioning masochistically.

'OK, not great. It was difficult for me at first, not like us, but I was lonely and as I said, you have been a bit detached recently. It's not a big deal, we've both been in this situation before, Clare, and got through it.'

It seemed so innocuous when he put it that way – though her gut was telling her otherwise. She had suddenly realised at that moment that life without him was beyond her. The bond between them was too deep. She hadn't felt the full force of it until now. She cried then, and they clung to each other, knowing something had been destroyed – shattered by the strength of the destruction. Finally they had made love again, desperately, almost in sorrow. They decided not to break up. He couldn't do without her, he said. The Kezia thing wouldn't last. He was confused, and he wanted them both. She agreed to leave things for the time being. The next morning she had gone back to her job. She was appearing in one play, rehearsing a second.

She passed the next few months in a trance. His treachery, for she knew that was what it was, absorbed every waking minute. It was as though discovering his perfidy had given her the cipher she had lacked over the past six months – for although he said it had been only two months, she knew he was lying. It must have started during the radio play. All the funny little things that had been inexplicable were suddenly clear. The hesitancy when she had phoned sometimes, his lack of interest in what she was doing. His eagerness for her to accept these parts, even though it would separate them for months. The nights when he had uncharacteristically gone for drinks after filming, and the lovemaking which had changed from warm comfortable desire to urgent, frantic sex. Why had she not realised sooner? Surely her friends had known? But he had been clever in covering his tracks. Even Diana had thought it was purely a friendship.

Clare continued to make the journey up on Sundays, longing for things to right themselves, hoping that she would find Kezia ousted. It didn't happen. He was there every Sunday faithfully to meet her. If she was in first she found herself doing demeaning things. Like checking the bed to see if he had spent the night there, and if so, whether he had been alone. She could never tell. The bed was always freshly changed, the dirty linen sloshing about in the washing machine. She would end up feeling cheapened even further by these insecure little detective games.

The pain between them was palpable. She took to inviting friends round for Sunday lunch so that she could get through the day. She drove back to Southampton on Mondays in a haze of pain. He still phoned her every evening, as was their habit when either was out of town. She drove him crazy with her endless questioning, both on the phone and when she came home on Sundays. There was nothing about this other woman that didn't interest her. He would answer her questions with a weary, almost bored look on his face.

No, he didn't want to marry Kezia. No, he didn't have any intentions of moving in with her. Yes, she wanted a child by him. No, he didn't, he had only wanted that with Clare. No, for the fiftieth time, he wasn't in love, he just enjoyed her company. She was a good companion. And he enjoyed her adulation too, thought Clare – and her youth, of course.

'What do you see in her? She's nothing special to look at, and Jenny says she talks incessantly – about herself – and laughs at her own jokes. Even when they aren't funny. How do you stand that?'

He tried to explain. Kezia was always in good form. She was fun to be with. She laughed a lot. She was witty.

'What does that mean?' Clare had asked him. 'Am I not witty?'

'No, you're funny, were funny.' What was the difference? All *she* knew was, witty was something she couldn't possibly be at this stage. But she was beyond reason by now. Her grief at sharing him had made her mad. Clare was surprised at the venom she was capable of: vicious, spiteful little jibes like 'How do you stand kissing her? She hasn't any lips.'

'That's unworthy of you, Clare,' he had replied.

And she agreed, apologised and cried yet again. She was bright and happy one minute, wracked with tears the next.

Most of her friends thought she was insane to tolerate the

situation, to allow him the indulgence of both women. They told her repeatedly to get out, leave him, stop tormenting herself. He wasn't worth it – no man was. The litany of advice was all ignored. Her tenacity at holding on to him on the basis of the merest glimmer of hope was equalled only by Kezia's. Those who knew Clare's rival were sure she would hold on like grim death. She meant to win this one. 'I've never seen her so determined,' a mutual friend told Clare.

Clearly Tim didn't have the ability to fight Kezia or, more importantly, he didn't want to. Kezia had contacts with all the right people. Her mother's success had ensured that. This impressed Tim. He hated being on the fringe. Kezia was his ticket to an inner circle. She wasn't a star herself, but she would be – and right now she knew a fair proportion of them.

Although Clare went out of her way to make sure that her path and Kezia's didn't cross – hard enough in that incestuous society – part of Clare longed to see her. Show me my rival. She had checked Kezia's picture in *Spotlight*, the casting director's bible. Kezia was listed under juvenile leads: a reasonably attractive young woman with a hard expression, nothing at all like Clare to look at. Clare had talked to people who knew Kezia, and relished any negative comments made about her. Realising, but caring little, that they might have been made to help her wounded pride, she stored them in her mind and rotated them over and over again, wallowing in the sordid little tales. She had never experienced jealousy before. The force of it left her reeling, unfocused, numbed. She hung on spiteful little snips of tittle-tattle. Making a nest of pain with these crumbs of discomfort. People told her, She's OK, not bad-looking, desperate for a man, likes older men. Her father was thirty years older than her mother. She really went for Tim. Has always been dumped before, slept around a lot, had affairs with anyone to get the part.

Well, thought Clare, why not, really? It had obviously worked for her. She was making a name for herself at only twenty-five, becoming quite a successful actor, a 'flavour'. And yet Clare hated herself for such sisterly disloyalty.

Their mutual friends expressed surprise at Tim's choice. 'What can he possibly see in her? She's so conceited' was the oft-repeated phrase. Yet Clare knew it mattered little that Kezia evidently wasn't too popular. The fact was that Tim wanted her, and for once, the opinions of others didn't matter to him. He was prepared to give up the ten years with Clare for this compliant and adoring woman. His ego needed it.

If she truly was as dislikeable as Clare's friends thought, what did that say about him? Despite his assurances to the contrary, he appeared to be getting more and more involved. Perhaps they were alike, he and his new woman. But Clare mourned his loss and talked forever about how wonderful he was, and how incomplete her life would be without him.

Nonsense, her friends said. Utter tripe.

'He's nothing at all, my love,' said Paula. 'Nothing at all. You need to move on, Clare, forget him. Let her have him. You're worth ten of him: I know them both, and they're perfect for each other.'

Finally, she could not endure the pretence of living with him any longer. On the last night of her play, she decided not to return to the flat and instead to move in with her close friends Bill and Julian.

She went gratefully – worn out by grief. And true to form they had clucked over her, mollycoddled her, cooked her meals, and gossiped endlessly about Tim and Kezia. Gradually they made her see that there was no way back and the only thing to do was to cut her losses and leave forever.

Her pain floated around her. She could feel it. She expected everyone could see it, touch it. She had never felt so raw, so unprotected. She was offered the part of a madwoman in a new play in one of the fringe venues, a short run. She told Julian that she thought she got the part because the director hadn't realised that she *was* mad, not acting, during the reading.

'Well, darling, at least you haven't lost your sense of humour,' he said. 'You should take it, it'll do you good. Keep you busy.'

She took it. Diana thought it would 'go'.

It *was* a success. Tim dutifully sent flowers and a card, and came to the opening night. Kezia had been stashed away for the evening. At the party afterwards it seemed like old times. Their old friends surrounded them. Clare was the hit of the evening. Infected by it all, Tim had been attentive, affectionate. He was a great man for the occasion.

'Come home with me,' he said. 'I've missed you.'

They went back to the flat together and he made love to her, but the magic wasn't there. The drink had obscured the truth for a brief spell, and when they got into bed she felt it had been wrong to hope. She lay beside him, her pain wrapping her tightly, repelling him as he brushed against it. She felt she was almost drowning in the void between them. That was when she decided to leave London and return to Ireland.

Next morning, when she told him of her decision, there was something close to relief in his voice. 'When will you go?' he asked.

'When the play finishes.'

'Who will you stay with? Brid?'

Brid, her older sister, had the largest house of any of her family members.

'No, with Daddy.'

'Come on, Clare, that's crazy. You'd go mad in that little house with just Tommy for company. Christ, the two of you argue all the time.'

This was true. Tim had become adept on visits over at keeping the peace between her dad and herself. 'Henry Kissinger', Tony had nicknamed him on one of the Christmas visits. Clare had always loathed Henry Kissinger but right at this minute she had a higher opinion of him than she had of Tim.

Until she said it aloud to Tim, she hadn't seriously considered that she would actually do that, go back to Belfast. She came to believe that this was the only solution: to go back to the family home and build up again from there. That, truly, was her only hope of healing. Then, hearing herself say it, as if she had it already planned, focused her thoughts somehow. The word became the reality and the following few weeks were spent telling friends.

The incredulous looks only made her more certain that this was what she had to do. Her stubbornness surfaced with a vengeance.

She stayed in the flat the week before she left. Tim was there a lot. It seemed as if he was there to see her off the premises. They didn't sleep together that week, with the exception of her final night. That had been a total disaster, ending in a row when she had asked if he intended moving Kezia in when she left.

'No,' he said coldly. 'I don't think so. She has her own place. She may stay the odd night.'

'I don't want her here, looking at my things, making love to you in our bed, on bed linen I bought. I don't want her here.'

But she knew that would happen. He was just too cowardly

to admit it. Her heart ached with the weight of his deceit, his moral cowardice.

Diana's reaction when told of Clare's decision to move back was comical. 'Sweetheart, you can't be serious. Back to that ghastly Trimble person and Gerry Adams and all those awful braying voices? All that endless marching?'

'It is where I come from, Diana.'

'Yes,' she wailed, 'but I was just starting to forget, and now you've reminded me.'

From anyone else, Clare would have found this offensive, but she excused Diana. That's how she was. And she was a good friend. She had been supportive despite being caught in the middle of the whole morass. Representing both Tim and Clare had naturally made her a bit of a piggy in the middle. She was an amazing woman, a huge personality, and a total parody of a theatrical agent. Tim and Clare used to chuckle that she was really an actor playing the part. No one had found her out yet. But it was effective role-playing – it got results.

Diana was a large woman. One would not have chosen the word *fat* to describe her. She dressed only in black to compensate for her size. Expensive designer clothes. She had long, chestnut-coloured thick hair, which she wore improbably in a series of velvet Alice bands of different colours. They were entwined sometimes with gold, or with glass beads. It was her trademark. Tim used to joke that they kept her hair on. She was never seen with 'naked hair'.

She was good-looking rather than pretty, with a booming voice. She smoked incessantly, and ranted about the mean-spiritedness of nonsmokers like Tim and Clare who forced her to smoke in their garden or had barbecues rather than indoor events so that the question would never arise.

She had signed them both at the same time. Diana was just starting up on her own as an agent, after getting her reputation with a large management company. Clare and Tim had liked her irreverence and her dynamism, and she had been good for both their careers, guiding them towards roles which in most cases had been good choices. There were lots of Irish parts in the late eighties, both on stage and on telly. Clare had been marginally more successful in those early days, but at times the balance had swung to Tim. They had each wanted the other's success, though, and there was no true competition then.

That only came later, when Clare's star began to wane. People began to get fed up with Irish plays. The Irish question was done to death; a new slant was required. It duly arrived in the form of newer playwrights, like Martin McDonagh, and Conor MacPherson, but they wrote for young women or very old ones or, more usually, men. It was hard for Clare to establish herself as anything other than an Irish actress, even though she was good at accents.

This was why, on Diana's advice, she had taken the job in Southampton: one part in *The School for Scandal*, and two other parts playing Englishwomen in English plays. It had meant rehearsing during the day and performing at night for six months solid, but she had hoped it would be worth the graft. Diana had promised to get as many casting directors as possible down to see her. The six months were going to change things. Clare hadn't expected the change to be quite so dramatic.

Get a grip, Clare told herself. You're in Belfast now. How could she expect to move on until she stopped all this endless obsessing about Tim? It probably wouldn't cease until she'd spoken to him. She dialled the flat number again. This time the phone was picked up.

'Hello,' Tim answered.

At the sound of his voice her heart leapt. She tried to sound calm. 'Hi, how are you?'

'Fine, how's Tommy? Are you still speaking to each other?'

'He's great, and we're getting on OK. He hasn't thrown me out yet. Look, I was going to come over next week to see

Diana. Can we meet to discuss the house?'

'Are you staying here?' A hint of what – nervousness? – in his voice? She did still have the keys.

'No, I'm probably not.'

'With Julian and Bill?'

'Maybe, probably with Paula, but we *should* meet. We really need to sort things out about the flat. Can we at least talk about it?'

She knew he couldn't really afford to buy her out. They had no option but to sell, but obviously he was reluctant to do that. It would be impossible for Tim to find as good a place for the amount he would have available after the division of the spoils.

There was a pause, and then Tim spoke, hesitantly, searching for the right words. He hadn't rehearsed this one. 'I'm glad you called. I'd love to see you when you're over, and it's still your place too. You know you can stay when you want.'

Liar, she thought.

He cleared his throat, always a bad sign. He was about to tell her a lie. 'I may have good news – I think I will be able to buy you out after all.'

Clare was taken aback. She felt confused by the suddenness of it all. She tried to inject some enthusiasm into her reply, but her voice was flat, dulled. After all she had been the one to propose that he should buy her out.

'That's great news, but how?' she asked. 'Did you get a film part or something?' He couldn't have – Diana would have told her. Or maybe that was why Diana hadn't talked to her when she called.

There was hesitancy in his voice when he answered. 'No, but I think I may be able to borrow the money.'

'Who from?' Clare knew everything about Tim's circumstances. There was no way, careful as he was with money, that he would be able to find fifty thousand pounds without selling. 'I don't understand, Tim, who from?'

There was a small pause, a heartbeat long, and then he

spoke, sounding unsure. 'I've been to the bank manager. It looks like I may get this drink ad I'm up for, and there's a chance of a telly series. So he's agreed to lend me the money. I can have it for you in about a month.'

Lying, lying, he was lying. She could read him so well.

'I thought you'd be pleased,' he added lamely.

Her voice was shaky, but she managed to tell him that was great news, great. 'Well, maybe we can get together and discuss the details when I come over. We can go through the paintings and bits and pieces as well.'

He didn't argue. They said their goodbyes and she put the phone down. She was trembling and near to tears.

Her father walked in, the paper under his arm. 'A cup of tea, love?' He glanced at her shrewdly. 'I saw Father Lorcan, outside the church. He thinks you're great. He was saying you're a quare help to them. You're going round tonight?' He pointed to the paper. 'Look, I backed a horse for you at five to one: Theatrical Agent. Isn't that what that one with the voice who phones you is?' He glanced at her and went on. 'I don't know how it'll do, mind you – it's against Frankie Detorri's mount.' She knew enough now, from listening to him, to know that this was one of the top jockeys. 'But sure, you never know yer luck. If it wins, there might be enough for a round of drinks. I'm feeling lucky. I did it a pound each way.'

He was making the tea and chatting away to her, boiling the teapot on top of the stove, making sure it was well stewed. She had got used to the strong stuff these last weeks.

'That's the way tea should taste,' he'd say. 'Look, sure you could trot a mouse on that.'

Clare gulped it down gratefully and was just about to phone Diana again when the phone rang.

Clare picked it up, expecting Diana, but it was Paula. It was unusual for her to call during the day, to interrupt her writing. Something must be up. They chatted for a few minutes and then she came to the point.

'Listen, Clare my love, I just thought I'd tell you this in case you hear it elsewhere. Kezia' – Clare's heart jumped at the sound of the name – 'Kezia has got the lead in a *huge* telly series for Granada, and apparently is getting loads of dosh for it. I met Bill and Julian and they had seen Tim, and he told them that he and Kezia were going to move in together full-time, and he hoped that you would let her buy you out.' Her voice trailed off. 'Clare? Are you there? Look my love, I'm sorry to be the bearer of bad tidings and all that, but I thought you'd better hear it from me. I told Julian I would call you straight-away. Are you OK? Clare? Say something!'

'I'm fine. I don't care really, perhaps it's for the best. I need to get him out of my life for good.' Clare heard her voice echo in her head. She felt weak.

Paula paused for a moment, then said, 'Look, you're not to brood about this. I've said this before. He's not worth it. You're worth ten of him. Anyway, we can talk all weekend. I'm coming over to see you on Friday. I've got a cheap flight, OK? I'll call you tonight.' She made a kiss sound and was gone.

Clare put the phone down. She was glad her father was there, or she would have thrown it out the window.

The bastard, the lying bastard! How could he have thought for a minute she wouldn't find out? Surely, he must realise she was still in regular contact with loads of mutual friends. How did he expect her to believe his lies? He was such a bloody cow-ard. Her anger almost choked her. The thought that this wo-man would be living in the flat they had so carefully chosen together ... the place they had decorated with so much care and love. It made her feel wretched, sick to her stomach.

She could barely meet her father's searching gaze. But he sensed her mood, patted her on the head, and said cheerfully, 'Well, love, what about making me one of those curries to-night, eh? It's been a week since the last one.'

Grateful for a change of thought even, she agreed and went to check what she would need for the task.

The invitation to dinner a few nights later was a welcome diversion from the relentless angst. Tommy had encouraged her to get out. She could see he was starting to worry about her. So when Maura Oliver had rung to invite her, she accepted with pleasure. The dinner had been perfect as always. Maura, her hostess, was one of the best cooks she knew. There were ten people seated on the elegant balloon-back chairs around the Olivers' large Victorian table. The room was lavishly furnished, in soft coral shades, yet it managed to be both stylish and understated. Her generous and welcoming hosts made formal dinner parties – which Clare usually hated – an enjoyable and pleasant experience.

Clare hadn't seen the couple since her return. She had called them a few weeks ago to say she was home for a while. Maura had asked her tonight because the Olivers' eldest, Robert, had just had a part in a film, and caught by the bug, had decided to make a career of acting. Clare suspected that his decision had created quite a family drama. She had caught a hint of something from Maura on the phone: reluctance to discuss the reason Robert had left Oxford, evasiveness as to why he had changed career midstream. But whatever it was that had influenced his decision to follow a career on the stage, they were obviously supporting him, making the most of it. Clare was their sole connection with that world, hence the invitation.

The other guests were three couples nearer to Maura's age than Clare's. Married couples of course. The Noah's Ark rule applied here too.

She had known the Olivers from her university days, when she had babysat for them. Their house had become a second home, and getting to know them eased her path into the ways of the middle classes. She had remained a friend over the years, and they had followed her career with interest.

John had rarely been there, in the early days. As a young man on the way to the top of his profession, his family time was limited. His application had paid off handsomely. He was a successful barrister now, a QC for more than a decade – and, more importantly, well respected. Maura and John had had only two small children when she first knew them, but there were now five. Robert, nineteen, was the eldest and the only son. The 'baby', Sophie, was now eleven. Four girls and a boy, attractive like their parents. She had enjoyed seeing the girls tonight. They had been handing round the nibbles before dinner and telling Clare all about Robert being on the telly.

They lived in Cultra, in Northern Ireland's green belt. There had been a gradual exodus from south Belfast during the eighties, when the IRA had taken to shooting judges and lawyers who crossed their paths. Catholic judges had been particularly targeted. So a move from south Belfast with its accessibility to the Catholic housing estates was pragmatic.

They had reached the pudding stage in the meal. Clare had eaten too much, but was still trying to fit in Maura's perfect crème caramel. She had been placed beside a man who worked as a planner. God he was boring. He seemed to find everything he said worth repeating. His name was Mervyn Clark. His wife Joyce was a teacher at a boys' school.

It had been hard work. Mervyn filled Clare in relentlessly on his life. He was busy busy busy these days. There was so much development. Belfast was mushrooming. Laganside. The Waterfront. Had she walked along the river? Had she seen or been in the new pubs on the water's edge? It was truly remarkable. Belfast was becoming the Venice of the North. 'The Celtic Tiger has nothing on us,' he assured her.

Mervyn had a rather strangulated Northern Irish accent. As he honked and brayed his way through one yarn after another, Clare was reminded of Philip Larkin's description of the Belfast voice as 'an argot of motor horns'. Mervyn did, however, mention one thing that caught her fancy. He was in the middle of some long-winded ramble about the position of pedestrian crossings. His job, he explained, was to determine the 'desire lines'.

'Desire lines?' Clare repeated. 'What are desire lines?'

'Well,' Mervyn began to explain. 'There are places in the road where people naturally *wish* to cross. That's where the planners situate the crossing. When they don't get it right you find that there's a certain spot where people tend to cross anyway. Like in a park. You come across a path worn away.'

Clare liked the phrase. It seemed too exotic, too poetic for something as ordinary as planning, but Mervyn assured her it was the accepted term.

The conversation drifted to the standard of contemporary art in Northern Ireland. Maura and John had an impressive collection, and Mervyn desperately wanted Clare to know that he knew this. He also was a knowledgeable collector, and clearly felt in his element. He brayed wetly in Clare's left ear, telling her who was who in the Northern Ireland art scene. 'Basil Blackshaw, Neil Shawcross, Colin Middleton, T.P. Flanagan, Tom Carr, Ross Wilson, David Crone, Rita Duffy,' he intoned.

She felt like answering, 'Pray for us.' It sounded like one of the litanies she had learnt as a child at the novena.

Her smile hurt: she could feel the muscles in her jaw seize up. She looked round for a bit of moral support and caught the eye of Robert Oliver, who was grinning widely at her obvious predicament.

He leaned across the table towards her. 'Do *you* collect art, Clare?'

'Hardly! As you should know, or will find out promptly, they don't pay actors that well.' She smiled, realising she had been a bit short with him. 'I mean, if I could afford it, then I'd love a few original paintings, but I'm afraid my budget permits just framed posters at the minute. When I'm rich, darling! Though that seems most unlikely at the moment, with ne'er a starring role in sight.'

Mervyn seemed to take this as his cue to advise her what to look out for when these mythical riches arrived. He droned on about his various purchases, and his extraordinary eye for a bargain. Apparently he *scoured* – he emphasised the word with satisfied glee – all the auction rooms. There was no stopping him.

He caught the eye of his wife opposite and she nodded her head vigorously, dutifully. Clare suspected she had heard this particular conversation of Mervyn's in one form or another before. She seemed to know when to nod her assent without appearing to listen.

'Oh yes, I've a quare eye for an art bargain though I say it myself. I've had some great finds. We're invited to all the openings,' he said – as if this was something remarkable.

Clare groaned inwardly, and asked him brightly if he had other interests besides art.

'Oh,' he said, beaming at her question. 'Funny you should ask. I've been doing a bit of the amateur drama recently. Just played the lead in a Ray Cooney. Heard of him yourself?'

Was there anyone in this bloody country who wasn't an actor of some sort? That was probably what was wrong with the lot of them. They all thought they were starring in some B western.

Fortunately at this stage someone initiated a move towards

the drawing room, and she took the chance to escape from boring old Mervyn and plumped herself down beside Robert, who had got great craic out of her obvious discomfort.

'God, where did they dig him up?' she asked.

'He plays golf with Dad. Isn't he a pain in the arse? Mum plays tennis with Joyce. She's nice, though. She coached me for GCSE French.'

Clare hadn't run into Robert on any of her last few visits to the Olivers'. He had been away at university, or perhaps out and about with his friends. He was a clever boy, she knew, and had got phenomenally high exam results and an exhibition to Oxford to read Law. So it had surprised her to find that he had dropped out of college and was hoping to make a full-time career of acting. He had managed to get an Equity card in a remarkably short period, by landing the lead in a TV play made by BBC NI. It had obviously given him too much hope and ambition too soon, but he'd have to find that out for himself. She wasn't about to get into the role of dampening his hopes at this stage.

Robert had been a few months into the second year of his law degree when he quit. As the only son, it had almost been a given that he was to follow John to the Bar. Knowing Robert, as she had since he was about three, she felt very comfortable with him. He had grown into a rather attractive young man. Not necessarily to her taste, too pretty for her, but he had the sort of looks that were currently in vogue, good juve lead looks. He'd look well in a Calvin Klein ad or a beer commercial. Well, at least he had an engaging personality. He was easy to talk to, and she found herself responding to his charm.

It had been a while since she had relaxed in the company of a man, and possibly because she found this one unthreatening, she did just that. He had that eagerness about his new profession that she had lost over the years, reality having set in. He wanted to know everything she could tell him. He was hungry. He'd always followed her television career, he told her earnestly.

'Surely you mean lack of it,' she grimaced. 'At the moment anyway.'

'No, *really*.' He was gazing at her intently. 'It was knowing you that got me interested in acting in the first place. We used to be so thrilled as kids when we saw you on the TV. There's our babysitter, we'd tell everyone. I expect you're sick listening to all of this all the time.'

Despite herself, she was flattered. 'No I'm not. To tell you the truth I haven't done much telly in ages, except for a small job a while back. I've been working mainly in the theatre. I actually prefer it, but the money's not great. Unfortunately the gaps between jobs are too long.'

'What was the television part?' he asked, gazing at her with admiration.

'Oh, just a small part in *The Bill*, and that was over two months ago. In fact, it's going out this week, and I'm hoping that someone out there will see it, think I'm wonderful, maybe give me a very big part in something else – though I doubt it.'

'Why do you doubt it?' he said. 'I think you're brilliant.' He smiled at her; he had a beautiful smile. 'And you're gorgeous too.'

'Not in this I'm not, I'm playing a battered wife.'

'Well, just wait, something will come out of it. I bet I'm right.'

'I hope you are. I'll buy you a drink if it does.'

'You're on!'

At this point Maura was motioning for Clare to rejoin the conversation with the others. The port was produced and exclaimed upon. Mervyn practically had an orgasm drinking his. '1985! What a year.'

The remainder of the evening passed in a pleasant haze.

She was glad she hadn't brought her car, even if it did mean accepting a lift from ghastly Mervyn and mild-mannered

Joyce, who had been 'on the water'. So Mervyn could relax and finish off the port, Clare thought unkindly.

She gave them directions, and had a secret chuckle at what they must be thinking of her Côte de Peaceline address. They lived in south Belfast, so it wasn't particularly out of their way, except socially of course.

Living in London for almost seventeen years had made her blasé about the social distinctions. Actors in London were impressed with this address; she had forgotten the Ulster middle-class attitude was entirely different. Mind you, there was probably more true snobbery in England, but she rarely encountered it. Actors were classless. To be fair to Joyce and Mervyn though, they drove her home without commenting, and seemed intrigued that she had left London to come and live here.

She passed on the real reason, saying she was a bit fed up with London and wanted to be near her father. He was getting old, she explained.

'Fed up with London. I'm not surprised. Stuck in tubes every day, I couldn't bear it!' said Mervyn. And he began a peroration about the joys of living in Northern Ireland. These bonuses included the convenience to the sea, the affordability of good housing, the burgeoning restaurant life, and the joy of the new Waterfront Hall. Marvellous addition to the city, marvellous! He and Joyce were never out of the place.

'You should work for the Tourist Board, Mervyn,' Clare said, and was rewarded by a laugh of pleasure. She told them she was looking for a flat to rent until she could buy, and they promised to get a friend, an estate agent, to look out something suitable for her. Maybe she had been overhasty in judging them, she thought, as she watched the brightly shining lights of the BMW indicating their route out of the little street.

Clare turned her key in the door as quietly as she could. She was reminded suddenly of the late nights in her first year at college when the sound of her mother's voice calling, 'Is that you, Clare?' — the mixture of relief and anxiety in it palpable — would startle her on her way in.

This time Tommy was waiting up, sitting stiffly in his ancient dressing gown, a cup in his hand. She felt insanely peeved.

'Daddy, there's no need to wait up for me. I told you I'd probably be late.'

'I wasn't waiting on you at all. I got up to make myself some Milk of Magnesia.' He indicated the cup. 'I've that oul pain in my chest again. I think it's wind, anyway I can't sleep . . . Oh, Father Lorcan was down lookin' ye.'

'What did he want?'

'Sure, he didn't say, something about the drama I would imagine. He says he'll drop in tomorrow. And Paula was on the phone. God she never shuts up that one. Tommy this and Tommy that.'

'Daddy, you *love* her. You've remembered she's coming tomorrow?'

'I know, that's why she was ringing. She says she'll get the bus down from the airport and not to pick her up. I'm off to my bed. Goodnight.'

Clare drank three glasses of water in quick succession — hangover precautions. Paula wouldn't forgive her if she wasn't in form for her visit.

After several years of hard graft, Paula was now reasonably well established as a writer, and was just about making a living from it. Clare envied the way Paula had applied herself to this new-found career, with a vehemence she had never had in the days when she had been an actress. Perhaps she had found her métier. She and Clare had met years ago when both had been struggling actors. Paula had talent, and good looks, but after ten years of slogging it out and not getting into the top ranks she had quit and started to write, leaving the cattle calls to everyone else. Encouraged by a radio drama producer she was seeing, she wrote a sitcom for Radio Four. It was fairly naff, but well directed and had a few names in the cast, and women writers were in demand, so it was enough to get her noticed and get a few commissions going.

After this, she certainly developed an unerring instinct for sleeping with the next right person: someone who could commission or direct a play or screenplay of hers and help further her career. She hadn't managed yet to bag the big one, the Spielberg. The nearest she'd come to it, she joked, was her last boyfriend, who after he'd had a couple of drinks looked alarmingly like ET.

Clare was never sure whether to be aghast at Paula's

behaviour or to laugh at it, but she excused it in spite of reservations, because Paula was so up-front about it and so very entertaining and irreverent.

Tommy had met Paula once before, when she had come over with Clare a year ago, and despite his reservations about the outrageously affected accent, and her frequent use of the F word ('no call for language like that, not very ladylike') he had really taken to her. She had flirted with him nonstop and to Clare's amazement he had lapped it up, allowing Paula to buy him drinks in the pub, and to link his arm on the way home. By the time she went back to London they'd become firm friends.

Now she was here again, rushing in full of greetings, hugs and exclamations just as Clare was setting the table for lunch. Somehow she moved the very air with her arrival, filling it with her exotic French scent and her personality. Although she was of medium height, her legs were long and shapely, and always set off by a very short skirt. She never wore trousers, even in the depths of winter.

A mane of long, bright auburn hair, the colour out of a bottle, added to her allure. Though it was obvious to all who knew her well that she had a redhead personality, the trick was to guess which had come first: the hair colour or the personality. She had large grey eyes, and wore loads of makeup on them, which was just about excusable since her skin was clear and she left it clean and scrubbed. Her big wide mouth with its ready smile made her irresistible.

Today, she was wearing a leopardskin coat. 'Fake! It's fake! Don't worry!' she mouthed quickly as she plopped her piece of designer luggage on Tommy's presidential rug.

She must have made a striking figure in the little street; Clare could practically hear the mass twitching of curtains. Indeed, the taxi driver who had just deposited her at the door was taking an awfully long time to get his car restarted.

Clare and Paula hugged, and then she turned her attention

to Tommy, who had risen to his feet with a broad grin on his face.

'Well, Tommy, and how are you? You're looking fit as a fiddle and sexy as ever.'

'I can't complain. I have my health, thank God, and that's all that matters.' He eyed her up and down approvingly. 'You're well mended.'

'Oh don't!' she shrieked. 'I know that's your way of saying I've got fat. I'm going on a diet as soon as I get back to London. *No* more drink. But since I'm in Ireland I can't start yet. I know you'd all be insulted. Shall we go to the pub for lunch?'

They didn't serve lunch in the pub, and Clare had actually made some soup, but her father was up and had his coat on before she could open her mouth to protest. They made quite a trio in the pub, Tommy undoubtedly the man of the moment, arriving with a girl on each arm.

The few regulars eyed Paula with a mixture of awe and disapproval. She was enjoying it all immensely. After insisting on buying the drinks she sat down and threw her coat over the back of the corner snug and turned to them both. 'Well, Tommy, is it great having her back? You know all her friends in London think she's gone completely potty. I've been sent over to check out her mental stability.'

Clare looked at her father. He was thinking things over before he answered.

'Well now, Paula, this is Clare's home, and I'm delighted to have her here. I keep telling her this will always be her home. But sure you know what they say, a change is as good as a rest. Maybe this wee break will help her sort herself out.' He lifted his pint. 'Now if you girls want to chat, excuse me a minute, I'll just take my drink over to oul Jimmy there.'

The bright wide face beamed at them from across the bar. Paula waved gaily, then turned to Clare. 'Central Casting,' she laughed. Then she looked at Clare, her face serious, concerned.

'Well, how's it been, my love? I can't believe you've stayed this long. Have you heard from Tim since I talked to you?'

Clare shook her head. 'No, and I've been feeling too murderous to call him. I know it'll solve my problems about buying a place. But I feel so hurt that he lied to me about where he was getting the money for the other half of the flat.'

'Are you surprised? He's a man. They're all spineless gits! Anyway, how are you? You *look* good. Tommy seems delighted to have you here.'

'Daddy's been great. I actually don't mind being here, for the minute, but that's because I know it's just temporary. I'll go crazy if I don't get somewhere of my own eventually.'

'Clare, wise up. You can't seriously think of staying here. What will you do? For a living, I mean.'

'Well, I might give acting up entirely. I mean, you'd be the first person to tell me what a crap profession it is. I suppose I could always do something else.'

'Like what?'

'Like go back to Queen's. Do some postgrad work as a mature student, that sort of thing.'

'But it's only April; surely the term starts in October. What would you do between now and then?'

'Maybe some temporary teaching. Frances says I can put my name on some sort of list.'

'Well, I think you're crazy. You're simply running away. This isn't you, Clare. You've cast yourself in some distorted melodrama. You need to move on. Get over Tim. What do you want from life? Acting is a lousy career for a woman. You are at the mercy of too many assholes. So you either accept it and roll with it, or do something else. Close the book on Tim. You told me only last year you couldn't ever imagine having kids with him. That says a lot.'

Tommy came back over then, and they finished their drinks. The place was starting to fill up with Friday customers freshly cleaned up and ready for action, a serious night's drinking ahead of them. A smell that was a mixture of smoke, and sour beer wafted round them.

Clare had planned a night out with Frances and Paula. But in the meantime, there were two small houses for rent in the university area that Clare had appointments to view. And Mervyn, true to his word, had lined up a flat. She felt guilty about all the unkind thoughts she'd had about him. She wanted Paula's opinion, so they went back up to the house to get organised. She had to laugh as she watched Paula waving goodbye to the boozers as if she was off on a world tour.

It was the first time she'd had Paula to herself. Even though they spoke regularly on the phone, Clare always felt restricted. Her daddy worried about the bill. Besides, the phone was in the living room, so even if Paula called her, there was little in the way of privacy, and it wasn't the same as a good heart-to-heart. They were deep in conversation when there was a light tap on the door and Father Lorcan came in.

'Hello, Clare, have you got a minute? Did Tommy tell you I was in earlier? We were wondering if you had an hour to audition a few more Aggies tomorrow? Oh,' he said, suddenly seeing Paula. 'I'm sorry to intrude. I didn't realise you had company.'

Paula's face was a picture when Clare introduced him as Father Lorcan. They chatted briefly, and he accepted with a resigned look that tomorrow wouldn't suit and she would have to miss the auditions.

Clare explained that Paula was a writer, and mentioned the titles of some of her plays. To her surprise he managed to endear himself to Paula forever by actually having heard her last effort on Afternoon Theatre. Still, despite the apparent ease of the chat, Clare felt flustered by his presence, and was glad to see him go. She said goodbye, closed the door, and turned to Paula. 'Shite! Maybe I should have offered him a cup of tea. What's wrong?'

Paula was staring at her, open-mouthed, slowly shaking her

head. 'You know perfectly well what's wrong my love. Christ! If ever there was a reason to allow priests to marry. He's gorgeous.'

'Please, Paula. I have still enough Catholicism drummed into me to find that a bit weird.'

'Oh, for Christ's sake, Clare.'

'Exactly! That's who he lives his life for, so let's change the subject.'

'You're being a bit touchy here. Have I hit a nerve?'

'Please, Paula.'

'OK, darling, I'm just being naughty. But I might go to Mass with you on Sunday! I bet he looks just great in all the gear! And what kind of a name is Lorcan anyway? Lovely Lorcan, Lascivious Lorcan, Lecherous Lorcan.'

Despite herself Clare laughed. Paula was outrageous. 'God forgive you, Paula Miller, you're dreadful! Anyway, you know I don't go to Mass any more. Now, in case you've forgotten, you're helping me house-hunt and we need to ring Frances about tonight.'

The rest of the weekend flew. Belfast was a great place to visit. Paula was right, people seemed to want to impress. There was a feeling of trying to atone for the world's low opinion, something in everyone that spelled out 'We're OK, and we're not monsters; *like* us, please?' Visitors responded. They enjoyed the ritual, the courtship. Paula was wined and dined and entertained. Even Peter, Brid's rather stolid husband, seemed to come to life in her presence.

On Monday Clare regretfully took Paula to the airport, sorry to see her leave, the thought of being alone again making her feel vulnerable once more.

She decided to take the back roads to Aldergrove, across the mountain. It was a dank, miserable day. She was glad not to be getting on a plane. She drove under the wishing trees, a long avenue of trees which lined the country road. In summer, it formed a green frothy canopy. But now, the buds were not yet showing, and all that remained were a few straggly leaves that had held out against the winter's wind and rain. The bare branches showed like black bony fingers outlined against the ragged grey sky, the rain slanting through in sheets.

When they were children and drove under these trees, Tommy would tell them to make a wish, since the fairies had caused the trees to huddle like that, and they were flying round under the leaves at the top, catching the wishes as they flew up into the sky. Every wish they caught came true.

Clare told this to Paula, who was enchanted by the old yarn.

'I'll make a wish,' she said. 'That you'll come to your senses and come back to London.'

'It doesn't work if you say what it is out loud.' Clare said, and wished silently that Tim would love her again, but her wish fell to the ground and the deadness in her heart told her she had wasted a wish.

She returned via the motorway. Alone again, she had no need for the scenic route. She thought about Paula's visit, and reflected that the weekend had been useful. Apart from loving the company, she had, with Paula's guidance, made some progress. They had looked at some properties, and the flat that Mervyn's friend had set up she could have in two weeks' time. It was spacious, the best of the lot. The young couple, academics, who owned it were off to the USA for a year. The only problem was that they wanted her to take it for a minimum of six months. She said she would call in a few days. With Paula still insisting she should come back to London, she was unsure about committing herself.

Later on that afternoon, Diana solved all the wondering by ringing to tell Clare she had had an availability check for a film. It was being shot in Belfast and Dublin, and they wanted to see Clare for the part of a woman journalist, early thirties. 'The film crowd saw you on *The Bill*, dear, and you know how casting directors are: if you can play one battered person, you can play another. Sooo this film role is a woman who gets beaten up by her terrorist husband. Not a comedy as you can see. Lovely scene where she tells the chap, her lover, what she thinks of him – just pretend you're talking to Tim. It's a good speech, great dialogue. Pity you haven't a fax, but I'll stick it in the post. They've just faxed me the relevant pages. Anyway you're heavily pencilled in. Fingers crossed, they'll let me know tomorrow, and . . . hang on a second – there's a theatre part as well.' There was a rustling as she consulted her list. 'Are you interested in reading for a new play Lagan are doing? Rehearsals starting next week?'

'Yes, of course!' Clare was impatient with Diana. She'd asked her several times to fix up an interview with the theatre.

'Yes, this is a biggie, it's not a bad part actually. University lecturer falls for a terrorist. So darling, it's not great money, the theatre gig, but if you get it they'll pay your subsid. I told them you were merely over there on a visit. I think they're seeing the locals just as a courtesy. It's a new play. Great young director – you'll love him, Declan Costello? Certainly worth reading for, I think he's going places, and the writer has just won some award for his last play. It might transfer to the Bush or the Tricycle.'

The audition was the following day. Hoping fervently, as always, that she wouldn't be rejected, she went to see the director. She found him intelligent, funny, and easy to talk to, not that that was any guarantee, but it helped. The play *was* good, it was written from the Protestant viewpoint in Northern Ireland, something only starting to be covered now, a welcome break from a lot of the plays that people were starting to tire of. The part was, as Diana had told her, extremely well written.

Elaine, the young woman she hoped to play, was a lecturer who gets involved with a paramilitary leader. Clare thought she read well, and obviously Declan Costello thought so too, because to her amazement he offered her the part on the spot. This was a rare occurrence. She accepted, and they agreed he would have the theatre phone Diana to sort out the details.

Robert Oliver was sitting outside in the foyer when she came out. His face lit up on seeing her, and he was making his way over when his name was called. She wondered which of the parts he was up for. It might be nice to work with him. When she got back home, she phoned the estate agent and took the flat for six months.

Next day Diana called to say the film company wanted her as well. Maybe her luck was changing.

Tommy took the news well. 'I'm delighted for you; being out of work doesn't suit you. Mind you, I'll be sorry to see you go. I think I was beginning to get too fond of your cooking.' He paused, seeming to feel he had said too much, then added, 'You know that's an odd thing. My two sisters Jeannie and Maisie, God rest them, neither of them could cook. It was their natures, too sour both of them. I think it curdles the food. Your mother was a good cook; she was always in good form, you see. Ah well, they'll hardly be much in need of the cooking now.' He looked at her, suddenly an old man. Something tore at her. She swallowed, close to tears.

'Daddy I'll come over every now and then and cook a meal for you.'

'Now don't be making promises you can't keep. If you do get over the odd time, well and good, if not, sure haven't I managed well on my own these last five years?'

It was one of those awful bitterly cold days when she moved out, wet, dreich, raining sideways. Donegal weather – the only thing missing was the smell of peat. The dampness crept through her being like a wet fog. It mirrored her mood. Not for the first time did she feel she was insane even being here. She hadn't much to move, one journey took it all, and she almost burst into tears when Tommy suggested she take the curry spices.

The flat was lovely though. She felt very lucky to get it. Ground floor of a large house, so she would have use of the garden. The flat had three large rooms and a hall, French windows leading to the back garden and, at the front, a wide driveway. The couple who owned it had left all their appliances. It was worth the extra. Decorated in nice inoffensive colours, muted beiges, greys.

'A riot of greige,' Paula had called it, but that was easy to live with. Clare could add a few coloured cushions to brighten it up if she needed to. Paula had been very funny when she told her about the part in the play.

'What's the director's name again? Declan? Isn't that what the glamorous priest is called?'

'No, *his* name is Lorcan.'

'Well, they're all Gaelic to me. I noticed last night in a rerun of *Cracker* one of the actors, the nice one who killed himself, is called Lorcan. Honestly darling! Lorcan and Declan, sounds like obscene pastimes!' She chuckled wickedly at her own joke. She was delighted Clare was going to rent the flat, and she was right really – Clare knew she needed to get out of west Belfast. It had been good to come there and find her bearings, but she needed some independence now, and socially she would find it easier to get by on this side of town.

The flat was off the Stranmillis Road, near the theatre and the university, and best of all near the PE Centre. Apart from the occasional swim, she had neglected her exercise. Now she would be left with no excuse. Things were looking up. The drama group had met the night before she was due to leave, and she had gone along with a light heart, bursting in fact with good will towards them, her confidence boosted by her job, and the news that the film company had offered her the part as well. It was ever thus in this business, she thought – swings and merry-go-rounds. The drama group members had congratulated her and promised to take a special trip to see the play. Breda was familiar with the writer of course, and had seen his first play at a fringe venue during the Belfast Festival. She would have given them all a tutorial on new Irish writing there and then, if Lorcan hadn't suggested a sort of farewell drink.

The bar was unusually crowded. Tommy was already there with Jimmy having a wee one. There was a crowd of Germans who were over on some sort of tour of the Troubles spots – the murals (or murials as the locals called them), the Republican Plot, and all the other equally tasteless gems of interest to tourists. The Germans were chatting volubly to the locals. There had obviously been large quantities of drink taken, judging by the level of noise.

The dramaturgs, as Breda liked to refer to the group, edged their way into a corner near the door. Clare found herself squashed up against Lorcan, and could only hear what he was saying if he virtually talked straight into her ear. It was disconcertingly intimate: she was glad she was leaving the group. She was sexually disturbed by this man, and was unsure if he was aware of the effect he was having on her, or even if he was doing it deliberately, though she dismissed this thought instantly. She was starting to think like Paula.

After about an hour it all became rather wearing: the smoke was making Clare's eyes water, and the constant shouting across the din was making her hoarse. She made her excuses and left. She still had quite a lot of packing and sorting to do, and she thought she would make a curry for Tommy and leave it for him for tomorrow. She was glad the 'weemen' from meals-on-wheels were still coming three days a week. She promised herself she would try to get over at least one other day if she could find the time. She would miss him, although it was a relief to get back to some sort of independence.

There was a knock at the door soon after she got back. It was Lorcan. He seemed hesitant.

'I thought I might beg a cup of tea.'

'I'll put the kettle on. Did you get fed up with the din? I was hoarse myself.'

'No, I wanted to say goodbye properly. I didn't – I didn't feel we got much of a chance to talk there.' He smiled shyly. 'I've got used to seeing you.'

'Sure, didn't I say I'd come over occasionally, and I thought you were all coming to the play.'

'Well.' He paused and looked at her, his green eyes clouded. He had a rather endearing way of tilting his head to the side, confidentially, when he talked. 'I'm going to miss you. I mean I'm not sure how to say this, or even if I should be saying it at all, but I've enjoyed you being here. And anyone can tell that it's given Tommy a new lease of life. He's always talked so much about you. He's very proud of you.' He stopped, as if he thought he had said too much. His voice became hearty.

'So then I'll look forward to you coming back over to see the production. Though I'm sure that'll hardly be a priority,' he added hastily. He broke off, uncertain now, his eyes not quite meeting hers.

She was standing in the kitchen, the smell of onions making her eyes water. She turned away to make the tea, her whole being vibrantly aware of his presence. The feeling of desire washed over her ... she longed for him. Why? Why him? Was it simply that she hadn't been with a man for a while – or was it *this* man?

He was a priest for God's sake – for God's sake – she smiled at that thought and he asked her softly, 'What is it?'

'Nothing. I was thinking how I've had more curries since I got back than I had the whole previous year in London, and we have an Indian restaurant at the corner of our street.'

She made the tea and put a plate of biscuits out. Lorcan was in the front room watching something on TV. They were acting completely naturally, yet there was an air of unreality about it all. The atmosphere was heightened: she felt as if she were stoned. She was utterly aware of him, and the feeling was intensely disturbing. She drank her tea quickly, burning her mouth, and went back into the small kitchen, pretending to concentrate on making the meal. There was a garble of voices from the TV in the other room, the tap dripping, the sizzle of onions, the clink of his cup against the saucer. She had given him the priest's cup (or the doctor's) – Minton, a china she had bought while living there, just the one cup and saucer. She made a silent inventory of all the noises as she cooked. They didn't speak, until eventually she said from the kitchen, 'Would you like more tea?'

'Yes, please.' His voice smiled at her.

As she bent over to pour, her hair fell against his hand. He brushed it lightly, touching her face as he did. The hairs on her arms stood on end.

'You have lovely hair.'

'Thank you. All out of a bottle – the red glints I mean.'

'It looks very real,' he said, not believing her.

She laughed, 'Well you're right, but most people think I dye it.'

'They're only jealous,' he said, and then, as if realising the nature of the conversation, becoming suddenly alive to the fact that he was flirting with her, he finished his tea, said good-night, and left, closing the door quickly behind him.

Shakily, Clare sat down on the sofa. Her head was pound-ing; she could feel a pulse as if her brain was bursting. Her thoughts raced. She needed to be out of the way when her father came in, as he shortly would. He would know some-thing was up.

She abandoned the curry. She'd finish it in the morning. Next day she moved.

The pattern of her days changed then. Belfast seemed not all that different from anywhere else when she was working. Though the rehearsals were demanding, she enjoyed the chal-lenge of working again. The cast knitted well together, she liked the director. The script was good, and the writer was easy and open to suggestions from the cast. There was a good buzz, plenty of energy. It felt like the play would do well. Robert Oliver was part of the cast; it was his first stage play.

'You're a jammy bastard!' she said, laughing, when she saw him. 'It takes some people years to get started.'

They exchanged a few remarks about the dinner party and the dreaded Mervyn, and had a few laughs about her 'art collection'.

'You'll have to come for coffee and see it sometime,' she joked.

'I can't wait,' he said, gazing straight into her eyes, and for the first time she noticed something disturbing about him, but dismissed the thought quickly.

He was a positive addition to the cast. Gratifyingly, he was good. He took it seriously. He was playing a small part, but one that would get him noticed – he was killed at the end of the first act. Maybe he would do well. He certainly seemed to be on a roll. The play was called *Sticks and Stones*. There were six in the cast, two women, four men, no change there. But all the parts were good and – best of all – hers – was the lead. She hadn't worked with any of the actors before, but they seemed at the first reading to be a likeable bunch. No prima donnas, or stars. Declan Costello, the director, was full of energy and inspiration. She knew she was going to enjoy doing the show. Niall, the actor playing opposite her, was energetic and interesting. He was about her own age; she knew of his work, and thought she'd hear a lot more of him. He was originally from Dublin, but lived in London. His Belfast accent was brilliant. He lived with a girl from Andersonstown, he told them. Modestly giving her the credit for his ease with the accent, he sent himself up in an exaggerated Belfast nasal. 'Sure she coached me for the reading, so she did.'

Clare was called nearly every session, being in most scenes. It was hard getting back into the way of it all. She was left with little time to get over to see Tommy. She missed him a lot and phoned him regularly, but the phone definitely was not his medium. Three minutes, till the pips in his head compelled him to hang up. She would have to make time to go over. She sensed during her last chat with him that he was feeling a bit neglected; not that he'd say, but she could tell.

It was while she was in the pool during a free afternoon, the third week of rehearsals, she noticed a young man jogging around the diving pool wearing some sort of flotation device. It took her a second to realise it was Robert. She didn't see a lot of him in rehearsals since they had only one scene together and they hadn't begun intensive work on it yet. They were to go through it tomorrow, and Declan wanted them word-perfect. Off the book.

'What on earth are you at?'

'Oh, this.' He grinned at her and pointed to the belt. 'I hurt my knee jogging and this is good exercise.' He made a funny little bobbing move. 'Keeps me fit. Do you want to try? Go on.' He began to extricate himself from the belt, and attempted to fit it on around her waist.

'Leave it,' she said. 'I think I'll stick to swimming.'

'No, seriously, have a go. It's great.'

They were hanging on to the side of the pool together. It was too deep to stand.

She mentioned that she hadn't been back to see his parents. While they talked she was conscious of a growing feeling of discomfort. For some reason it mattered to her that her hair was wet and she was in a swimsuit. She was sure as well that she had red weals round her eyes from her goggles. Damn! Then she thought, Why the hell am I worrying about this? I'm a lunatic.

She took a long appraising look at him, aware that he was doing the same to her. They seemed to be able to talk more freely away from the others. She still hadn't totally overcome the feeling that she was a friend of his parents, and not of people of his generation, though that was changing gradually.

Robert looked good wet. Slim, skinny even, but with broad shoulders. His hair was light brown with sunstreaks. He wore it long, and his grey eyes were fringed with extremely dark, thick lashes. His nose was slightly off-centre – possibly it had been broken, but the flaw stopped him from having too-perfect looks, and added to his attractiveness. His teeth were white and even, and he smiled easily. The one physical attribute he lacked was height. He couldn't have been above five foot six – her height. He was undoubtedly a charmer, perhaps a little too much so.

She returned to her swimming, and was getting out to leave when he called her back and suggested a drink sometime, just the two of them. 'I live up here now. I've moved into a wee house in the Holy Land.' (This was so called because of the names of the streets: Palestine, Jerusalem, Damascus, Carmel.)

'I'd have absolutely no street cred if I still lived with the parents in Cultra now I'm an actor. So we're neighbours.'

He was chatting her up, she thought. Well, well, how funny. Doing their scene tomorrow would be interesting.

The cast rehearsed unceasingly from ten till six each day. Declan had a very clear idea of what he wanted, no faffing about. The writer, Iain, a self-effacing young man, seemed to leave most of the talking to Declan. The actors went through the play working almost sentence by sentence, wringing meaning from the lines and questioning motives until they saw each possible approach to the part they were playing. She got a buzz from it all, found Declan stimulating and fresh to work with. Some directors using this approach could come across as posers, but Declan had everything well thought out, and was inspiring, despite the extensive note sessions at the end of each day.

This part was a gem. Nicely complicated, it was the story of a woman in her thirties who gets involved, in spite of herself, with a terrorist she meets while tutoring in jail, and ultimately causes the death of a young man. The playwright had written the lines with such intensity that she felt they were her own words. She wanted to make a success of the role, to make it work for herself and for the production. Robert was playing the younger terrorist, whom Clare (as Elaine) ultimately betrays to save the skin of her lover – played by Niall. The argument and plot, although heavily political, were skilfully lacking in polemic. It remained to see how the Belfast audiences, sick of watching everyone else's portrayal of them, would react to it.

Robert's attitude towards her had altered somewhat since their meeting at the pool – he was now openly flirtatious. This wasn't out of place in the script, since in their scene together Robert's character attempted to seduce Elaine.

During the technical run she was standing at the side of the stage waiting to go on when Robert came up behind her and grabbed her. 'Good luck,' he said. 'You're a star.' And before she could reply he had kissed her roundly on the mouth.

She recounted the episode to Paula later that night.

'Well, my love, I'll resist the term toy boy, but if he asks you out, why not go for it? It would do your ego no end of good.'

'He is quite dishy, but he's only a child, and I'm a friend of his parents, for God's sake. What's wrong with me that the only decent men I seem to meet these days are either priests or teenagers?'

That was the first reference to Lorcan that she had made. Some deep feeling had still prevented her from discussing the incident of the hair with Paula, or with Frances for that matter: it would disappear if she spoke it out loud. Expressed in words, the memory would appear tawdry, commonplace. She still felt she had imagined it. Taken it out of her dreams.

Paula passed over the priest reference without comment. After she had run out of suggestions of rude things to do with young men, they laughed, then went on to discuss the usual topic: Tim and Kezia.

It was after midnight when they hung up, and Clare fell asleep at once. Rehearsals were exhausting, but so were conversations about ex-lovers.

Clare had worried throughout the rehearsal period that the play wouldn't be a success, so it was a wonder she was able to coax a performance out on the opening night. There had been a few articles in the local papers about her return to her home city to star in this new play. What if they hated her?

Her fears were groundless. To her delight, it was greeted with rave reviews, not always easy to garner in Belfast, as there was something about the people that grudged success. Clare was light-headed with relief, only then permitting herself to acknowledge how scared she had been of being in a flop. She hoped, as ever, that this success would lead to more work. She was thrilled when Diana, who had braved the ceasefire and flown over for the opening night, told her that the film job in

Dublin looked definite. A done deal.

The opening-night fun was enhanced by Diana's flamboy-
ant presence. She totally disarmed the artistic director, a dour
Scot, who had skulked around during the rehearsal period
barely speaking to the cast. He was pissed off that he hadn't
directed this critical success. She also dealt sweetly with Robert
– who naturally was on the lookout for a London agent. Clare
introduced them and mentioned that he would like to drop in
for a chat when he was next in London. Diana promised to
give it some thought when she got back, and get in touch with
him.

'Sex on a stick, darling!' she said to Clare. 'And young!
What age is he?'

'Nearly twenty,' Clare said. 'Sickening, isn't it?'

'Hmm, darling, looks like he's got the hots for you.'

Diana was also the soul of tact to Aislin, the other young
keenie in the cast (who was playing Robert's sister, a small
and thankless part). And this was despite the fact that Aislin
had her agent-seeking antlers out, and was committing the
unforgivable offence of asking Diana to sign her on the spot,
directly after the show.

'Ordinary,' Diana told Clare later. 'No stage presence what-
soever. She'll need more than an unpronounceable Irish name
to make it.'

Clare hadn't really been all that struck on Aislin, though
they had got along well enough in rehearsal. None the less
she felt a bit mean that she didn't defend her to Diana.

When the fuss in the theatre died down somewhat, Diana
invited the cast and hangers-on back to her hotel, the Europa,
in the centre of town. She had chosen to stay there even
though Clare had suggested the McCausland, a newer and
much nicer hotel.

'The most bombed in Europe,' Diana kept reminding them
delightedly, and generously treated them to several bottles of
rather superior champagne. Declan had the grace to change

their call for notes, from late morning to afternoon. He might have had a mutiny on his hands if he hadn't.

Clare, like the others, got extremely drunk on the champagne. But she managed, despite her state, to resist the drunken passes of Niall – not that they'd have been in a fit state. She had been keenly aware of Robert watching her every move the entire night, no girlfriend visible. At about three in the morning she finally managed to get herself together enough to order a taxi and go home before her head exploded, thankful that she hadn't brought the car.

Next day, she had only vague recollections of the journey home. She remembered the taxi driver telling her he was a Van Morrison fan, and 'Brown Eyed Girl' playing loudly.

As well as being a critical success, the show was a sellout, delighting everyone. During the second week, Clare came out into the bar after the performance and found about eight of the St Brendan's lot waiting for her. Lorcan wasn't with them, and she hated that his absence affected her so much, realising intensely just how much she had longed to see him again.

Breda, in her role as head girl of the group, apologised on his behalf. 'He was on the rota for the Royal Hospital last night and apparently didn't get any sleep.' Breda lowered her voice to a dramatic whisper. '*Two deaths!* He says to tell you he'll try to make it next week.'

Did Clare detect just a hint of satisfaction? Perhaps not, but she managed to swallow her look of disappointment and thanked them profusely for coming. They had loved the play, had had an enjoyable evening and had endless observations about performances. They were most complimentary about hers.

Seamus, who had brought his wife, had several criticisms about the leading man, Niall, and his interpretation of the role. 'Made him a wee bit ordinary, none of the menace you'd expect to find lurking below the surface. After all,' Seamus droned on. 'He was a terrorist, a mass murderer.'

The message was implicit: *he* could have done a better job. She was glad to say goodbye, but felt guilty as usual that she had somehow lost the feeling for real people, although the St Brendan's players only just about fitted this criterion. Tommy was her touchstone, her tap to reality. He would never lose the common touch.

When she went home that evening, she felt for the first time in weeks a profound feeling of sadness. She had been deceiving herself that the incident with Lorcan had been meaningless. Unconsciously, she had been counting the days until she would see him again, silently ticking them off. She had gone into the bar on her way out each night – not essential, although fairly standard for most of the actors. She had scoured the front few rows. She told herself that she had merely wanted to see him to normalise things, but deep down that was not so.

Lorcan O'Carroll had stirred something deep within her, something she did not want to acknowledge. Perhaps, she reasoned, it was largely the result of her general emotional instability, the break-up of her relationship. Ten years was a long time: one got used to being part of a team, thinking for two. It was natural, after all, her longing to have someone, and there was, too, the obvious lack of a sexual life, something she had always taken for granted. Maybe, she thought, she should take Niall up on his offer of a night of sin, an offer he jokingly renewed every couple of days. She still found Robert's attentions flattering. He was like a puppy mooning round her at the side of the stage, talking into her ear, flattering, and stimulating too. It was great for her ego but surely she would be insane to take him seriously. Niall was more her age, he wasn't exactly her usual type physically, but she liked him a lot. He was witty and great fun, so it didn't seem offensive in any way, this come-on of his, in fact it had become something of a running gag with the whole cast.

How, she wondered, had Paula, with *her* track record, stayed celibate since her last big affair almost a year ago? It had been three months since Clare had been with Tim and her libido was not yet subdued. Would that it were.

Paula phoned just as she was on her way to bed.

'I'm going to get into bed and I'll call you right back, OK?'

They chatted, and perhaps because of her mood, she told Paula for the first time about her feelings (fantasies?) about Lorcan. She was aware when she described him brushing her hair with his hand how erotic it sounded when said out loud, and how aroused she was repeating the incident.

'Christ, Clare, you old horror! Why haven't you told me this before? Didn't I tell you he fancied you. He is a gorgeous hunk of manhood. Do you think he's ever done it? Do you know anything about him?'

Clare felt irritated at Paula's flippancy, protective of him. She realised this was why she hadn't mentioned the incident before. It had been better kept a secret, but it was too late now. Paula was agog.

What did she know about him? What did one usually know about priests? was Clare's first thought. 'No, I don't know much about him really, just that he's been in the parish almost a year. One of the priests died, and besides I think the younger ones get moved about quite a bit. He's about my age, and he seems quite well read, and normal, except he's a priest, and, in spite of all the current publicity, I think most of them keep their vows. It's too much of a cliché – I feel embarrassed even talking about it to you. It's such a strong feeling of lust, it unsettles me. Anyway, you met him.'

It was true: telling Paula made her feel emotional. The mixture of the deep taboo and her obvious erotic attraction was best left undisturbed. Her growing desire for him warred with her sensibilities about his being a priest.

'When are you coming over?' asked Paula, interrupting her thoughts.

Clare was overdue a trip to London. Now would be the time to meet Tim, and sort some things out. She was almost ready to face him. She had a few days on the film, but that wasn't for a couple of weeks, after the play finished.

Sundays were a welcome break during runs. She had been invited over to Frances's for dinner, so despite her inclination to lie in until late afternoon, she went over to see Tommy around midday. She took a chicken to roast, and a good head of cabbage, another of his favourites, and some Bramleys for a pie. He had regularly extolled the virtues of cabbage to them throughout their lives, and earlier in the month had managed to enjoy some rather dubious-looking coleslaw provided by 'the weemen' when assured it was made from cabbage. Tony always used to joke that Tommy would be the only person who'd enjoy the food in Russia.

Tommy was pleased to see her, though as ever his greeting was understated. He kept her up to date with local gossip while she cooked for him, and he ate the lunch she served (his dinner, as he called it) with enjoyment.

'I still think it's unnatural the size chickens grow to these days. In my day, before they grew them in cages, they were a lot tastier. They were a luxury too, apart from a wee boiling fowl. A lot scraggier, mind you. They're as big as turkeys now. I read somewhere they have them on the pill, full of hormones or whatever.'

Clare decided not to rise to the bait. 'I deliberately got a big one, Daddy. I thought you could have it cold with a salad during the week.'

'Salad? Sure what would I be doing eating salad in the winter? Are you trying to finish me off?'

'It's spring, Daddy, actually.'

'Well,' he said dubiously, 'I suppose I could make a few sandwiches. Or I could mebbe boil it up for a soup. You know,' he went on, 'we should have asked the wee priest for a meal. They've only oul Minnie Madden cooking for them now up at the parochial house and I believe you wouldn't feed the pigs what she turns out for them. He's lost weight – failed away to nothing. I don't think he's at himself lately. Seems a wee bit depressed.'

Clare began to clear the table. He looked at her, understanding something suddenly, or sensing something. When she didn't speak he said almost nervously, 'I've asked him down for a cup of tea this afternoon. Is that all right?'

'Sure, Daddy, it's your house. You can ask whoever you like.' Her heart thumped in her chest, a strangled pain. She felt he could hear it.

'Anyway,' he went on, 'did you have a bit of a disagreement with him about the play or something?'

'Not at all, sure it's over two weeks since I've seen him.'

His blue eyes searched hers keenly. He knew. He felt it. His face clouded. He kept talking. 'He's been very decent to me, a decent fellow. It's not easy being a priest these days, all that television rubbish they've to put up with. If you ask me, it's all a lot of nonsense.'

Normally Clare would have challenged him on the vagueness of such a remark, but she let it pass and said she would bake an apple tart. She'd brought all the stuff, and they both left it there, knowing whatever it was hadn't gone away, and both wishing it had.

Lorcan rapped the door at four o'clock exactly. His face was friendly, but a mask, no feelings on show, so the conversation was easy. They talked about Clare's play and he promised to get along to the Lagan Theatre sometime during the week as it was the last few days of the run. The talk turned to the forthcoming St Brendan's Players production and how the rehearsals for *Dancing at Lughnasa* were going. Clare had a few uncharitable things to say about Breda's directing talents, and although Lorcan loyally came to her defence, Clare could tell he agreed with her opinion. Seamus's amazing Welsh accent came in for a bit of stick too, and a few chuckles.

'Ah, you're a dreadful girl, Clare, egging me on about poor Seamus. Sure he's a harmless fellow.'

Tommy feigned an interest, but talk soon turned to parish matters, to the obituaries. It seemed at least two people Tommy knew died every month.

Lorcan had been with one of Tommy's old cronies in the hospital when he had died earlier on that week. It always amused Clare to hear her father discuss death so casually. She wondered if it was just his personality, or his age, which allowed him this matter-of-fact attitude. She didn't contribute much, but was impressed by the ease with which the priest chatted to her father. She could see why Tommy had such a high opinion of him. She understood then that, it was precisely this, this ease, which was ultimately his seductiveness. As for desire, *that* feeling, she forcibly suppressed it. He was wearing a T-shirt – he was more muscular than she had thought – and she noticed the hairs on his arms, golden, soft, and had an overwhelming urge to stroke them. She busied herself in the kitchen, and made tea. 'Woman's work' her father used to call it until he realised that it put her in bad form. The apple tart was eventually produced, and the men embarked on a long complimentary conversation about the high quality of her baking.

'Mind you,' Lorcan laughed, 'you wouldn't want oul Winnie next door to know she had any peer in the apple tart field. Tommy would never get another slice from her!'

So he knew all the oul ones, Clare thought. She wondered that he didn't go insane visiting parishioners.

By the time he left, she was beginning to feel the whole surreal nature of the tea party. She wasn't having a day off at all. This had been her best performance all week. If Tommy *had* noticed anything, and something in her sensed that he had, he wasn't saying. They sat together and watched a bit of *Ski Sunday*, each flicking through the Sunday papers to avoid having a real conversation.

Finally he said, 'The play's going well then, eh? I see they said in the *Irish News* you were good. That was a nice picture of you. Put me in mind of your mammy. I cut it out for you. I might take a run over next week, but sure you know I can't be doing with all the fuss at my age, and sure you shouted at me for coughing the last time I went to see you.'

That had been almost fifteen years earlier, the last time she had appeared on a Belfast stage. She laughed. 'Don't worry, Daddy, you needn't bother to go. It's not at all what you would call a good play. Anyway it's full of bad language.'

'Well, could yous not leave the bad words out? I'm sure people would enjoy the show just as much if yous did.' He shook his head, making a wry face. 'But sure why would you listen to me?' This was all said matter-of-factly. He didn't expect a reply and didn't get one. She left around six and drove over to Frances's, looking forward to the evening with her friend.

Friday night's performance of *Sticks and Stones* had a sort of manic energy about it. Tomorrow night would be the last night, and consequently the actors all seemed gripped by an element of desperation, the sense that it was all going to be over, their success ripped from them, themselves returned to ashes. There was talk of bringing the play back: the houses had been great, and the critics from the broadsheets enthusiastic enough to leave the possibility of a London transfer on the cards.

Maura and John were in for the second time, and had brought several friends, 'Robert's fan club'. The others had had great sport slagging him off about it. He had been nervous but, his adrenalin up, he had given his best performance to date. Clare was glad for him: she knew that he really wanted to impress his parents, show them he was serious about acting. He had begged her to walk into the bar with him for moral support, so she had rushed to get changed, and they arrived down within minutes of the curtain call. There was a large, enthusiastic group in the foyer – the Olivers had brought quite a crowd, and they had all adored the play. Maura and John were obviously proud of Robert, there were lots of You were wonderfuls and kisses and hugs and congratulations.

The Olivers were going on to dinner at one of Belfast's bet-ter restaurants, and they invited Clare to join them, but she cried off, claiming truthfully that she was tired, and only too aware of two performances looming next day. There was a large crowd milling around, and when Robert and his fans had dispersed, she worked her way over to the others, who were standing directly at the bar. While Niall got her a pint of Guinness, she chatted to Cathy, the stage manager. About to sit on a stool at the bar, she sensed someone at her shoulder. She turned. It was Lorcan. He was alone.

He was dressed in a casual jacket, blue shirt and dark-grey trousers. His off-duty clothes. He smiled at her. 'You were great, Clare, the best. I loved it. Well done!' He spoke quietly, but with warmth.

It took her a moment to find her voice. 'Thank you, it was good of you to come.' The ritual reply. 'I'm glad you liked it, it's a good play, isn't it?'

They stared at each other mesmerised, not speaking.

Cathy, after giving Clare a meaningful look, turned to talk to Aislin and the others.

Clare looked around her, flustered, not quite in command of herself. 'Are you going to join us for a drink?'

'Yes, lovely. I'll get myself an orange juice.'

There was a moment of confusion as she tried to tell him she would get it for him, and then they joined the group. She in-troduced him as Lorcan O'Carroll, leaving out the *Father,* con-scious of the omission. He didn't mention it either, but then it might have seemed clumsy had he done so. Niall looked a bit aggrieved at first, as if to say, why weren't we told about him then? But then he seemed to relax, having decided perhaps that Lorcan wasn't a threat, and chatted away easily enough, touch-ing her on the arm possessively a few times.

The whole evening suddenly seemed exhilarating. She found herself sparkling, telling stories about the production, all the hairy moments. Lorcan was carried along on the tide of their gaiety and chatted with ease, appearing to enjoy this performance as much as the show. Eventually, when last orders were called, the consensus was to go and eat. They rang a few restaurants to ask for a late table and got one. It was assumed that Clare and Lorcan would join them, but he made his apologies, saying he had an early start.

'What about you, Clare,' said Niall. 'You coming?'

'No, I can't. I've just refused Robert and his parents: he'd kill me if I went somewhere else, and besides I'd better get home. I'm expecting a call.'

Niall rolled his eyes expressively. They said their various goodbyes, and Lorcan stood with her as she collected her things.

'Have you the car?' Lorcan asked.

'No. I don't live far from here.'

'Of course. I forgot, I'll drop you off.'

'It's hardly worth it.'

'Well, I go past your place anyway.' He stopped, embarrassed suddenly. 'Your father told me where it was, or you did.' For a moment he seemed flustered, but they walked out together and he drove her up.

It took less than five minutes. She invited him in to see the flat, trying to sound as casual as possible, feeling sure he'd refuse. He didn't.

There was something in her psyche, something ineluctable, drawing her towards him, creating this 'occasion of sin'. She recalled the phrase from her catechism. The feeling was one of horror mixed with fascination. She was acting out the man–woman ritual, all the time aware that there was a patina of normality, hoping that her real feelings were masked by the easy friendly chat between them. He made all the required polite observations about the place, and showed no sign of wanting to leave. She made some coffee eventually, though it was the last thing she needed, and sat opposite him on the beige sofa. He sat down in an armchair, perching rather on the edge of it, not relaxed though sounding perfectly at ease.

'Why don't you sit back?' she said. 'You look uncomfortable.'

'No, really, I'm OK.' But he did as she suggested.

She noticed he had long legs. She met his gaze for the first time. His pupils were huge, black luminous dots pulling her in. His eyelashes were long, spiky. He hid behind them, almost coquettishly, she thought.

God, I want you. I want to submerge myself in you, she thought, and her head spun. 'Would you like milk?'

Someone else seemed to be speaking. Another voice, not hers.

He nodded. As she leaned over to take his cup, his face turned upwards, and their lips almost touched. She felt his breath warm against her cheek. She kept her head still, expectant, feeling an overpowering urge to press herself to him, to push her mouth against his. She could feel his desire,

Almost at once, as if seared, he pulled away. He looked up at her, suddenly coming to his senses. She saw fear in his eyes. Was it fear? Something – she wasn't sure what. 'No, maybe I'll not have another cup. I'll go. I'd better.'

'Yes, I think so, I think you had.' Her hurt made her voice come out coldly.

He stood up to get his coat, his back to her. She was trembling, befuddled.

They walked to the door and then he turned to her his head lowered. 'Please forgive me Clare, I don't know what to say. I'm very confused. I'm losing the picture a bit. I thought I could always have handled things if ever I were attracted to a woman. I mean, there have been other times when I thought I was, and I thought I had, indeed, managed to overcome the feelings. But it was as nothing to this.' His voice was just a whisper.

Somehow the use of 'as nothing' touched her, moved her. She started to cry.

'Don't, please.' He reached out to her, awkwardly putting an arm round her, patting her shoulder.

'I feel as if I've led you on, made this happen. It's my neediness, my pain over Tim. I'm so sorry.' She was sobbing quietly now, feeling a mixture of relief and fear. The tears were for everything really, a release. She knew she didn't want him to leave.

'Sit down for a minute, Lorcan, please. It's OK, nothing will happen. I don't want to be alone just yet, please?' This pleadingly. She blew her nose and stopped crying and looked at him.

He said nothing.

'I mean could you stay a bit longer, are you allowed out this late?'

He laughed, and sat down again. 'Sure there's no one keeping tabs on me. Father McLean and Father Cahill will be long in their beds, and Minnie only comes in at seven. I'm not on call tonight either, Father Lynch is.' He got up and made more coffee then, and sat beside her, on the settee.

She talked to him honestly about Tim, outlining quickly about the break-up, about Kezia.

He asked if there was anyone else yet. 'What about Niall? Was he a boyfriend? He certainly seemed a bit flirtatious, proprietorial. He made me feel I was trespassing.'

She smiled, pleased that he had noticed. 'No, we're just mates, we're lovers in the play. I guess we're just playing the parts a bit off-stage as well. I expect I should have told them all you were a priest, but the words just wouldn't come out.'

'I understand, I'm afraid I didn't want you to, and of course I could always have explained that myself. No one asked me about myself though, so I thought it best not to say anything.'

She laughed. 'That's actors for you – only interested in themselves.'

'Perhaps in this instance it's just as well. I felt dishonest, mind you, a bit of a phoney. God forgive me, but I wanted them to think there was something between us. I wanted to feel how it was, sitting with a woman again, seeming to be with her.' His eyes clouded, he looked down. She wanted to hold him. 'I should talk about this to someone, but I can't bring myself to. I know the official response to it all would be to send me away, perhaps to another parish, and I'm happy where I am. I don't want to leave, and I don't want to stop seeing you.'

They talked then. She wanted to know him better. She asked him all sorts of questions about his life, a part of her shocked at the ease of the intimacy. He told her that he had kept his vow of celibacy despite temptation, until now – although increasingly he thought that it wasn't a realistic vow, and that priests should be allowed to marry, have relationships. 'An awful lot of the bother the Church is in now, with child abuse cases, could have been prevented if priests were allowed a normal sex life.' He frowned. 'It's hard to be sure, but perhaps the solution would be to make celibacy optional. Have the monastic orders keep it, and the secular priests choose. It's been hard for me, believing, or rather accepting, the celibacy all this time to find others – even our bishops – haven't.'

'Yes, I suppose it must be. Maybe they'll change it soon.'

'I doubt it. Not with this pope anyway.'

He had been ordained for nine years. He was from a small town in Tipperary, one of seven children. His father had a small sheep farm, and kept a few dairy cows; both his parents were still living, in their late sixties now. His brothers were all married. There were two younger sisters still at home, and one sister married, living in England. He was the middle child. She listened avidly as he painted a picture of a large, reasonably happy Irish Catholic family. He had gone to boarding school – they all had – and from there he had gone to University College Dublin to do Sociology. While there, he had had a philosophy tutor who had impressed him deeply. The man was a priest, and an astute theologian. They became close friends, and spent a lot of time talking about religion. Gradually, he had felt himself drawn to the priesthood. He decided that perhaps he had a vocation. He had gone to Clonliffe College, a seminary in Dublin, and lived there while he completed his degree, going in to UCD with the other seminarians for lectures. It had been strange at first. As a group they tended not to mix much with the other students, eating together and travelling in together each day, keeping their distance. 'The clothes at first, were a barrier, and then we were allowed to wear civvies, but even then we still didn't blend somehow. Maybe we had the look of chastity wrapped round us.'

Still, he had enjoyed the life and decided he did indeed have a vocation. This was his second move since his ordination. His first had been a small town in rural Ireland. He loved west Belfast, admired the people, their humour, and their ability to cope throughout the Troubles. He'd made a lot of friends.

Clare listened carefully. He was so serious about it all, so good. She felt ashamed that she had ever lusted after him. It was hard for her though, living in the world she did, to recognise that there were still people who were so innocent, for that's what he was really. She had to ask him, and eventually did, had he ever been with a woman?

He laughed. 'Yes, of course I have. I had girlfriends right up until I started at Clonliffe, until I began, you know, to study for the priesthood. It took me ages to stop looking at girls, or women if you like, and stop mentally undressing them.'

Clare was intrigued 'Was it hard?'

'Of course, but we were told it would be. In a way, we were more fortunate than the priests who had gone before – at least there was some acknowledgement, however vague, that we had a sexual nature. It was discussed, though not too much – probably not enough, to be honest.'

'And,' he added, 'don't forget I was nineteen. I'd had girlfriends. I was mad for sex. I was just never lucky enough to get a girl who would let me go the whole way.'

'Did you ever kiss anyone?'

He roared with laughter. She was insanely pleased to get this response.

'Clare, don't be daft, of course I did. I mean, I went out with a girl practically all my first year at UCD. Angela her name was. She wouldn't let me do it, though I wanted to. She did too but was scared stiff of getting pregnant. We did everything but. She left me in the end,' he said wryly.

'Why?' she said, wondering how anyone could ever leave him.

'For an Engineering student called Matt. I used to feel murderous towards him when I saw them together. Anyway, I eventually learned to offer it up.'

'For the souls in purgatory or what?' Clare joked. She knew all about *offering it up*. That had been the nuns' war cry at school, though there were of course two interpretations of this phrase.

He laughed, as if he'd read her mind.

'So how did you know that the priesthood was the right decision?'

'I suppose I didn't really, but it seemed gradually to beckon, to steal up on me really, and once I accepted that, sex was out of the question. Mind you,' he added, his eyes smiling, 'I've always had an eye for a pretty girl.' The use of the phrase made him seem very gauche.

But being celibate had not been an undue strain, he said, until now. Until he met Clare. He looked at her steadily, making her blush. 'It took a very special person to make me think of breaking my vow.'

His faith had remained strong, and he liked the pastoral side of the priesthood. He'd a desire to help people. He would probably have gone into social work otherwise. His mother had cried when he told her he was becoming a priest, but the family had accepted it as his informed choice and were proud of him. They were good Catholics, after all. And there were plenty of others to provide his mother with grandchildren.

'One of the lads at Clonliffe with me was an only child. He said it broke his mother's heart not to have grandchildren, but to tell you the truth I think he was gay.'

She liked him confiding that to her. It made her feel closer to him.

He told her he had thought about her a lot after first meeting her in the pub with Tony. 'I knew of you before of course. Tommy had talked about you so much. He's so proud of you, and I had a picture of you in my head. I was startled to find you so beautiful. I kept hoping you would come along to the drama group – especially after we met in the pub. I didn't think you would, though, and I prayed that I could put all thoughts of you out of my head, but I'm afraid I wasn't too successful.'

'I only came because of you,' she said, only now allowing herself to acknowledge that was the case.

After she had come to the drama group the first time, he said, he simply couldn't remove her from his mind. He told her it was as though her picture was fixed firmly in front of his eyes. Even before tonight, he had been thinking of talking to his confessor about his feelings for her, they disturbed him so much. Perhaps that would still be best. This happened. The Church was more aware these days. There was a counselling service. All very discreet. There were always priests who found the rule hard to keep. But he had decided against it, because he knew they would move him away from the 'occasion of sin' and he wasn't ready for that.

All the time he was talking, Clare was conscious that he was somehow trying to exorcise her and it was working. He *was* calming; his soft lilt was hypnotic, soothing. By the time he left, they both, she felt, had reached an explanation of their mutual feelings that was satisfying, if not entirely truthful. He hugged her tightly as he left as if he was squeezing all the sexual desire out, hugging her into chumminess.

Maybe it would work for him, she thought, but it made her want him more, he felt so good. It had been a release of sorts, though.

At two o'clock she went to bed and dreamed of having mad, passionate sex with him. Then she slept soundly.

She awoke early next morning, threw some things into her bag, and headed for the pool.

Saturdays were awful, the main pool packed with kids with bright plastic armbands, the diving pool full of silly boys jumping on top of each other and splashing the swimmers. Kid Soup. She persevered. The swim revived her, though she'd only had one drink the night before, and felt relatively fresh.

As she swam she turned the conversation over in her head. The episode with Lorcan seemed sorted, somehow. She felt sure that when they next met, all would be fine. She had dreamt it all, enlarging it, exaggerating it in her mind. Last night had felt like a cleansing, a confession even. She chuckled at that thought. The one thing it had done though, she thought ruefully, was make her feel sexually awake again.

She didn't want to think that way about Lorcan. She would simply torment herself. She needed a distraction: maybe to-night she'd let poor old Niall seduce her − all she needed was a good night's sex. A sort of grand finale to the play. Let's hope he was as good a lover as he kept telling her he was. They had established a fairly good friendship throughout the course of the play, and, under ordinary circumstances she might even have fancied the man. Perhaps a little romantic interlude would be good for both of them. It would certainly be a lot healthier than lusting after a priest. She turned things over in her mind as she did her usual thirty lengths; the swimming, as always, calmed and restored her.

Last nights can be one of two things: special − electrifying even

– or flat and depressing. This one had all the right ingredients, and the cast went for it. The audience, even though it had the Saturday night curse of 'ENTERTAIN US' wafting from it with every grudging clap, eventually caught the mood, and the evening was magical. They had several curtain calls.

The Lagan Theatre had a tradition of 'buffets' on the last night for cast and friends. There was a late-night bar. After a few jibes about her 'handsome mystery friend' from the night before, Niall resumed his flirtation. For an actor, he was surprisingly thick-skinned. In fact, he was a total extrovert, and behaved the way most people expect actors to behave, although the rest of the cast was shy if anything. He was flying tonight, in great form, amusing her friends, and paying attention to her as if he had been partnering her for years.

When the others had gone, she stayed on and drank with the cast, although Robert, she noticed, had been somewhat subdued and was the first to leave. She wasn't sure what the expression on his face had been, but he didn't join in a lot of the banter. She thought he had been quite snappy to Niall at one point, rude even. Not that Niall was in any state to notice. He was all over her, chatting like fury, flirting outrageously, making her feel great. She felt alive and desirable again.

Eventually, drunkenly, she allowed him to walk her home, and almost dispassionately, after a practical chat about protection, surprising given the amount they'd had to drink, she agreed that he could spend the night. She had a lost feeling deep down. A longing that she knew he couldn't fill. But he could assuage some part of it, and so she made a deal in her head. It was all right to do this, to have each other. They had a mutual need. Still, when they had finally made it into the bedroom there was a heightened sense of unreality about it all. In a way it was as if they were still on stage. He even made some nervous little jokes when they finished, asking, 'How was it for you, darling?' Yet somehow, perhaps because of the night that was in it, they managed to satisfy each other, and even enjoyed it.

It was nearly one o'clock the next afternoon when they finally surfaced, feeling poisoned with drink. She felt a bit unsure about the whole episode for a minute, but the feeling passed, and after large doses of Solpadeine, they made a sort of brunch, and chatted like old friends. Niall was off back to London tomorrow, and their paths had never really crossed before. Unless the play was revived, it seemed unlikely that they would in the future. She thought that if that were to happen, this would be a bond rather than a gulf between them.

She wasn't due on the film for another week. Although the part was a small one, it was for Channel Four, so it would be a useful addition to her cv. The director, a young man of twenty-three, had won an award for his first short film, and this was his first full-length feature. She didn't get enough chances like this. She was looking forward to it.

She knew that she should use the week to go over to London – there were still so many things to sort out with Tim – but the thought of all the palaver oppressed her. She felt unable to face him just yet. She decided to leave things a few days. Then, if she could get a cheap flight on Thursday or Friday, she would go and see how things were when she got there. She was aware that she had promised Paula she would come, but Paula would understand if she couldn't get it together.

In the meantime, she would go over to see Tommy, spend a bit of time with him. She missed him. Missed his dry, quizzical look, and absurd view of life. Above all she needed a hug. Not that he would offer one, but he always responded when she asked for one, holding her tightly and asking gruffly, 'What would you be needing a hug for at your age, eh?'

It was a crisp fresh day, and she decided the walk across

town would do her good. Belfast wasn't really a city; you could drive from one end to the other in twenty minutes. The walk into town took her almost half an hour. She loved walking past Queen's University. The place always had an emotional effect on her, its smooth green lawns offsetting the wonderful redbrick Gothic building. The diamond-shaped leaded windowpanes glinted and flashed in the sun, making the building sparkle. The magnolias in bloom in University Square were voluptuous, and intoxicating: her favourite trees. She breathed in their heady scent as she passed.

She walked down past the Victorian terrace, past the English Department, remembering fondly her own self-importance during her first few months there, the sheer pleasure of having made it from Kinsale Street against the odds. She'd been the first from her family to go to university. Brid had opted for St Mary's, preferring not to leave her close friends from school. It had made more sense anyway – Brid had always known she would teach.

Clare had wanted to get out of Belfast to go to university or drama school somewhere else, but financially it wasn't possible. Her parents had done their best – it was a hardship for them to allow both girls to go off to college. The ones in the street on occasion had remarked about the 'two big girls, well over working age, still at the learning, and not an extra penny coming into the house'.

She turned down Botanic Avenue. This area had changed dramatically too. The regulars, groups of crusties and students, were overwhelmed now by new bars and coffee houses, all serving a clientele who drove cars with alloy wheels and talked incessantly into mobile phones. Nauseating. It was getting as bad as London.

The crusties hadn't quite been forced out though. She passed a group of winos at the corner of one of the streets. Though the wind was a cold northeasterly, the clear sunny day obviously had induced a celebratory mood. They heckled her good-naturedly, and she gave them her loose change. She was amused to see a woman walk past and give her a filthy look for her 'good deed'. It was Breda. When she recognised Clare, she stopped to talk.

'Well, is the play finished then?' She smirked at Clare. 'Hmm, I must say it did very well. You were very good, though it *was* a good part.'

Clare smiled. 'Yes, you're right, so it was, Breda.' There were always those who thought parts played themselves.

'Did Father Lorcan ever get across to see it?'

Clare's heart leapt. She hoped she sounded casual enough as she answered. 'Yes, he was there on Friday night. I think he enjoyed it. I saw him afterwards – he waited to say hello.'

Breda was one of those women whose feelers were always out, brushing up crumbs of information which, gathered together, made for a large slice of gossip. 'Hmmn,' she said. 'If you ask me he's far too good-looking for a priest, that young man. I hope he doesn't end up getting himself into a sticky situation.'

Clare could feel the blush creep up over her entire body. She met Breda's gaze. Brazenly she stared at her. Her heart was now pounding. It had managed to break free and had stopped somewhere near the top of her throat. 'What do you mean exactly, Breda?'

'Oh nothing. I just think we should treat him with more respect. Things might be a lot more relaxed these days with them wearing civvies and going into bars and all that. But they are, in the final analysis, men of the cloth. If you ask me, I think he's a bit too familiar. He should keep his distance.' She sniffed the air to emphasise her point.

Clare was furious. God, what an old bitch! The implication was obvious. She heard herself say calmly, 'I'm sure he knows what he's doing. After all, the drama group are all adults – as is he – and I'm sure he just fits in with the mood.'

'Well, perhaps you're right,' Breda said, and as she moved

to leave, she asked Clare casually, 'Anything else lined up?'

'Yes, a film for Channel Four actually,' Clare replied with some satisfaction, and was pleased when Breda looked suitably impressed. They said their goodbyes. Clare couldn't believe how shaken she had been by the conversation.

The road into town from Shaftesbury Square was nick-named inappropriately the Golden Mile, though she could see nothing golden about the ghastly rash of fast-food joints which had sprung up over the last decade. They even had a McDonald's: she hated McDonald's – as far as she was con-cerned their only contribution to posterity was supplying the entire world with clean toilets. She passed a series of tacky buildings all outlined in either blue or yellow plastic, at odds with the Victorian redbrick. She recalled coming this way from Queen's years ago, her senses alert as she passed each parked car, the constant fear of car bombs making her vigilant. It was so different now. Even the way the people walked was different. There was a carelessness to their gait. The restaurants had pulled chairs and tables out onto the pavements, and these were filled with people enjoying the rare sunshine.

Clare thought over her conversation with Breda, at the same time replaying in her head the various nights at the drama group. Had there been any indication that there was a 'buzz' between them? She didn't think so, but then these things were hard to judge. Well, it was sorted now. For good – she thought. None the less, Clare felt adrift somehow. She sud-denly had a desperate desire to see Lorcan again. She longed to hold him tightly once more. Maybe he would drop into Tommy's. No, it would be better if he didn't. Oh God! Why was everything so bloody complicated?

She was still mulling all this over by the time she reached Kinsale Street, pleased with herself for walking all the way. She looked up at the church at the top and wondered if Lorcan was there right now. The church spires seemed to her like two accusing fingers.

She had phoned to say she was coming, and Tommy had bought buns. Huge currant squares. Flies' graveyards, they had always been called when she was growing up. He'd made a plate of tinned salmon sandwiches as well. He was delighted with himself.

'I got three tins for the price of two,' he said. 'I like the John West's red, you can't beat it. That other oul pink stuff would turn your stomach.'

She struggled through three 'big ignorant slabs' and was relieved when Tony came in to help her with the rest of the plate. He was on his lunch break.

'All right, kid? We enjoyed the play, thanks for the tickets. We couldn't stay afterwards though. The wee one had a cough and the babysitter's only thirteen. Cheers, da.'

He took the mug of tea Tommy handed him. She knew it was more likely he hadn't had the price of a drink, or that Sally had wanted to leave, but she accepted his excuse. They had been great chums as kids. There was something touching about him. His cheerfulness and sense of humour were a veneer for something vulnerable, bruised. He didn't have it easy, in and out of various jobs, never quite finding anything to satisfy him. The Troubles had hit him hardest of all. The girls had all managed to clear out, but he had been left smack in the middle of things trying to raise a family and avoid either joining the IRA or becoming yet another victim of the UFF. There was a piece of graffiti at the bottom of the street. He used to quote it frequently to her. 'Is there life before death?' Meaning it somehow.

Yet he hadn't wanted to leave. It always surprised her how rooted the people in this small huddle of streets were. Living out a destiny they accepted as their lot in life. Apart from her mother, she'd missed Tony most when she first moved to London. He hadn't been married then and was still living at home, working as an apprentice electrician, the first in his line of 'interesting' careers.

When they had cleared the plate of sandwiches, Tommy patted his stomach and announced he was going to have a wee lie-down.

'You should be getting back to your work, son,' he said to Tony. He liked to keep him on his toes.

'That fellow doesn't know what a day's work is' was a favourite rant of Tommy's. Tony, not relishing the usual lecture about Tommy's own long days as a checker in a bakery, dutifully got up to leave on cue.

Then, as he was walking out, he turned to Clare, remembering something. 'You know that wee lad was in the play with you? The one who got done? Lives in the Holy Land?'

Clare nodded, interested. 'Robert Oliver?'

'Aye, that's him. Well, Frankie and me are doing a wee job for him, a bit of painting and double-glazing. The frames were rotten though, so we had to get new windows made.'

'What about him?'

Tony paused for dramatic effect. 'He has a picture of you in his bedroom.'

Clare looked up at him. 'A picture of me?' she echoed.

'Aye, a big black-and-white one, framed like. You know, one of those actress ones you have, like the ones they put out front in the theatre.' He smiled appreciatively at her. 'Obviously got good taste, eh kid?' He paused as if something had just struck him. 'He's a bit of a weirdo, isn't he? Isn't his da a lawyer? We were wondering how he could afford all the work on the house at his age, and, ye know, being an actor like.'

There was no doubt about it: this town was a parish. She looked at Tony.

'Well, don't go digging the arm in because you think he's well off.'

'C'mon, kid, what d'ye take me for? Anyway, I'm sure his da's the one paying the bills, and he's hardly short of a bob or two.'

She laughed and began to clear the dishes. She called after Tony as he left, 'He's not a bad fella. I've known him since he was three. Tell him you're my brother, won't you. I probably won't see him for a while, now the play's finished.'

She was wrong though, because when she got back from swimming next day, there was a message on her answerphone from Robert.

'Hello, Clare. Well, you managed to wriggle out of our drink nicely. Any chance of one now I'm on the dole? It might cheer me up.' And he gave his number.

On impulse she dialled it. To her surprise he was in, and answered immediately, sounding absurdly pleased to hear from her.

'Imagine Tony being your brother? I knew he seemed familiar somehow. Anyway, I miss you terribly. You were the best thing about doing the play.'

'God you're really full of it.' But she was tickled all the same. 'When are you taking me for a drink?' she asked.

'How about tonight?'

They agreed to meet at the new, pretentious-looking hotel on Botanic Avenue, the one with a torso climbing out of the upper walls. She was glad to have something to do. It was always a bit odd the week after a play finished. She had a constant feeling of thinking she should be doing something and not quite knowing what. It always took her a few days to stop checking her watch, thinking she should be on stage. He probably felt the same.

'There's a dress code, love.' The man on the door shifted uneasily as Clare met his gaze.

'What are you talking about?' Clare asked.

'No jeans allowed.'

'Oh, for Christ's sake, who thought that up? This is the twenty-first century, you know.'

But the bouncer was adamant. He made a rueful face and shook his head bouncer fashion. 'It's more than my job's worth, love. No jeans allowed.'

It really didn't seem worth arguing. They were both wearing jeans.

There were several other possibilities within walking distance, so she was surprised to hear herself say, 'Let's just get a bottle of wine and go back to the flat.'

Robert was quick to accept. 'Good idea. I'm a bit fed up with pubs.'

Clare almost immediately wished she had kept her mouth shut. Robert got progressively more flirtatious on the walk to the off-licence, but she went along with his mood, despite the young man in the wine shop on the Stranmillis Road eyeing them with open curiosity. They were definitely giving out signals. They could still go to the pub. They each bought a bottle of wine and left.

'Maybe we *should* go to the Bot,' she said.

'No, let's not, it'll be bunged, and I want to see where you live. Anyway,' he added, 'I know everyone in the Bot. We wouldn't get a chance to talk.'

She suppressed her doubts. Nothing would happen. They would have a drink – that's all. They walked the rest of the way in silence, and after a few yards he tentatively took her hand and she let it lie in his limply, not actively taking his. She was making it seem casual, natural, but somehow letting it happen, not holding back. This in itself seemed somehow an indication that the evening was taking a certain turn. He followed her into the flat, and after an appreciative look around he sat on the settee and watched quietly as she found two glasses, lit the gas fire, and got some cheese from the fridge, and crackers from a tin. She placed them on the table in front of him, an offering. Her thoughts were scrambled. She tried to work out her motives for being in this situation with Robert, but she didn't feel like being that honest with herself. Perhaps by bringing him to the flat she was just acknowledging the fact that she felt at a disadvantage being seen with him. He did look awfully young, and he turned heads. She felt visible in his company. When she had seen him from across the street waiting outside, it had brought home forcibly how young he was. And besides, if her motives for accepting this date were clearer, even to herself, she would feel more relaxed.

At any rate, she felt more aware of her appearance than she normally did. Pathetically, she had spent longer than usual on her makeup, in an effort to look as if she wasn't wearing any. Why was she doing this? Behaving recklessly by accepting a date with Robert. Was it all a diversion? Some pathetic attempt to keep herself from admitting Lorcan's effect on her? Because she knew that this, this being here tonight with Robert, *was* only a diversion, the equivalent of having a snack when she needed to eat a meal. And yet she was colluding in some way with whatever plans he had. She didn't really want to think too hard about any of this, preferring to hold her moral breath for now. She was certain John and Maura would be scandalised. And they would be right to be, she thought.

Her thoughts tumbled. She could see her feelings mirrored in his eyes.

The goblets were large. She had bought them in town the week before. He poured the wine, almost filling them, and toasted her, putting on a silly upper-class-twit voice. 'To us! To tonight!'

She wanted to laugh out loud, but thought it might hurt his feelings. He seemed to be taking it all so seriously. The glasses clinked.

They chatted in a desultory fashion at first, avoiding the bigger topics, about her being in Belfast, about his being there. He was ready to move now to London or Dublin. Diana had been as good as her word and called him this morning. She would take him on, proving infuriatingly that it was always easier for males. And of course being attractive didn't hurt, although Clare had to admit he could act as well. He was going over to London on Monday to see Diana, stay a few days. She had said she would arrange for him to do the round of casting agents, whatever. He was plainly excited about it all. He wanted to know what it would all be like, what would be expected of him.

Clare wasn't really in the mood for talking about London, so she shifted things back to *Sticks and Stones*, whether there was a chance of it transferring still, and if they'd both be in it. They talked about the play, the cast, what Declan had been like as a director. The conversation had that meaningless quality that sexual tension brings. They were talking for the sake of it, and once this was accepted by both, they began to relax into it, to enjoy it. The shape of things seemed predetermined, as if whatever they decided, fate had already finalised the details, and they were simply following the plan. They were going to sleep together. She could feel it, he could too, and until then they stalked each other, verbally, mentally, enjoying the ritual, the search for a way to justify the deed before it was done. To smooth the path they had stepped onto.

She felt alert, fired up, animated. She was enjoying Robert's company. He had an ease with women rare in one his age. She had worked with younger actors before and tended to agree with Paula, who claimed to find all men under thirty dull. 'Nothing to contribute my love, even in bed.' And she of all people would know. But Robert had grown up in the company of women. He had four sisters, and being the oldest was used to having his way. Spoiled.

He flirted with her by staring at her, meeting her gaze. Few people did that, and she found it disarming. Yet there was a quality behind his gaze that unnerved her. She wiped the thought, thinking perhaps it was her own guilt reflected in him.

Eventually she said, 'I haven't got around to asking you before. But why did you give up Law, leave Oxford and move back? You've never said. And Maura and John haven't exactly been too forthcoming about it.'

He grimaced. 'I know, I ballsed up badly. They've been great, actually. I just hated Oxford. I didn't really want to do Law for starters, and it was rare being from here, being Irish. I felt my accent was wrong. I didn't know the right people. The first girl I got involved with actually left me for a lord!' He looked at her balefully. 'I was smoking too much dope and it was doing my head in. I'd got into it in a big way in India during the summer. I spent three months there. I would get these really black moods.'

He stopped, waiting to see the effect of his words. She kept listening. After a minute he continued, enjoying the release. 'I uh . . . sort of lost it one night, got into a brawl with a tutor, ended up in hospital, hearing screaming in my head.' He sighed deeply. 'Not a pleasant time really. Parents called and all that. Dad came and fetched me back. A bit messy.' He took a deep breath. 'Soooo, Ms Murphy, I came home and spent two months recuperating from what is commonly known as a nervous breakdown or collapse, and a friend of mum's – she's called Jane Durham – you know her, don't you? –'

Clare nodded.

'– she works in the Beeb and heard they were looking for an eighteen-year-old for a part in a drama being made here, a local writer. I read for it, and got it. I'd only acted at school before. It was cool, really got me fired up, so after that I went up for about ten other things and finally got the part in *Sticks and Stones*. Lucky for me eh?'

His hand touched hers. They had finished the first bottle of wine and she felt quite tipsy.

'Mum and Dad are so glad that I'm doing something I like. Siobhan's doing Law, and loves it. She can go into the family business. It's sexist expecting me to.'

He grinned endearingly as he spoke. His eyelashes were long, and when he looked down they brushed his cheeks, so appealingly. He'd perfected this look, she thought cynically, and then dismissed the thought at once.

'It can happen to anyone, you know,' she said eventually. 'A breakdown.'

He nodded. 'I know that, and I'm much better. The folks are buying the house; it's an investment. Prices are really shoot-ing up here now. And I'm rent-free the first year. I feel so much happier now being back, doing this. Everything seems so much lighter now. There was a woman, Helen. She did my head in. She rejected me, you know – after leading me on for ages. Then she made all these stupid accusations. Wishful thinking on her part mostly.' He touched her hand affection-ately. 'I'm happy tonight, and I'm glad I finally know what I want to be when I grow up. Hard to follow in such illustrious footsteps as John Oliver's, you know?'

Clare nodded sympathetically. She supposed it *was* pressure of a sort. She had never had it: as her father often said to them all, The only way is up!

Robert sipped his drink. She could tell he was relaxing now, enjoying telling his story. 'After the telly, I was going to try for RADA and I may still, but maybe Diana will get a few people to see me.' He sat back, aware he had been talking a long time. 'What about you? You haven't really moved back for good have you? Mum and Dad don't think you'll stay.'

She thought about it for a moment, and shook her head. 'No, I expect I won't. You know, I suppose, that Tim and I have split up. I'm getting over that, and I just wanted to be here for a while, do something different.'

The nibbles gone, they were both still hungry, or possibly they were stalling. She phoned for a pizza, but somehow when it arrived they had no appetite for it.

He brushed her hand softly, deliberately, sensuously, with his long fingers. 'I've wanted you the whole time during rehearsals and during the run. Didn't you guess?'

'No, I didn't, not at all. I thought I was a mate, I guessed you just felt comfortable with me.'

'No, Clare, believe me. I can't stop thinking about you. I am really drawn to you.' He pulled her hand and placed it on his crotch. She pulled it away at once, finding his action shocking, naïve. 'Look, that's what you do to me. It's embarrassing.'

She wanted to delay things. She wasn't ready. Not drunk enough.

He laughed. 'Sorry, am I being gauche?'

'A bit. Anyway, just relax, we're not going anywhere.'

As the wine disappeared, so her doubts inevitably drowned in the swell of sexual desire enveloping them, pushing every other thought away. She made the case out for and against: to allow him to continue flirting and possibly end up in bed with him, or to stop now, before drink became the arbiter of reason.

Clare had shocked even herself by having the one-night stand with Niall. She had never been promiscuous, although she knew that the definition was a variable one. Her sense of loss since Tim and she had split had been colossal. She missed the intimacy most of all. That special connection with another human being that only sexual intimacy could seal.

While she had been in London and things had been going badly with Tim, she had shied away from any sexual encounters. The episode with Niall had been out of character but justifiable: good, even necessary for her self-confidence. She knew intuitively that anything sexual with Robert would be madness. Yet here she was, quietly considering it. Surely she was losing her mind? The person she really wanted above all was Lorcan O'Carroll. That was the true source of this longing, her overwhelming desire for *him*. This was a diversion. She turned her thoughts back to the present. She felt as if her brain was split in two and she was having an ongoing argument with herself right now.

I shouldn't be doing this. Well, why not? This is wrong, but why? He likes me. I like him. I feel so stupid. I'm older. I should be responsible. He's just a baby. Well he's not, he's a man. He's travelled, so he's obviously not a virgin.

They chatted a while longer. He had quite a sense of humour. Eventually she said, 'Do you want to come to bed?' and that was that.

It seemed so simple, so direct. She was surprised at her own boldness, but somehow he had willed her to make the move. And something in her wanted to make the sin her own. If she thought of her motive, and she had chosen not to, she was doing something wrong to stop herself from doing something even more wrong. This was as far from sleeping with a priest as she could get.

Robert was an enthusiastic lover, eager to please. His energy was exciting, and she was satisfied quickly, a combination of the newness of it all, and the fact that for all her worldliness she felt she was committing a sin. He was half her age, he was the son of friends. Clare could imagine Maura's reaction, and in some perverse way this heightened the pleasure. He spent the night; there was something raw and urgent about him, a neediness that she had never experienced before, but she put it down to the age gap. He seemed inexhaustible. She was high on desire, and felt more alive than she had in months. There was no point, she thought, in allowing the guilt to intrude just yet. There was plenty of time for that, and they weren't harming anyone. Age gap or not, they were both single. He grew more confident each time he took her, and she gave herself totally. His passion was like a balm, enveloping her, making her whole again. She had missed feeling like this, desirable and sexy. By rejecting her, Tim had reinforced any hang-ups she had had about how she looked and felt. This was her cure, her elixir. It felt good. She let her body take over.

She didn't mind, therefore, when the night became days and, apart from visits to the shops for food, they spent the time in bed, fielding phone calls and acting like teenagers – well, he was one, she supposed.

Nothing beckoned until the weekend, when she had to go to London. Nothing else was planned. The answerphone was on. She had bought one as soon as she moved in. She had the actor's paranoia about missing the big part, and she let the machine pick up her calls. Paula sounded as if she had an idea something was going on when she rang, but was fobbed off with a promise of a 'chat' later in the week.

For the first time since she had been a student, Clare was living purely for the moment, and had forsaken all thoughts of the consequences of her actions. The feeling was intoxicating: as if some force other than reason possessed her. Robert delighted her. She revelled in his gaucheness, in the act of fulfilling for him his fantasies of her. Admittedly there was a strong sense of impermanence about it, but Clare chose not to dwell on that; she forgot her natural hesitancy, and abandoned herself to the passion. She was raw from the sheer physical workout, but it was satisfying pushing herself sexually like this, their eagerness for yet another sexual high driving them on.

But by Thursday morning, she felt somewhat stir-crazy. They had been holed up long enough. She needed to go and see Tommy, and see how he was. He hadn't been in the couple of times she had taken a break to phone him. Reality was setting in, and for Clare at least the sexual euphoria was dying down. She brushed away the misgivings. It was usually the men who felt like this. She promised Robert that they could get together next week when she returned from Dublin. She would phone him when she knew where she would be staying. She was still of a mind to go to London first – the encounter with Robert had given her a gloss, a shell with which she felt she could deal with Tim. She had the aura of a woman desired, not the wretchedness of a loser. But she needed to be decisive if she was to keep to any of her original plans. If she was going to go to London at all, this week of lotus-eating had complicated her travel arrangements, since she had to be in Dublin on Monday. She phoned and reserved a flight to London on Friday.

After Robert left, she tidied the flat, changed the bed, and tried to get her head back together. It had certainly been, for her at least, a fairly outrageous three days. At lunchtime, she drove over to her father's feeling a bit tired and washed out, but oddly at peace for the first time in months. Tommy was sitting in the small front room. He looked up with a grin of pleasure when she came in.

'I've the tea on,' he said, eyeing her up and down. 'Well you're looking a bit more like yourself.' He brought in two mugs and poured out the treacle-like tea, 'So the play's all done now. Well I'm sorry I missed it, but Brid and Tony enjoyed themselves, thought you were great, and Father Lorcan said you were smashing too. He wanted me to go over with him, but I wasn't at myself. Have you been away on a wee break?'

'Yes, staying with friends for a few days, out and about, catching up with things, getting a bit of exercise.' She was surprised at the ease of the lie.

'Well, I had a wee bit of a scare earlier in the week. I woke up with pains in my chest, thought it was indigestion at first, but when it didn't go away, Winnie made me phone for McCann. He said I might have a touch of angina. I've to go to the hospital for tests next week. Told me to cut out the butter and cut down on the smoking, but sure what's the point of that at my age, eh? If I'm going to die I might as well enjoy the bit of time that's left to me, eh?'

She was alarmed. Remorse flooded her. 'Oh, Daddy. That's awful! Why didn't you phone?'

'Well I did, but you had that oul machine on and I feel like an eejit talking into it. It's OK. I got Tony. He was down in five minutes. He said he'd tell you.'

'Well, he didn't.'

Oh God! Now she thought about it, there *had* been a message from Tony to call him. And she'd ignored it, thinking it was nothing untoward. The truth was she had been too wrapped up in her own physical needs. And at the back of her mind she knew she hadn't wanted to see Tony because he was still working in Robert's house, and she didn't want him to know any of the reasons Robert hadn't been home. A flicker of this crossed her face.

Tommy looked at her searchingly. 'I'm all right. McCann told me not to worry myself. He's given me some tablets. I'll be startin' to rattle I'm taking that many of them. I've to stick one of them under my tongue – the taste of them would sicken you.' He made a face. 'Father Lorcan has called down every day. Brid has been clucking round me getting on my nerves. Peter even came over, though to tell you the truth, if you weren't feeling great that fellow'd finish you off. He could bore for Ireland. Winnie has been in with three apple cakes. You'd think it was Hallowe'en. I've been hiding them in the back of the fridge – you may take one of them over with you.'

'Daddy, I'll move back in. You shouldn't be on your own.'

'Ach, don't be stupid. I'm all right. I've to take it easy, but sure that's all I do anyway.' His blue eyes regarded her calmly, and his next words were spoken softly. 'You know, Clare love, I wouldn't mind if I *was* to go now. I'd be happier if you were settled, but I've had my three score and ten, and I miss your mother. I wouldn't mind joining her at all.'

Clare felt the tears well up. She cleared away the cups and plate, and excused herself, saying she was off up the street to buy a paper. 'Can I get you anything?'

'No, I'm grand, I've the *Irish News* learned off.' He broke off, changing his mind. 'Well, mebbe see if the *Tele*'s in early. I don't get it delivered any more. Two papers a day, too expensive.'

The church was big, impressive. She had spent a large part of her childhood within these walls. You didn't have to be particularly religious to do that. It seemed the done thing when she was growing up. The ornate altar to Our Lady of Perpetual Succour with its gilded gates and Byzantine icon was one of the more popular altars. She walked towards it now, not quite sure why she was drawn to it. The church was almost empty at this time of day, save for a few old women, heads reverently bent, who knelt in silent prayer, watching her from under clasped hands.

The altar was festooned with flowers. It was a local custom for brides to send their bouquets down to Our Lady's altar, and there had obviously been a spate of weddings. She counted four garish efforts, tasteless except for one, which was a rhapsody of brightly coloured freesia, her favourite flower. Tim had always sent her a bunch on opening nights. The smell was evocative.

She knelt at the shrine, placing the two newspapers beside her, then cupped her face in her hands, and tried to pray. Her heart felt like stone. The words of a prayer she had learned by rote years ago floated to the surface.

'Remember, O Most Gracious Virgin Mary, that never was it known . . .'

The Memorare, it was called. As a child, she had often recited it when she had wanted something from God, saying it through without a breath, as if somehow that made it more effective. Wearing it out during exams. She had tried to conjure it up during her mother's illness, the prayer a desperate last plea to God, to anyone, to whoever answered prayers. She knew it would be hopeless though. Perhaps that was why it had failed.

Her mother's prayers had always worked – for others. In the end, they hadn't helped her. 'Never mind, it's God's will. Sure we all have to go sometime.'

Clare still felt the pain of those words.

The marble coldness soothed her. She knelt until her knees began to hurt. Her mind was blank, her thoughts suspended. Then she gathered the newspapers and left, stopping self-consciously to dip her hand in the holy water font on the way out. Under the statue of St Anthony she stopped, then emptied the change from her pocket into the box beneath it. In gold letters it said: FOR THE POOR, ST ANTHONY'S BREAD.

St Anthony, patron saint of the lost and found, stared impassively. He had the child Jesus in one arm, a book and a bunch of lilies in the other. One of his feet had been rubbed away to nothing. A smoothed-out hollow attached to his ankle. She had rubbed it herself countless times on her way out of church. It was satisfying, comforting. The days she forgot would unsettle her, like stepping on a line in the pavement, not on the tile. No one had ever explained the reason for this ritual: perhaps there wasn't one. She touched it now, storing up another talisman. She needed them. She was lost, and she wondered if St Anthony could find her. She needed someone.

Apart from Brid, who was the most traditional, the other Murphy children had largely given up the practice of their faith, having lost precisely that. The church was still potent though, compelling, redolent of childhood. Just going in and smelling the place was oddly comforting. When they were young, she and Frances would sit in the seats in one of the side altars during Sunday Mass, so that they could talk to each other without being told off by the nuns who sat in the main body of the church. It all seemed so long ago. It was long ago.

Lorcan was talking to someone in the car park as she was leaving. The familiar twinge hit her in the gut. She was getting used to feeling like this around him. She waved, and then decided to stop. He was wearing his priest's clothes; they made him seem more formal, and different, she thought.

He was obviously pleased to see her. He greeted her with a broad smile. 'Well, Ms Murphy, you're looking well. You're over with Tommy I take it?' He made no reference to the fact that she had come out of the church. 'I thought you might have been over earlier in the week.' His tone changed. 'I suppose Tommy has told you of his wee episode?'

'Yes, I feel terrible! The neglectful daughter – I can't think why neither Brid or Tony came over to get me.'

'Tony thought you were in London when you didn't call him back, and Tommy didn't want to make a fuss. I'm sure you know that about him a lot better than I do.'

He looked at her searchingly. 'How are things?'

She couldn't meet his gaze: she felt, ridiculously, as if she'd been unfaithful to him. 'Oh fine, I've just been visiting friends and so on.' She fiddled with the newspapers as she answered him. 'I'm off to Dublin next week to do the film. I'm supposed to go to London tomorrow for the weekend. I should maybe cancel my flight in case something happens to Daddy.'

'Well, he seems a lot better, and I've been looking in on him every day now.'

'I know. You're very good.'

'Ah, sure he's great craic. It's no bother.'

He moved to leave and then turned back to her and said hesitantly, 'There's a rehearsal of the drama group tonight. I mean we wouldn't expect you to come round, but maybe –' he paused, flustered – 'maybe you could join us in the pub afterwards and hear how the play's shaping up. Bring Tommy if he's feeling up to it. It might do him good to get out for a bit, and I'm sure they'd all love to see you.'

'Maybe I'll do that.'

She was suddenly anxious to get away. His look made her feel transparent. She had a strong sensation that he was seeing into her soul, and somehow knew what she had been up to all week. She said her goodbyes and went back down to the house. Filled with the whole idea of him.

'Well, were you printing those yourself?' Tommy asked when she arrived.

'I went into the chapel for a minute.'

Tommy looked at her quizzically, 'What? Are you prayin' for me now, eh? Well, *did* you say a prayer for me? I'm not on the way out yet, love, don't you be frettin'.'

I'm the one who needs the prayers, she thought. Had she prayed? She had tried to, but she'd lost the knack. She had sent her thoughts and wishes somewhere. Heavenwards perhaps or – like Claudius – had hers too remained below?

There was still the problem about the weekend, about the trip to London. She had left things with Robert fairly loose, and felt unsure how she would deal with all that. Her emotional life was a mess, a mire, Tim, Robert, Lorcan. The sane thing to do was to go, see Tim, and tell Robert it had been fun, but mad, senseless now she'd had time to contemplate it, an aberration. What had possessed her? She was sure Robert would think better of it all when he'd had time. No one need know. She wouldn't even tell Paula. It was over, that was that.

Lorcan, well, she couldn't even begin to think about that. It was too overwhelming.

Brid came in then, so the kettle went on for the second time, and yet another pot of tea and the bloody apple tart were produced. She wondered how the people round here didn't spend the entire day running to the loo, flooded as they were with tea. In a way she was glad to see Brid: perhaps the family bond was stronger than she thought, and the looming mortality of Tommy made them draw closer.

Understanding that they might want to talk, Tommy announced he was going out to collect his winnings. 'I suppose yiz'll be working out the funeral arrangements. Well all I can say is, you can shove me in a couple of them black bin bags and bury me in the Hatchet Field. That'll do me rightly. Now I'm away round to the bookie's, I had 50p each way on Angel of Death.' He grinned at them, enjoying their response. 'I think it might have won, ye never know. Anyway, the walk round will brighten me up.'

He left and they carried the cups and plates into the small kitchen, falling naturally into a routine of washing and drying. Brid spoke first.

'Where were you? Did you go to London?' Not waiting for an answer she went on, 'You know, Doctor McCann says he needs to take it easy, stop the smoking, but sure you know what he's like. I've been worried sick about him. I asked him to come over and stay with us till he's feeling better, but he won't budge.'

'Brid, he's far happier here. It's better if we just make sure one of us calls to see him every day. I can manage most days after next week. I'm doing the film then. I *should* be in London this weekend, but that can be cancelled. It's just that I'd like to get things sorted out with Tim. About the flat I mean.'

'It's really over then? I thought he'd be over here after you. He always seemed keener than you.'

'Well, things change. I suppose we grew apart.' Clare said ruefully. 'He has a younger model now, a trophy for losing his hair. I expect I didn't appreciate him when I had him. Perhaps we should have got married years ago.' She attempted a cheerful grin.

Brid snorted. 'I wouldn't say that. Marriage isn't all it's cracked up to be either.'

Clare laughed. 'God, Biddy, you never change do you? Maybe you're right, I'll get over him. I've no choice really. I expect I'll get used to the single life eventually.'

Unexpectedly Brid moved across awkwardly to the sink and gave Clare a hug. Clare was touched, Brid was so prickly, any show of affection was rare.

'You know I'm here if you need to talk. It's not often my independent little sister shows that she hasn't everything under control. Go to London, sort yourself out. Daddy can put up with me for the weekend.'

They chatted easily after that. By the time Brid left, Clare felt that something significant had taken place. Her mood was lightened.

She phoned and paid for the flight to London the following morning, Friday. Then she prepared a meal for herself and Tommy, who had returned from the bookies £8.55 richer. She decided that she *would* go to McAuley's for a drink and Tommy had promised to treat her with his winnings.

He was a popular figure in his local. He had always been a great man for buying a round when he was in the money, and now he had only his pension, he was reaping the benefits of his legendary generosity. He still bought the old cronies a few wee half 'uns now and again, when the odd treble came home.

He and Clare had been in the pub since about half nine. It was nearly full, but they had found a corner with a few spare seats which they were keeping for the drama group. Most of the regulars had heard Tommy had been unwell, and sent over drinks. After about half an hour there was hardly any space on the table. It was as if the perceived wisdom was that he'd be better off drinking himself to death, rather than waiting for a heart attack to finish him off. Clare had asked for a whiskey, and found herself staring at four more.

The St Brendan's crowd arrived almost at closing time. There were about ten of them, led by Breda and Seamus. Lorcan came over at once. He laughed when he saw all the drinks lined up in front of Clare and Tommy.

'Goodness, Clare, we'll have to carry you home if you finish that lot.'

'I'm only having the one. I have the car with me,' she said

regretfully. 'But my order seems to have started a chain reaction.'

'Why don't you have one yourself, Father Lorcan?' said Tommy. 'It's an awful pity to waste it.'

To her surprise he agreed, and Seamus, after some coaxing, was persuaded to have one as well. 'Bad for the voice – whiskey,' he said, taking a hefty sip.

Billy – Mr Pigeon Fancier – went up to the bar to get a round for the others. They shuffled up and squeezed in beside her. There was hardly any room, and she found herself seated between Tommy and Seamus. Lorcan was sitting opposite her. She couldn't avoid looking directly at him. The atmosphere felt charged: the man was mesmeric and she found herself checking for his reaction every time she spoke. She wanted him badly.

She dismissed that lustful thought, changing gear in her head. She didn't need any further complications in her life. Not one like this anyway. The thought wouldn't go away, though. Her hormones must suddenly have kicked in after months of celibacy. She was starting to think like a slut. She laughed at the idea.

Lorcan looked at her quizzically. 'What's up?'

'I wish I hadn't brought the car,' she said. 'I just feel like having a few drinks.'

Tommy patted her arm. It was a rare display of affection from him: the few whiskies had helped him unwind, and he was in expansive form. He had probably been a lot more worried about his health than he was letting on to them all, she thought. The drink was working on her too, she was beginning to feel mellow.

'Sure, drink away, love. It'll help your nerves. The bed's still there. Winnie changed the sheets for me. You can always stay the night.'

Lorcan smiled, saying nothing. He was still nursing the whiskey she'd given him. She had the other three in quick succession, unusual for her, and downed a pint of Guinness before the place closed.

Later she was to look back on this evening and realise that it was the turning point, the moment when she stopped trying to fool herself. She knew without a shred of doubt, with total clarity of thought, even allowing for the drink. She knew this was *it*. Whatever she had felt for any man before in her life, whatever she had previously thought was love, fell very short of this emotion building now for Lorcan. It was disturbing.

Lorcan walked with Tommy and herself to the door, and refused Tommy's offer of a cup of tea, standing instead at the step to talk to her. Tommy seemed oblivious of any subplot, and went in to put the kettle on. She felt exposed, as if there was some sort of window into her soul. Her mouth moved unconsciously, imagining his kiss, trying to draw it from him, wanting his mouth against hers. They looked at each other, saying nothing, the air between them charged.

Then Lorcan surprised her by asking her directly, 'Shall I go and get my car and drive you over?'

Yes, she thought, yes please. She didn't want him to leave, not yet. 'But it's out of your way,' she said.

'I'm going out anyway, to the hospital. As soon as darkness falls, people start thinking they are going to die, but a quick visit helps quell the fears until morning. Well, sometimes it does.'

'I hate hospitals. They're spooky places at night,' she said, thinking of her mother.

He touched her arm, and she had a sensation of the hairs standing up, a thrill.

'Clare I'd like to drive you home. OK?'

'Yes, that would be great. I don't think I'm in any state to drive.' Surprisingly, though, she did not feel drunk.

'I'll be back in a few minutes.'

He walked up the street towards the church. She went in and had a cup of tea with Tommy. About ten minutes later

Lorcan arrived at the door, and after a quick goodbye to Tommy they left. Lorcan held the car door open for her and she got in, noting he was dressed in his priest garb. He saw her looking and said, 'Yes, I'm afraid a quick change was needed. It's more reassuring for them to see me in my gear.'

She laughed. They chatted easily on the way over, and when they got to the flat, he turned off the engine and looked at her. 'I'm so glad you came over tonight. I enjoyed the pub. It hasn't been the same without you. It's hard for me to stop thinking about you.'

'Did you ever get around to talking to anyone? I mean like you said you would.' She felt awkward mentioning it, but he answered immediately.

'No, I'm afraid I didn't. I've prayed about it a lot, though. I suppose I thought if I didn't see you, it would just evaporate – my feelings I mean. But I'm being naïve, I know that.'

She was tempted to tell him then that he had permeated every waking thought of hers and that even three days of glorious sex with a young, good-looking man hadn't helped a bit. But she bit her tongue, realising that it would be a selfish remark and would only worsen things.

'Thank you for the lift,' she said instead. 'Goodnight.' On impulse she leaned across and kissed him briefly on the cheek. His skin was soft, warm. He made a little sound, an intake of breath. She wondered if she'd been too daring, but he smiled at her, touching his cheek in acknowledgement.

He started the engine again. 'I'd better get over there, it's getting late. You'll be back over to see Tommy?'

'Yes, I'm off to London tomorrow morning, back late on Sunday night (I'll have to come and get the car from Daddy), then down to Dublin on Monday to do the film. I'll be back on the Sunday.'

'Good Lord,' he interjected. 'You have a busy life.'

'Not really. In this job it's either a feast or a famine.'

'Well, I'll maybe run into you when you're over next.'

Suddenly she wanted to know *when* she would see him again. She needed a date, something to look forward to. 'Maybe you'd come and have tea with Tommy and myself next Sunday when I get back. Daddy thinks oul Minnie Madden has you half starved.'

He laughed.

She loved the sound of his laugh – it made her heart smile.

'Well,' he said, 'put it like this: she's not exactly Delia Smith, but she fairly shoves the calories into us. So it's far from starved we are. But I'd be delighted to come. Maybe Tommy could persuade you to cook one of those amazing curries he's been on about.'

'Curries on Sunday! Does the Church allow that?'

They were both laughing now, she hadn't felt this happy in ages. They agreed a time, and she reluctantly opened the door and got out, skipping up the steps to the flat without looking back. She heard him drive off and she went in. It was time to talk about these feelings to someone. She dialled Paula's number.

As she listened to the number ring, her doorbell sounded shrilly, startling her.

Her first thought was that Lorcan had come back. She put down the phone and opened the door. Robert stood on the doorstep. She stood there staring at him. 'What do you want?'

'That's not a very welcoming response, is it? Aren't you going to ask me in?'

'Of course, come in. I'm sorry – I'm just in myself. I was over at Daddy's.'

She was interrupted by her phone ringing. She moved over and picked it up. Robert sat down on the settee and waited. It was Paula.

'Darling! I almost broke my neck getting to the phone – I was on the loo and then you hung up – I dialled one-four-seven-one. *Well*,' she drawled. 'Everything OK? I hope you've a good explanation for being incommunicado for three days!'

'Listen, Paula, I can't talk now. I'll call you later. Are you going to be up for a while?'

'Yes.' Paula was puzzled now. 'What's up Clare? Is everything OK? Can you talk?'

'Not right now.'

'Don't worry, call me as soon as you can. Doesn't matter how late, all right my love?'

'Yes, thanks.'

Clare put the phone down. Robert stood up and walked towards her. His arms were around her in a trice and his lips buried in her neck. 'God,' he moaned. 'I've been going crazy all day thinking about you. Can we please go into the bedroom?'

Clare disentangled herself; he was holding her so tight it actually hurt. 'Robert, look, I'm sorry, but I'm really tired, and I'm going to London tomorrow and I've packing to do.'

'Oh I see.' His eyes blazed. 'Who was that in the car with you? I was waiting for the past hour across the street. I expect I'm only one in a long line, is that it?' His lip curled unpleasantly.

The look on his face frightened her, but she decided she was being ridiculous. She'd have to remain calm. So she took his hand and led him back to the settee, her heart pounding.

'Listen, Robert.' she spoke quietly. 'That was my Daddy's priest. Daddy had a slight heart attack earlier this week – while we were here with the answerphone on. They couldn't reach me, thought I'd gone to London. You knew I was going over to see him today. I told you this morning. Anyhow, I had a few drinks while I was over and left my car there. Father O'Carroll was kind enough to drive me home.' She looked at him squarely. She wondered how she could sound so cool. Part of her was ashamed at her sangfroid, but she was worried. How much had he seen?

Robert put his head in his hands. 'God, I'm sorry,' he mumbled. 'You must think I'm an idiot. Is he OK?'

'Yes, he's fine. His doctor has told him he has to take it easy. But I'm afraid it's sort of knocked the romance out of me a bit.'

'Of course, I understand.' Then he added pleadingly, 'Could we not just go to bed and sleep?'

'Look, I'm sorry, Robert. I don't mean to be hurtful, but I really just want to be on my own. I've a lot on my mind. I'm seeing Tim when I'm in London, and I've the film all next week. I promise I'll call you when I get back. Please?'

'Well, all right. Maybe I can see you in London. I know I'm not due to see Diana until Monday, but I changed my ticket to tomorrow, so we can at least travel together. What flight are you on?'

Her heart sank. Christ, what on earth had she been thinking of these last few days? She had brought this on herself.

'I haven't paid for my ticket yet, but I'm provisionally booked on the twelve-thirty British Midland,' she lied.

'Great, well, I'll call you first thing in the morning then.' And he left reluctantly, looking pointedly in the direction of the bedroom.

She locked and bolted the door behind him, made a cup of camomile tea, and took it into the bedroom. When she had undressed and got into bed, she dialled Paula and told her the lot. She enjoyed the yarn herself – she felt it made her seem alive again.

Paula was a great listener, but then it was an interesting story, Paula was also reassuringly nonjudgemental. She was fascinated with the whole saga. 'I'm so pleased to hear you talk about someone other than Tim, my love, but he does sound a teeny bit obsessive to me, you've turned the poor child's head.'

'He'll probably forget all about me when he moves to London. To be honest I don't know what my motives were. It was so stupid of me.'

Paula laughed. 'Try lust! That should explain enough of it, fuelled no doubt by a few scoops of vino.'

'God, Paula, what am I going to say to him tomorrow morning. I feel as if I've taken advantage of him.'

'You'll think of something. What flight are you on?'

'The ten-thirty.'

'Right, then you'll be gone when he phones. Call him from the airport and say you had to get an earlier flight – an audition or something. Listen, I'm exhausted, and I've a grotty lunch at Channel Four about a script that they are probably going to reject, so I'll not be here when you come, but I'll leave the keys in the usual cubbyhole. OK? 'Night, darling.'

Clare found it peculiar to arrive back into London and not to be going home. She was one of the millions of visitors now. The place seemed so crowded compared to Belfast, the tube from Heathrow packing them in at every stop. She was pleased she had been on from the beginning and had a seat, although she was far from comfortable, squashed beside a fat, sweaty young man with earphones pounding away, destroying his hearing. Her suitcase, having started on the floor, was now on her knee, so she was unable to read. She looked around at the various faces. Of course, no one spoke. If this were Belfast, they would all be chatting away like mad. She had found it disconcerting when she first went home, this habit Belfast people had of talking away to complete strangers, but she had got used to it again. She smiled at the idea of suddenly starting a conversation with the woman opposite her, but she remained silent. She had little recollection of ever having talked to anyone on the tube, even while stuck between stations. Still, London gave her a thrill; it would always remain a special place to her, and she supposed that she would move back eventually, when everything was sorted. She had outgrown Belfast.

It was just one o'clock when she arrived at Paula's flat. Paula had left the keys as promised, and Clare let herself in. The flat was comfortable, small but tastefully furnished: one large room with a pull-out sofa and a futon. Maximum use of space, but she felt at home there. Paula's large black and white cat Oscar eyed Clare solemnly from his usual vantage point on top of the fridge. A note from Paula urging her to help herself to 'whatever' and saying that she had invited Bill and Julian round for a drink later was propped up beside the phone.

Clare pushed Tim's number. Kezia answered. Clare was thrown but she managed to stammer, 'Hello, it's Clare. Is Tim there?'

'No, he's not. Can I get him to call you?' In contrast Kezia sounded unfazed, relaxed, languid. She had a husky, affected voice – an actressy voice. Clare had thought of acquiring one years ago, and then decided she'd get more mileage out of her own accent.

'He'll be in around six. He's doing a voice-over. Perhaps we'll get to meet properly while you're over,' she added suddenly.

Clare was shaken. This was the conversation she had imagined in her head. She was finally talking to Kezia, who was living in *her* house. The worst was happening.

'I don't see any point,' she said. 'I've nothing to say to you.'

'Well, I know Tim hasn't stopped caring about you because he's with me. It's been awful for the poor darling – sometimes I catch a glimpse of his face and he looks anguished. You two were together such a long time. *I* feel awful about it *too*. I feel so sorry for you.'

Clare listened to her calm, assured tones and couldn't think of a reply. All the sharp biting remarks she had rehearsed in her head for months turned to ashes in her mouth.

Kezia continued, obviously on a roll now. 'In fact I don't think he meant to fall in love with me as deeply as he did. It's just one of those things. I think you and I might as well meet: I'm not going to go away. He thinks we would like each other actually, we obviously have the same taste in men.' It was her attempt at a joke. She wasn't sounding quite so confident now. Clare's silence had unnerved her.

'Ask him to call me please,' Clare said. 'I'm at Paula's; he has the number, thanks.'

She was on the verge of tears when she put the phone down, but she collected herself. It was inevitable that they would at least have to talk on the phone, and really, she reasoned, her quarrel shouldn't be with Kezia. Tim had obviously made himself available. He had stopped loving her; if not they would still be together.

She was emotionally wrung out. The day hadn't started well, with prima donna tactics from Robert when she had called from the airport to say she was getting an earlier flight. She had explained the decision as Paula had suggested, unexpected job interview. He hadn't believed her, but she really didn't care. She took his number in London; he was staying with a friend and she promised to try to see him. She was grateful when she could truthfully say she had no more change and anyway her flight was being called. She had thought the whole Robert business over, while on the plane, and felt she had screwed up pretty badly. Her emotions about Lorcan and Tim had clouded her judgement. She would have to extricate herself from the affair with care. She just had not reckoned on his taking it all so seriously. She had a sickening feeling it wasn't going to be easy.

As for Tim, she needed to give herself some space there too. It was all too raw. It had been her life for almost ten years. It hadn't *all* been bad, just the leaving. It was all obscured now by the bitterness of the break-up. Tim was essentially a good man. He was kind to women, he knew how to treat them – as they wished to be treated, equally. He was a supportive partner. As good a cook as Clare, and better at ironing. He was loving and attentive, and she should have married him years ago. He had wanted her to get married on her thirtieth birthday. Now, she thought, here she was just a month away from her thirty-eighth. The years had flown. Maybe they would have had children by now, be a family. But then who was to know what would have happened? Marriages break up too.

Meeting Lorcan at this point in her life was confusing too. It was hard to look at it dispassionately. Her instincts told her that her attraction to Lorcan would still have been this strong even if she had still been with Tim. It was so alarmingly forceful. But she couldn't be sure: it had happened at a time when she was emotionally volatile, and circumstances had caused her to doubt her own judgement. She phoned Diana's mobile to say she was on her way, and went outside and hailed a cab. She was working, after all – she didn't feel like braving the tube again.

Diana was her usual ebullient self. They met in the Ivy. It was conveniently near Diana's office. It was also somewhere Clare used to go with Tim when they had money. She liked the place. He probably took Kezia here now, she thought. Diana ordered a bottle of Chablis, and Clare accepted a glass gratefully. They talked shop mostly – Clare had resolved not to bring the conversation round to Tim, being sure Diana was heartily sick of it all.

And what could she say, really? It was all a *fait accompli*. The conversation with Kezia had at least convinced her of that. There was a smug triumphant tone in Kezia's voice that let Clare know she had been truly ousted.

She concentrated on the food, and tried not to laugh at the fact that one of Diana's shoulder pads had worked its way down her front and made her already expansive bosom simply enormous. They had just finished eating when Diana turned the chat around to Robert, catching Clare off guard for a minute.

'Isn't he a sweetheart? I've no one on my books around his age. What is he, eighteen? Haven't got his cv yet.'

'No, he's nearly twenty actually.' Clare suddenly minded the two years. Eighteen was just too absurdly young.

'Well, a *baby* at any rate. Yes, but he's good though, very *promising*. He's coming over on Monday, staying the week, actually I've managed to get him a few interviews. I think he should do well. Seems quite keen, phoned *and* wrote to me the day after the play, but I didn't mind for once because I think he'll be good. Whatever *it* is, he has it. Don't you think?'

'Yes, yes,' said Clare, 'I'm sure he has. He's keen all right.'

Diana picked up the tone at once. 'Don't you like him?'

'Yes, I do, of course I do, he's a great lad, delightful. I've been a friend of his parents for years. Sorry, I was thinking about something else,' she said hastily.

'Oh, Tim?' Diana sighed.

Clare didn't correct the misunderstanding.

'Well,' Diana said, obviously not wanting to engage her on the subject. 'You seem in much better form, you look better too. I'm sure this weekend will convince you it's all for the best. I knew all you needed was a few good jobs, darling. More wine?' She nodded towards the waiter. He came at once. Diana never had any trouble in getting good service.

When Clare arrived back at Paula's, she phoned Tim's number again. He answered this time. He agreed to meet her the following day at the flat. Paula, who was home by now, offered to go with her, but Clare felt she had to face this alone.

They chatted about it that evening over a meal. Bill and Julian had come over for drinks, and ended up staying for dinner, which of course was cooked by Bill, who worked wonders with the ramshackle odds and sods he found in the kitchen. Paula made no secret of her distaste for the task.

Several bottles of wine had been drunk, and naturally the chat had encompassed everything, from Clare's fling with Robert, to the ongoing saga of Tim and Kezia. Bill and Julian had taken gossip to an art form. The subject of Lorcan was *not* on the agenda; even Paula hadn't been taken into her confidence on that.

They were agog at the idea of Robert. Julian was teasing her to call him right there and then and ask him over. 'Go on then, sweetie, if you know where he's staying. It's simply not fair to keep beautiful young men to yourself.'

Bill cut in then, slipping into his limp-wrist routine. 'Darling, we'd be *awfully* good to him, just think of it. We could launch him into London society.'

Julian was roaring with laughter.

'You must be joking,' Clare retorted. 'I'm having enough trouble clearing my conscience as it is!'

'Yes, can you imagine?' Paula was shrieking by now. 'First telling his parents that you took him to bed and debauched him, and then that you introduced him to two of your gay friends who were going to look after him in London. Yes, I bet they'd love that. His father would probably have you interned.'

It was an evening of great hilarity, and though part of her felt disloyal to Robert, she enjoyed it so much. She felt like taking their advice and moving back straight away, but she'd see how she felt when she saw Tim tomorrow. That was why she was here, after all. Lately, when she'd been having fun and feeling back to normal, she had begun to realise that, the last year, she had been what her mother would have called 'a droopy drawers'. It was good to feel that she was getting back to her old self, even if she couldn't sustain it all the time.

Paula insisted on leaving her over to the flat to meet Tim, and would have come in with her, but Clare assured her once again that she'd much rather do it on her own. She had to face him eventually. He had said he'd be there all Saturday afternoon, to just come after lunch. She had thought of going there earlier and perhaps surprising him with Kezia, but it was a stupid notion, and fortunately she had thought better of it. The experience would be too demeaning and she wasn't ready to see them together – not yet.

She had keys, but rang the doorbell anyway. She wasn't sure what she would be walking in on. She assumed he would be alone, and he was. Her heart lurched when she saw him. Part of her longed for him to take her in his arms and say it was all some ghastly mistake, to kiss her the way only he could. Their mouths fitted so well together: she remembered the first time they had snogged, the feeling of his mouth being the one made just for her. But that was the stuff of cheap novels, this was reality. In the short term, the best she could hope for was to feel indifferent to him. Maybe, eventually, they could reconstruct an uneasy friendship, but it would be hard.

He smiled, looking a bit abashed – his vulnerable look. *He* wasn't immune to *her* either. He offered coffee and was obviously going to take the cue for his mood from her. They had always done that when they were together, set each other's moods. She used to think this was unusual, but neither had ever had the power to cheer the other up. Extraordinary really, in a relationship that had lasted so long. She couldn't remember if it had been like that at first; then, just the sight of the other or being together was a good enough recipe for joy. Latterly it had been different, even before Kezia's arrival on the scene.

'Where is she?' Clare asked. 'Does she live here now?'

'No,' Tim replied evenly, his mouth tight, his neck stiff in that way he had when he was being patient, trying not to lose his temper. He answered Clare as if he was translating from another language.

Men do that a lot anyway, she thought.

'I've told you, she has her own place, but she stays here a bit. If you agree to a price, then she'll maybe sell her place, and move in, but not until then. And of course we would do it all properly, get it valued and all that.' He looked uncomfortable.

'How do you know you'll still be together?' she rejoined.

'I don't know that,' he continued in automaton mode. 'But we can only live from one day until the next, can we not?'

His tone jarred with her. She knew it was defensive, but it

was wounding. He doesn't love me any more she thought, and it was painful.

'I don't want to sell right now!' Clare said suddenly, surprising even herself. 'It's too soon. I don't feel like starting to divide things up, making piles of yours and mine, ruining our home.'

She could feel the tears well up, and Tim, knowing the signs well, immediately interjected. 'OK, OK, OK. *Fine*. There's no rush. You were the one who wanted to sell out, remember? It wasn't my suggestion. It's just that I can't afford the entire mortgage on my own, and I'm sure you can't either.' His voice softened and he touched her arm. 'Clare, sweetheart, I'm sorry it's all ended like this, but we can't go on waging a war of attrition forever. It's not as if I've sprung it all on you. You've been in Belfast almost three months.'

'I know, I know,' she said wearily. 'You're right, I just find it hard to take. I expect I was still hoping we might work it out.'

'Yes, but we haven't.'

'You're in love with her, then?'

'I'm not sure, what does that mean, *in love*? I don't know, perhaps I am. It suits me now, *she* does, I mean. We suit each other. She's like me – contained.'

'You mean I'm not?'

'No, not at all, I mean, she doesn't have your confessional urge. Sometimes I feel you're like a running tap. Your emotions just pour from you.'

God, she thought, English bastard. Compared to the rest of Ireland, I'm self-contained, cold even. 'So is that what you like about her, her self-containment?' she asked.

'Yes, she doesn't feel the need to analyse everything as you did. It suits me better now.'

What a recommendation, she thought, but she dismissed the feeling. She had loved him for over ten years. He couldn't be that bad. She should pull herself together really. God knows when she would be over in London again, and they had to make a start sometime. Why not now? It was as good a time as any – she needed to let go.

He looked at her steadily. 'What do you want to do? Shall we leave it or not?'

'Well, I expect you're right,' she said. 'We'll have to do it some time, so let's have a look at the spoils.' She had meant the remark to sound light-hearted, but she could tell from his reaction that it had instead sounded caustic, sour. She couldn't ever get it right with him any more. Things were too far gone between them; the damage was irreparable.

With an aching heart, she spent the next few hours helping him to sort through their joint possessions. Neither of them was in form to argue, or claim any thing in particular. They were efficient, like two volunteers organising a jumble sale. There was a heaviness about them both: she could tell that he was unhappy too, but he had that male ability, at least she thought of it as more a male thing, to be unemotional, matter-of-fact, efficient. He would have made a good surgeon, she thought. Part of her, too, was detached from it all, watching in quiet horror as all the smaller furnishings in the flat, photo albums and other precious mementoes of their last ten years, were moved into piles. She had to be. There was no other way to get on with it.

They both resisted the temptation to dwell too long on the framed photos of their happy moments together, poses that mocked these painful proceedings. They decided that Clare could have all the frames, the photos removed, shelved to become vague memories of their last ten years. It was so maudlin, so melodramatic.

They had agreed that he would pay her something for the curtains and larger furniture; things like sofas. It struck her then that the best thing would have been to let him have the lot. In the end it would have been more satisfying. Clare looked around at the piles on either side. It was hard to believe they were dismantling it all in an afternoon.

Finally they had both had enough. She was meeting some friends at the National Theatre, and she was sure he had to see Kezia, though he gave the impression of having all night. At times he could be a cool customer indeed.

He promised to pack all she had selected and bring it over to Julian and Bill, who had agreed to store it. She knew she could trust him to do this. He was honest with everything but his heart, she thought. When she was leaving, he said, 'Mum and Dad were asking about you. I said I'd ask you to call them.'

'Have you told them?' She genuinely loved his parents and had missed the contact. They had embraced her fully as part of the family – sad, really, the fallout from break-ups, she thought. She felt bad that she probably wouldn't see them again. They were both approaching retirement. She would call them when things settled.

'Yes, and they've taken it badly. You know how much they like you.'

'Have they met *her*?'

'No, of course not,' he said tersely.

'What do you mean, of course not?'

'Clare, for Christ's sake, I'm not totally insensitive. Give me a break will you? They'll meet her eventually I suppose. There's no rush.'

'No, I expect not – just the rush to leave me I suppose.'

'We were drifting apart long before I met her.' He spoke in a measured voice, as if he was stating a known fact.

She felt like cracking something over his skull. She hated his superiority, his ability to sound reasonable about the unreasonable. Liar, she thought. Fucking *liar*. But she said, 'Well Tim, you *have* to think that, don't you?'

He said nothing.

She felt wretched when she left, bruised, depleted, but as the day progressed she felt lighter, more focused, and she wondered why it had taken her so long to get to this. She would move on now. She had shed a skin. She was a survivor and she knew with certainty she'd make it without him. The pain would take a while to shift, but she'd get through.

She met Paula at the Cottesloe. The play was good. She enjoyed it. Meeting the cast afterwards was always so much easier when the play had been a success and the cast could be faced without the mask of too bright smiles and false congratulations. It was an Irish play by a hot new playwright, and there were quite a few people she knew in the audience, and a lot of them in the bar afterwards. It could have been awkward seeing old friends, but the security of having just finished a play, and having work to go to, helped. Acting could be such a bitchy and insecure business (though Clare was aware that actors didn't hold the monopoly on either bitchiness or insecurity). Compliments were not always given graciously, but tonight the overall opinion was favourable, and the buzz good. Clare had the extra dimension of the Tim and Clare saga to contend with. There were a few people present whom she knew were still in touch with Tim, a few friends of Kezia too, pointed out by Paula. But the subject wasn't broached, apart from a few sympathetic *How are you*s. No direct mention, even from very close friends. She suspected, however, that she was under observation. She knew she was looking well. Her move back to Belfast had become a talking point, made her interesting again, for a while at any rate.

The evening passed in a flurry of chat and drink, and she was glad she'd come. Now and again Lorcan would flit through her mind, and her face must have registered this, because Paula mistakenly accused her of thinking of Robert. 'Darling! You're looking impossibly smug now. Dare I say, like someone who's had a surfeit of young flesh! I'm jealous.'

Clare couldn't get Lorcan out of her mind, and the following morning she called her father at a time Lorcan might possibly be there. He wasn't. She was tempted to ask if Tommy had seen him, but she didn't dare – her father was no dozer.

'You needn't be worrying about me,' he said. 'I'm grand. Brid has practically moved in. She's putting my head away. So don't be fussing. Just you get on down to Dublin and do yer filum.' He always gave the word the extra vowel; it managed to make it sound ridiculous. 'Sure, aren't you lucky to be getting a part in a filum at your age?'

Great, Da, make me feel good! she thought. 'Oh,' he said as she was about to hang up. 'Tony was looking your number in London, that wee actor fellow he was doing the job for has lost it. Are you not supposed to be seeing him?'

'Did you give it to him?'

'I did of course, I gave him the number you left. He phoned Tony to the house and all, so I knew it must be important.'

Her heart sank.

Paula, lounging with the Sunday papers, a hangover and a cup of coffee (they had been very late last night) looked at her askance when she reported this. 'Oh dear – a teeny bit obsessive, our Robert? Well, my love, we'll just screen all the calls. You're leaving tomorrow anyway.'

'Thank God. You know, I'm sure it's all got to do with the excitement of getting an agent, and I expect he feels that's all tied in with me. I'll wait until I'm back from Dublin to call him. I think that would be best.'

All the same, Robert was beginning to worry her.

Dublin had changed dramatically over the years that Clare had lived away from Ireland. She didn't get to go there often enough, but it was one of those places she felt truly at home in. She always left Dublin feeling it was too soon to go, with a sense that she was missing something. There was a tremendous buzz about the place now. Compared to Dublin, Belfast had the feel of a small town, lacking the cosmopolitan edge.

The streets were full of young people, a multiplicity of tongues and accents, making it seem so much more European to her than London. The newly redeveloped Temple Bar area was vibrant, teeming with people. It was stylish, this inner-city enclave, full of cafés, restaurants and pubs. New European architecture reclaiming the old rundown buildings and yet retaining the old world feel of the narrow streets. They were making the film there. The South of Ireland was a haven for filmmakers now, something to do with the tax laws, and you could tell that the people were used to film crews. They barely got a glance from most of the passers-by.

The film crew and the director were young – very young, she thought wistfully, but she wasn't going to allow herself to indulge in *what if* thoughts. She was here now, and she was happy with the opportunity to be in the film. She had to suppress a grin at the crew, though. It was all such a cliché. Lots of eager, impossibly thin young women running round, posing, and talking loudly into mobile phones. But they were getting the job done, and the enthusiasm was infectious. The director knew exactly what he wanted, which was a relief, and he was good. It was a low-budget film, but it was full-length, and despite the fact that there was no money in it, at least for the actors, she felt convinced it could as always lead to something else.

She was staying in a genteel boarding house, Stor-mo-croi, on the Drumcondra Road, as were the other members of the cast who had less than a week on the production. These were three young lads who were full of the joys of film. The leads were staying in town. The company had obviously got a deal on the lodgings. She didn't mind not being in the centre of Dublin, and she was able to park her car at the back. She wasn't sure why she had brought it in the first place – the trains were regular enough – but at least she could leave any time. Stor-mo-croi was like a set for a film. Although it was clean, and beautifully kept, the place hadn't been redecorated for years. It was pure sixties: early motel with holy pictures. They all loved it, because it was comfortable above all else and because the decor gave them all something to talk about in the van on the way in, in the mornings. They had long hysterical conversations about the crocheted Spanish ladies that discreetly covered the toilet rolls, and the little gingham knickers sported by the African warrior ornaments that lined the mantelpiece in the lounge.

The lady of the house, Mrs O'Leary, was up early every morning with full cooked breakfasts ready for them at seven, despite their earnest entreaties that there was catering on site.

'Ah no, I couldn't do that, sure yis have paid for it.'

And so they staggered through the first of two breakfasts. Clare enjoyed coming back there in the evenings: it gave her time to think. The three lads would go off with the crew for a jar, but she decided she'd wait till the Saturday to join them. She was determined not to look ragged on film, and any alcohol the night before a shoot made her look like a vampire. So she was being sensible for once.

Tommy sounded in fine form on the calls to Belfast. It struck her that he was a bit more forthcoming on the phone, as if his recent brush with illness had made him more in need of the contact. Again she had the reassurances that Brid was over, and some news: her younger sister Monica had phoned – she was thinking of taking a trip home.

'I suppose,' Tommy complained to Clare, 'that Brid one has phoned her to worry her about my health. I told her not to be coming on my account, sure the two of them haven't two ha'pennies to nip their arses with, but sure none of yis ever listen to me.'

Reading the subtext of this, Clare realised that he was secretly delighted that 'the wee one', as he called Monica, was coming home. He was moving towards an acceptance that he wouldn't be around for long, putting his affairs in order. It was heartbreaking, but she cheered herself up with the thought that his slight heart trouble might just be a warning, and he'd outlive the lot of them. His family were long livers, her grandmother had made it to ninety.

The night before Clare was due back, she phoned Tommy and Lorcan answered the phone.

Her heart almost stopped. 'Lorcan? What's up? Where's Daddy? Is he OK?'

'Clare? Hang on, Tommy's just here. He was pouring me a cup of tea and asked me to answer the phone. Here he is.'

'I got an appointment for the big heart doctor in the Royal on Monday. Brid is taking me. She's bought me a clatter of new underwear to go. She's afraid me old trunks would let her down. Do you want to hear Father Lorcan's news?'

Lorcan came on the line again. His voice made her heart beat faster. He told her that the production of *Dancing at Lughnasa* had just won at Ballymena and was through to the finals of the Ulster Amateur Drama Festival. There'd be no stopping them now. Breda was ecstatic, and Seamus, he told her, was fervently hoping for Best Actor. She resisted the temptation to make a snide comment: she wanted him to like her, and anyway, the group deserved their success, they had worked hard, so who was she to carp at it? She and Lorcan had a quick chat about the group, and she said she hoped she would see him when she got back.

'I can't wait,' he said simply.

When she put the phone down she skipped about, exhilarated. She couldn't wait to see him again.

She finished filming on the Saturday, and had her drink and night on the town with the cast members she had befriended during the shoot. The following morning, after Mrs O'Leary's monster meal, she packed up her little car and drove home.

She reached the outskirts of Belfast at one o'clock, and decided to drive straight to her father's. She would go and get something for tonight's meal: the shops were open on Sunday, and she was sure Lorcan would have remembered her invitation.

As soon as she pulled up at the door, she knew something was wrong. Tommy's outside door was closed and there was no one in. She still had her key, so she let herself in. She called upstairs, 'Daddy?'

No reply. There was a strange stillness about the place, though it all seemed normal. She ran through the house, her heart in her mouth. No, he'd gone out. Maybe he had gone to Brid's for lunch. But she had a sickening feeling it was something else. She went out into the street and rapped Winnie's door, then realised that this was Sunday, and Winnie went to her nephew's for lunch. She went back in and called Brid – no answer. So she got into the car and drove straight to Tony's. Sally was there, surrounded by kids, looking harassed. She knew at once why Clare was there.

'Clare, love, I'm awful sorry. Your daddy had a heart attack this morning. Tony's with him now. He's in the intensive care in the Royal.'

Clare didn't know how she managed to drive to the hospital, she was trembling so much. All the way, which was only a short mile, she chanted inwardly: Oh God please don't let him die, I'm so sorry for wanting Lorcan, for thinking like that about a priest. Oh God forgive me please. Please God don't let him be dead when I get there. Don't let him be dead. Please God please.

She parked the car on the Falls Road and raced into the hospital. She ran in the Accident and Emergency entrance and down the escalator to the admissions. The place was dingy, despite or perhaps because of the fluorescent lights. There were a few people sitting about looking ill at ease. She gave her father's name to the receptionist and was directed to the Coronary Care Unit. She raced down the main corridor, following the signs. Coronary Care. Turn right, Coronary Care. Hospitals filled her with despondency. She hated them. She had spent a lot of time in them during her mother's illness. Sick sad days, full of fear and futile hope. Her mother had died in this hospital, on a Friday. Five years on she remembered the evening vividly, each sequence frozen in her brain.

She had been at home, alone, in the flat. Tim was on stage. She'd been getting ready to go to meet him after the show when the phone rang.

It was Tony, sounding shaky. She knew at once, although she'd been home the week before and her mother was weak, but fine. She certainly hadn't seemed close to death.

Clare's last words to her, even now she heard the sound of saying them. Remembered the crooked way her mouth went, the prickle at the back of her throat in an effort to stop herself from crying. The quiet smile on her mother's face as she looked at her. 'Mammy, love, now don't be going and dying on me.'

'Would you go away out of that! I have no intentions of dying, go off and do your job,' said her mother. 'I'll see you in three weeks.'

That was it. A nightmare trip home for the funeral. Tommy solemn, dark-suited, bereft, pointing to the still, waxen face of her mother in the coffin. The pale lifeless hands, with blue veins visible, the rosary beads knotted round. She touched them, for the last time; there were little ridges on her mother's nails, which needed cutting she had thought.

'There's your mother, Clare. She looks peaceful doesn't she?'

The Irish had a gift for death. Excelled at it. The leaving was all. The ritual. The hoards of relatives, all remarking on the fact it took a funeral to bring them together. Wondering who would be next. The often-repeated phrase 'It's happy for her.'

'It's not happy for us!' she had shrieked at one point to someone who said this, and there had been a momentary hush as the heads shook, and then the words 'God love her', 'Upset, beside herself', were muttered from one to another and she was handed yet another cup of tea.

Please God! she pleaded, as she pushed through the plastic swing doors at the entrance to Coronary Care. Don't let me have to face it all again, not yet. Well-meaning as they all are don't let me see them again, not yet. The close cousins, the not so nice cousins, the standoffish cousins. The strange comfort in having them all there, all the aunts, all the uncles, all fifty-six of the first cousins who still lived in Ireland. A number that when quoted to friends in England had caused astonishment and mirth.

Tommy don't die on me, she prayed, please. She chanted it like a mantra as she approached the nursing station.

'My daddy! My daddy! Tommy Murphy,' she blurted to the nurse.

The nurse was sympathetic, but brisk. 'Yes, he's in the first cubicle, he's very ill. The doctor has spoken to your sister and brother; they're in with him now. You can go in for a minute.'

There were no windows in the ward. Instead it was brightly lit by garish overhead strip lights. Brid and Tony were sitting at the bottom of the bed, their faces drawn. Her father was lying white-faced, his white hair slicked back, his eyes closed. He had a drip in his arm and a plastic bag at his side collecting his urine. He seemed to be wired to a machine beside the bed. The monitor had a green neon line and it beeped constantly, Brid was staring at it fixedly, as if she was willing it to keep him going. Clare suppressed a sob.

Tony put his arm round her and motioned her towards the door. 'C'mon kid, let's go outside for a second.'

She tiptoed out in front of him. He hugged her; he was crying and so was she.

'Oh God, Tony, I don't want him to die. I couldn't bear it if he died.'

'Don't be daft kid, he won't die. Sure he's a fighter, he might pull through. He's surprised us before.'

Brid came out. She too had been crying. She held on to Clare for a minute. 'They said his blood pressure is still very low, and his condition is still serious.'

Clare interrupted. 'Is he unconscious?'

'No, the nurse said he's just been given a lot of morphine. He's sleeping it off. He has to be allowed to rest, and only two of us can be in with him. Peter's taken the boys to his mum's. I can stay, can you?'

'Of course. Brid, did you phone Monica?'

'No. I thought it was too early. What time is it there? Middle of the night. Maybe we should wait to see how he is.'

Tony looked ashen. If anything happened to her father, Clare thought, it would hit him hardest. He saw Tommy every day, and although they complained about each other nonstop, Tony idolised his father.

He said, 'Brid talked to the doctor – he was your year at Queen's. He says to bleep him when you arrive.'

'I'd like to go back in and sit with him for a while,' she said. 'Can you ask them to bleep the doctor?'

Brid nodded and went over to the nursing station.

The doctor arrived a few minutes later, and she moved outside away from the bedside to talk to him. She remembered him – she had gone out with a medical student at Queen's for a while, and this was one of his friends. The name hadn't reached the surface of her memory, but he held out his hand. 'Bernard McEnroe.'

'Of course, Bernard, nice to see you.'

They nodded, awkward to be meeting under these circumstances.

'Clare Murphy, you haven't changed. I see you on the TV from time to time. Your poor daddy, he's fighting away there. You never know – he could pull through, but he's had a big one. I'd say, a lot of damage to the heart. We'll have to see how he does over the next twenty-four hours.'

He had a nice, easy manner, she felt comforted by him, glad that Tommy was not in the care of a total stranger. They went back in to their vigil. Tony went home to freshen up and see the kids.

Brid and Clare sat together quietly, watching the machines bleep, and the green line rise and fall; occasionally they talked softly. Now and then Brid would touch her father's hand, hoping for a response. It felt icy. All around them the nurses – there were three of them – quietly and efficiently tended to the other two patients, coming over to check on Tommy every ten minutes or so, rearranging his pillows. Tommy lay still, pallid. Tony came back early in the evening and let Brid go home. Their father lay quietly, no change in his condition. Every couple of hours Bernard would appear, check Tommy's functions, and give them a progress report.

Clare wondered if he ever went home. She assumed he had a

wife and family. At one point she couldn't stop herself, and asked, 'Bernard, do you think he's going to die?'

Bernard's face was grave. 'It's not certain, but I think you should prepare yourselves for that. I'm off duty now,' he said. 'I'll see you in the morning.'

By late evening, Brid was back and was standing outside convincing Clare she should go home, or even up to her house for a few hours' sleep. Clare decided to go up to Kinsale Street; Tony promised to phone or come straight up if there was any change.

The house was quiet; it felt as if it too was waiting, keeping vigil. She was about to go into the back room when she suddenly had an urge to get into her father's bed. She lay on top of it; it smelled of him, it was comforting, and despite herself she dozed off for a few hours. She awoke, feeling stiff, about five-thirty and called the hospital.

Her father's condition was stable. What did that mean exactly? Over the years of the Troubles there had been so many medical reports on casualties. Condition stable. Critical condition. Not seriously injured. Medical jargon. She thought about it all as she hurried back to the hospital. Brid met her as she arrived at the Coronary Care Unit. She looked excited. 'Daddy's been awake for about an hour and the nurses say there's been a great improvement in his condition.'

They both went to the bed and their father had indeed opened his eyes. Tony was smiling nervously, talking quietly to him. At breakfast time, Bernard McEnroe arrived, and pulled the curtains round the bed and asked them all to leave for a while. The sisters and brother paced anxiously outside.

When Bernard finally came out again he was smiling. 'Well,' he said, 'it looks like he's decided not to leave us just yet. Let's give him another twenty-four hours and we'll see how he does. He's strong for his age and obviously he's put up quite a fight.' Bernard's bleep sounded as he was talking, and he excused himself, saying as he left, 'You can go in now. I'll see you later.'

Tommy gave Clare his toothless grin. His voice sounded weaker. He looked like an old man. Not her daddy.

'Well, Clare love,' he said, in a low voice, 'they're making an awful lot of fuss over me, saying I had a heart attack. I don't agree, I think it was that oul pastie I got from Alfonso's. I think it didn't get the whole way down, it was that greasy.'

Brid put her schoolteacher look on. 'Clare, you know Dr McCann told him to cut out the greasy food. He listens to no one!'

Tommy made a face behind Brid's back.

Clare gave him a hug: he smelled of tobacco and Lifebuoy soap and above all of himself, his Daddy smell, familiar, comforting. She pulled a chair up to the bed. 'You will have to take it easy for a while. You gave everyone a bit of a scare.'

Brid turned round to look at Clare, her face troubled. 'There's no talking to him: he mowed our garden last Sunday as soon as Peter's back was turned,' she snorted. 'One word from us and he does what he likes.'

'Well, Brid,' said Tommy, 'yourself and Peter had my head turned, whether Peter would do it or you would. I thought I'd get it done and let yis whinge away.'

Clare took his hand, squeezing it gently. 'Daddy, you really *should* try to take it easy, we don't want anything to happen to you.'

'Ach, will ye give my head peace. Nothing will happen to me. They're going to keep me in – it'll save yis having to drive me down to my appointment in the morning. The wee nurse says they'll take me down in a wheelchair.'

'Listen to him,' said Tony. 'He's them all organised and he's only in.'

'Anyway,' Tommy continued, 'it's not my heart, there's nothing wrong with my heart. It's in here.' He dug his finger into his chest at his breastbone. 'In here, feels like indigestion.'

He clasped the left side of his chest, dramatically. 'This here is your heart.'

While he was speaking, the neon green line suddenly sputtered, evened out, and dropped off the monitor. The screen darkened. Blank. Black.

It seemed that they all stopped breathing simultaneously. There was a moment of stillness. The hum of the other goings-on in the ward seemed to Clare like some dreamlike buzz in another part of her head. Tony almost broke her hand squeezing it. Brid stifled a sob.

Then Tommy continued talking. 'I don't see what he means about taking it easy. I spend most of . . .' He tailed off. All three of his children were laughing helplessly, and tears were running down Brid's face.

Tommy stared at them. 'In the name of Jesus, are yis right in the head or what? What's so bloody funny, eh?'

Tony pointed to the blank monitor, choking with laughter. 'You're clinically dead, Da.'

'Does that mean yis have to sit cackling like a pack of hyenas at the bottom of my bed? Begod, I'm sure them wee nurses think yis are nuts.'

The nurse was over in seconds. A tube had disconnected, and she fixed it.

Later, when Tommy's children all talked about it, they agreed that the whole thing had taken less than a minute, but it was a preview. Clare thanked God it wasn't to happen yet.

By late morning, Tommy was sitting up having a cup of tea, and they were beginning to feel slightly in the way. The young doctor, who was a competent, reassuring fellow, said he seemed stable enough, so Clare allowed herself the luxury of going home to have a shower and something decent to eat. They'd had a few excursions down to the dank underground cavern that was the hospital visitors' cafeteria, but she hadn't felt like eating. Now she was suddenly ravenous. She stopped at the garage on the way over and bought herself some eggs, milk, and tomatoes. She fancied an omelette. She cooked, had a shower, ate, and got ready to go back to the hospital. She didn't use the phone, she wanted to keep the line free in case Tony, who was staying with Tommy, needed to call. She still couldn't believe he was OK, not just yet. She had told Brid that she would call Monica and let her know about her father.

Lorcan was sitting with Tommy when she got back. His face was grave, but he managed a smile for Clare. Neither Brid nor Tony was there.

'You poor thing, this wasn't great news on your homecoming. Mind you, he's looking a whole lot better than he did in the middle of the night.'

'Oh, you were in?'

'Yes, Brid told me I'd just missed you.' He looked fondly at Tommy. 'I think he's going to have to promise you all to cut down on the lawnmowing and the fluid. Isn't that right Tommy?'

'Sure, there'll be no fun in living then. What do they want me to do, eh? Sit like an oul lad all day long. No smoking, no drinking, and no moving. Sure where's the fun in that? I'd be better dead!'

'Daddy, they just mean you to take it *easier*. Dr McEnroe was saying you're very active for your age, you just have to slow down a bit.'

Tommy snorted his disagreement.

Lorcan got up to leave, 'I'll let you two have a chat. I'm back down in an hour or so. I'll pop my head round the door then.' And he was gone.

'Lovely fella that,' said Tommy. 'He's got a nice way with him, just treats everyone the same. Not like some of them, too full of themselves to bother with the likes of us ... Well?' he asked Clare. 'Did you ring the wee one?'

'Yes, I did, and she's coming home.'

'Now what's the point of that?'

'Well, she was coming anyway, Daddy. She's just moving her trip forward.'

'Well if anything happens to me, there's no point in her coming home for a funeral. A waste of money, if you ask me, I'd be just as happy thrown into a bin bag and buried in the Hatchet Field.' He warmed to his subject. 'Do you know how much oul Johnny Cassidy paid for his wife's coffin? Nearly a thousand pounds. Have you ever heard of anything as stupid? Sure, who'll see it when it's all covered in dirt? Don't they only bury it!'

His indignation was preposterous. Clare didn't know whether to laugh or cry.

'Sure we're all going to go sometime, love, and I've had a good life. There's a limit to the amount of enjoyment you get walking up and down to the post office and round to the bookie's.'

Tommy was out by the end of the week, frailer, diminished somehow. But though he might have been weaker in body, he was still giving out about everything, and only with great reluctance did he agree to stay with Brid for a week. Monica was arriving on the following Sunday, and if he was to move back to the house, then Clare thought, she'd better go over and get the place into shape.

Somehow when she was staying there it hadn't been possible. All the attempts to fix things up were met with comments like, 'Can you not leave well enough alone,' and 'Sure who'll see it, and would you not sit down and stop fussing, you're making me dizzy.'

She asked Tony to redo Tommy's room from one of his endless pots of leftovers, no matter what the colours were. If her father could live with Winnie's curtains, he could live with anything. The rest of the house wasn't too bad, it would do. Whether Tommy liked it or not he was going to be rehoused within the next year or so. The street was virtually the only one left standing in the area. She decided she would get her father a duvet. He'd been sleeping under blankets for years. Probably since the war, she thought ruefully, as she pulled them off his bed. He said he liked the bit of weight. 'So fill the duvet with bricks!' Tony quipped to her when she told him this.

The room she had stayed in was fine, bearable – despite the peach-and-green decor. Monica could have that. Knowing Monica, once she had spent a few days with Tommy she'd be out gallivanting anyway. Catching up with all her old mates.

Clare went over to Tommy's every day and cleaned the place from top to bottom. She enjoyed sorting out cupboards, going through Tommy's meagre possessions. It was therapeutic. Not that he had much. He had a habit of giving stuff away. She remembered one summer while still a student, she was working in the States, and she had come home to find he had cleared out all her winter clothes. He'd given them to the St Vincent De Paul. 'Sure you hadn't worn them for months,' he said when she kicked up a fuss. 'They were cluttering the place up.'

She spent hours gazing at old photographs, stored in an untidy heap in an old biscuit tin. There weren't all that many. Her parents hadn't had a camera when she was growing up. The photos of the children seemed to be mainly school photos, and pictures of the annual visits to Santa's Grotto. Two, three, four eager little faces, surrounding a series of Santas. Fat ones, thin ones, sour ones. No attempt was made to pick a matching Santa each year!

Events like their first communions were there, all three girls in the same dress. Clare had hated having to use Brid's short dress. She had wanted a long one with sticky-out skirts and lots more frills, but she did what she was told, and wore the hand-me-down. And there was Tony, looking angelic but scruffy in his communion photo. Her mother was so ashamed when the photo came from the school. He hadn't been wearing his communion suit – he had forgotten to tell her they were having the photo taken, and he was dressed in a grotty pair of shorts and a T-shirt. And to make matters worse, the teacher had put him in the front row because he'd been one of the smallest.

There was the odd snap of a day trip to Helen's Bay and, of course, the three weddings. There were cameras galore by then. Well, there'd hardly be a fourth wedding now! Lots of colour snaps of the family. Brid's stiff formal affair – with Peter's awful mother Fidelma trying to smile. *Her* parents, looking apologetic. Brid looking, well, resigned really. Tony's lower-budget version of the same and then, most surreal of all, Monica and Al, with their two oldest kids, holding hands on a windswept Pacific beach, with Clare and Brid as bridesmaids, petrified with cold. It had been St Valentine's Day. Tony hadn't been able to afford the fare out and had missed it. Tim was in a play and couldn't come. Peter had opted out with excuses of work and kids, so Brid and Clare had flown out together to San Francisco for the event. A gay priest, a close friend of Al, had married him and Monica, and they had written some outlandish declaration of love, which they read to each other. Brid had spent the entire time worrying it wasn't a proper wedding. Clare got too drunk or stoned to care. The three Murphy girls had spent most of the reception crying anyway because it was so soon after their mother's death, and because well-meaning friends of Al kept playing maudlin Irish music to make them feel at home.

Clare sorted the wedding photos into boxes. One of the heartbreaking things was that several of the early family photos had been defaced – by Brid, when she was about thirteen. She was looking through them one night, decided she was ugly, and cut her head out of a lot of them. Her mother had sensibly kept them anyway. One in particular, taken before Monica was born, struck Clare. The three of them again at Christmas: Clare smiling, posing for the camera, Tony angelic on Santa's knee, and Brid apart from the others, faceless, a forlorn hole on a little body, wrapped up in winter clothes, fists clenched tightly, with a parcel from Santa tucked under her arm. Clare wished she were closer to Brid. She expected it was her fault that Brid was always a bit stiff with her. At school, according to the nuns, Brid had been the sensible one. Clare had been the flighty one, the 'giddy goat'.

She was in and out of Tommy's for the entire week, working on the house, and did not as much as glimpse Lorcan the whole time. She gazed longingly in the direction of the church as she arrived and left each day. She had hoped he would call in. He knew her car. Brid told her that he had been to see Tommy once and had phoned once to check how he was. Sometimes she would just stand at the door and look up the street towards the church. Willing him to appear, hoping none of the neighbours would come out and engage her in the interminable conversations about Tommy's progress. He didn't appear and they invariably did.

Winnie was the worst offender. 'How is he doing, Clare love, eh? Sure, isn't he lucky he has Brid – and yourself too,' she would add hastily. 'Right enough, Brid did quare and well for herself didn't she? I believe her house is gorgeous. Would she not have him to live permanently?'

'No, Winnie, she wouldn't!' Clare would reply with as much patience as she could muster. 'And you know he'd hate that. He likes being here, in the street, with his friends, and –' she would add, if she was feeling charitable '– you know he misses the craic. And yourself too of course.'

And Winnie would smile her crazy smile, and ask her the same questions next time they chatted. The loop had obviously only one programme setting.

As promised, Tony came and decorated Tommy's bedroom, in a sort of ghastly fawn shade. Innocuous enough, she supposed. He did it, surprisingly, in one day, with some roller contraption that seemed to cover everything quickly, including himself. He looked like he had a sort of measles complexion. Job complete, he obviously felt he had at least earned himself a few jars. She went with him down to McAuley's. The pub was quiet. It was a bright summer evening and the doors were open, a real case of caution to the wind. They were chatting about things generally, both feeling as if they'd been through it over the last while. Glad that Tommy looked and felt better, and talking of organising something for Monica's return. Clare was looking forward to seeing her, even if the circumstances weren't as she would have wished. She was just finishing her drink and about to leave, when Lorcan came in. He smiled over at them, and then went up to the bar. He was with an older man whom she vaguely recognised.

'That's Charlie McCann, runs the young lad's football team,' Tony told her when she asked. 'I think Father O'Carroll trains with them now and again.' He looked at her, inviting further comment.

She finished her drink, and said nothing.

Tony continued.

'I think they're playing in the club final this weekend. M'Da'll be sorry to miss it.'

'Why don't we have another drink Tony. Here.' She handed him a fiver. 'You go and get it.'

'I thought you said only one?'

'Yes, well – I've changed my mind.'

'Suits me. I'm in no hurry.'

Tony went up to the bar to get it. She fiddled in her handbag trying to look as if she needed something, trying not to look in Lorcan's direction. She caught the eye of oul Jimmy and hoped fervently that he wouldn't come over to ask about Tommy, but he stopped Tony on the way back from the bar instead.

Tony handed her the Guinness, jerking his head in the direction of the bar. 'I suppose I would be wrong in thinking you have a wee bit of a notion of that fellow, Clare?'

'Oh for God's sake Tony, don't be so bloody stupid!'

'Ye needn't bite my head off. I only asked. As a matter of fact, to listen to him talk, you would think he'd a notion of you.'

'I'm sorry,' she said, regretting snapping at him. 'I feel a bit tense. Yes, I do like him, but he's a priest, and my life is complicated enough.'

They finished their drinks and left. Lorcan smiled and nodded goodbye to them.

She couldn't believe how disappointed she felt that he hadn't taken the opportunity to come over. She felt wounded, sore, and she realised that she had been yearning for him. Yes, that was the only word for it really, yearning. As soon as she got home, she dialled Paula's number, but there was no reply. She needed to tell someone or she'd go crazy, she thought. So she called Frances and told her everything, from the initial conversation with Lorcan, including the hair-touching episode, to her three-day fling with Robert.

Frances, after an initial gasp, listened in her usual sympathetic way, and assured Clare that it was all stress-related behaviour. Just think of all she'd been through recently. Tim finding someone else. Her daddy having a heart attack. Leaving her home in London and moving back to Belfast. That's all it was, a reaction. She'd be fine; she'd get over it. They arranged to see each other. Clare was about to hang up.

'I hope I'm not being too outspoken, Clare, you know I find the whole notion of celibacy ridiculous, but the complications of getting involved with a priest, especially in west Belfast and with your father as ill as he is. If it all came out, it would kill him. Mother of God, Clare, have you taken leave of your senses? I mean the Robert thing was crazy, but he'll probably get over it, move on to someone else.'

Clare didn't speak.

'I've annoyed you, haven't I?'

'No, Frances, you're right, I'm insane. But thank you for listening.'

Clare went to bed, but even after unburdening her soul she couldn't close her eyes. At four o'clock she was sitting in the kitchen watching the dawn break, thinking about Lorcan. It didn't stay dark for long in June in this part of the world.

The night before Monica arrived, Clare went over to leave some things in Kinsale Street. Brid was bringing Tommy over the next day. He'd been feeling a lot stronger, and was getting impatient sitting around Brid's place. He wanted back to his own house, he said. He needed to get things sorted for the wee one's arrival. Monica was getting in around noon, and Clare and Tony were going to get her from the airport. Clare hoped it would all go according to plan; her state of mind did not stretch to contingencies right now. She had had two upsetting phone conversations with Robert, and three notes from him through her door. It didn't seem to register with him that she wasn't interested. She had only managed to pacify him by saying she would meet him for a drink next week. He'd been back from London for over a week, he said, and wanted to talk to her about the possibility of moving there. Diana thought he'd get far more work if he were based in London. The sooner the better, Clare thought.

Kinsale Street was looking good, wee palace status. It was getting late by the time she had finished everything. She would buy a bottle of wine on the way home and watch a bit of TV, perhaps get a chance to catch up on things with Paula. She was locking the door on her way home when she turned to see Lorcan.

'Clare, I need to speak to you. Can I follow you over?' He sounded upset.

She nodded numbly. As she drove home she agonised. Every possible thing he might be going to say to her was flitting through her head. He'd told the bishop, he hadn't meant it. He was going to ask her to leave him in peace. He loved her, he didn't love her. He was moving to another parish. On and on the thoughts scrambled. She was nearly ill by the time they reached the flat. Prepared, for now at least, for whatever he had to say to her. She'd exhausted every possibility. He parked directly behind her outside the door; it was rare to get two parking spaces so convenient. He said nothing, simply following her to the door.

She walked ahead of him and opened the door of the flat, her hand unsteady, her heart in her mouth. She walked in and switched on the lights. When she had closed the door, he walked over and switched the lights off again and, reaching for her, clumsily put his arms around her. She held her mouth up expectantly and his lips fell on hers. It was bruising, rough, at first, and then he seemed to steady himself and his breathing slowed, and he began to kiss her gently, exquisitely.

His mouth explored hers, building the kisses, more urgently now. She responded, quickening the pace again. She began sucking at him, opening her mouth wider, trying to cover his with it. Rubbing herself against him, feeling him hard against her leg. At one point, she thought they were about to fall on the floor, but he managed to steady himself somehow, knocking the calendar off the wall behind them. His mouth was covering hers, as if to take her into him. His teeth pushed on her lips. She was excited. She wanted him, she was wet, ready, and he hadn't even touched her. His hands remained locked behind her back squeezing her, barely letting her breathe.

After a few minutes she broke away and whispered, 'Shouldn't we go into the bedroom,' wondering if that was the right thing to say, afraid speaking out loud would make him regain his senses, because now she felt half crazed with wanting him. She had stopped herself thinking about what all this meant, she wanted him inside her.

She took his hand and they stumbled into the bedroom, still in darkness: a pause would be fatal. Her thoughts tumbled and swirled. She began to undress, fumbling with the various bits and pieces of her clothing, until she was naked. Then realising he wasn't doing the same, she stopped and, reaching down, undid his fly. He was hard, and she couldn't manage it easily.

He was wearing a belt and this added to the awkwardness. He didn't help her, it was as if he was paralysed, but he allowed her to guide him into her. The intensity of the feeling was over-whelming, she came almost before he was all the way in, as did he. Only then did he allow his hands to caress her body, gently, tenderly, making a map of it. As if to find out where he'd been. He held her close. He was still fully clothed. He was trembling, and it was a full minute or so before he spoke, and then to say, 'I love you Clare, God forgive me. I love you.'

She couldn't compute it right now, couldn't feel, couldn't focus. The enormity of it all was too great. She wanted him again, and turned to him, desire bursting from her. She wanted him to hold her, reassure her.

But he was agitated, restless. He sat up and whispered quietly, 'I should go now, I have to get back.' He sounded confused. He didn't move, he was holding her tightly, as if for protection.

She reached over and turned on the light and they blinked at each other, and seeing herself naked, him clothed and dishev-elled, the absurdity of it struck her and made her want to laugh. But she heard herself say calmly, her voice coming from somewhere else, 'There's hot water. Why don't you clean up and I'll put the kettle on.' And reaching for her dressing gown from the back of the door, she went into the kitchen.

He took ages in the bathroom. She had scoured the cups, made the tea, and cleaned the surfaces and straightened the room. She wondered if he was OK, if she should knock.

But finally, out he came. His hair was wet, his face shiny, and he looked so insecure, she had to stop herself from touch-ing him. He looked at her worriedly. 'Can you get pregnant? I mean that was very irresponsible of me, I don't know what to say. I couldn't stop, I mean, I didn't want to stop. I'm glad I didn't.' His words came in a rush. 'I hope it wasn't too . . .' He trailed off. 'Well, I don't have the words really.' He smiled apologetically. 'Are you all right?'

She made a face in agreement. He was right; there was

nothing to say. At least she felt unable to think of anything appropriate. She reached for him, and he moved to her side, sat down and took her hand in his, stroking it.

'Your tea is cold.'

Not letting go her hand, he reached for the cup, and drank it in one gulp. 'I don't want to leave you, but I really should go. I have to go to the hospital. I'll come over in the morning, after Mass.' He looked sheepish when he said this. 'I have to say Mass at nine. It's Sunday,' he added unnecessarily. 'Let's not talk now.'

She curled in his arms, eyes shut. Wanting him to stay, willing him to stay.

'I'm sorry I have to go,' he repeated. 'I know it's awful timing.'

He knew what she was thinking.

He held her gently and tentatively kissed her eyelids, little, mothlike kisses. He seemed more controlled now. 'Don't worry, Clare, I love you. It'll be all right. We'll be OK.' He put the cup down, stood up and, feeling for his keys, walked to the door. She watched him go, unable to move.

After he'd gone she thought of calling Paula, and then decided she wouldn't know how to begin to tell her it all, or if she was ready to. She knew sleep wouldn't be easy, but she decided to have a bath and go to bed. They'd talk when he came back in the morning – if he came back. The impact of what had happened was just beginning to sink in.

She slept fitfully, getting up in the middle of the night to make some camomile tea. Her thoughts were insistent. She wasn't sure what would happen now, but she knew she hadn't had enough of him. The intimacy had come before the knowledge, yet she felt she would love him more as she knew him. It was hard to separate it all, to strain out the messy bits of her life prior to meeting him. Hard to sift and find the gems, which she felt instinctively were there. Did the fact that he had lost his virginity mean he had just wanted *her*, or just wanted to lose it? How did the whole incident tally with his vocation? The questions tumbled round her brain. Morning came, and she rose, exhausted, to shower and get ready to meet Tony.

The phone was ringing shrilly as she finished showering. It had been ringing on and off as she showered, and she was willing herself not to climb out dripping and answer it, hoping that it wasn't bad news about Tommy, hoping it was Lorcan and he would call back. It rang again. She wrapped herself in a towel and answered it.

Robert's voice jarred, completely the wrong person.

She suppressed her irritation and tried to sound light-hearted.

'Hello. How are things?'

'Miss Murphy, I'm beginning to feel somewhat paranoid. Are you avoiding me?'

She laughed. 'Don't be silly, you know I've been busy. I've been sorting out Daddy's house, and my sister Monica is coming home from the States. I'm picking her up at the airport in an hour. It's been frantic since I got back from Dublin.'

'How's your dad?'

'He's much better, moving back into his own house today. Look,' she said, relenting a bit. 'I'm sorry about the way things have gone, but I think we were both a bit insane those few days, and it would be madness to let things go any further. But we do need to talk things over. Why don't we meet later in the week for a coffee and have a chat?'

There was a silence, and then he backed down graciously. 'OK, that's OK. Let's do that. I'll call you later in the week.'

She was so grateful, she sounded overenthusiastic in her goodbyes. God, what a fucking mess.

She had heard no word from Lorcan by the time Tony arrived to take her to the airport, but she wasn't going to start obsessing about that. She'd too much to think about. She felt sure she'd hear from him later. For some strange reason, all the normal neurotic thoughts she could have about a man didn't seem to apply here. She knew he'd be in touch. She felt secure about that. Making love to him had calmed her, completed her.

Tony's car was a wreck like her own, but roomier and deemed appropriate, since Monica had a tendency to belong to the everything-but-the-kitchen-sink school of packing. She would have brought all the hand-me-downs for Tony's ones and muesli and coffee beans. Giant jars of salsa and God knows what else. They drove to the airport under the wishing trees, both remembering Tommy and all his yarns. There was a strong feeling that this was a fragile time for all of them. Their father meant so much. It was as if since the death of Kathleen, their mother, he had held them all with some invisible thread that got stronger each year, pulling them closer to him and to each other.

Monica's plane was late, and then there was some palaver about picking up luggage which had been checked through.

Clare pushed her tiredness to the back of her mind. The day had only started. Monica arrived looking paler and thinner than Clare remembered her. She was tired of course. They took her straight to Tommy's. They were to eat at Brid and Peter's and then bring Tommy back home.

Clare helped Monica unpack, and lay down on the settee and daydreamed about last night while her sister bathed and readied herself. Clare didn't feel like going home to change. She could have done without it all, and she was sure Monica would have preferred to go to bed, but Tommy's near miss made her feel the importance of the occasion. They took a taxi to Brid's. Monica had brought some good Californian wine for Brid and Peter, which saved them having to stop to buy any.

Tommy was thrilled to see the wee one, while protesting that they had all made a fuss about nothing and he would be proved right yet. 'Nothing wrong with my heart. Bad indigestion, probably what oul Jimmy calls it – one of them hideous hernias.'

It felt good to be together again. Brid had gone to enormous trouble. Sally and Tony's five were included. The children were fed first, and then the adults sat down. Tommy, playing the patriarch, seemed genuinely thrilled to have them all there. They had all the crystal out, and the best china. Clare felt a surge of love for her older sister. Everything had to match up. Her old bat of a mother-in-law did not help Brid's feelings of inadequacy. Peter had provided some fairly classy wine and the meal was excellent. Brid was better at the plain things, like roast lamb, which they were having. Monica wasn't a vegetarian any more, which was a relief. She had recently gone back to eating 'murdered animals', she told them, because her children had been corrupted by 'Happy Meals' and the like, and she had got fed up with organic lentils. 'The time required for extra bowel movements was enough to put your head away!' Monica could be very droll.

The phone rang in the middle of the meal, and Brid went into the hall to answer it. She returned and announced, archly, that it was for Clare. 'Father O'Carroll, if you don't mind. I told him you were in the middle of dinner.'

Clare went into the hall feeling apprehensive. She picked up the phone.

'Clare, I'm really sorry for ringing you there. Look, I know this is crazy but I don't have your home number, and I remembered you'd all be there. Today was impossible. Can I come over tonight? Are you all right?'

'Yes, yes, and you can. I'm fine now, I'm glad you called. I want to see you.' She gave him her number. 'We're in the middle of dinner, but I'm going home afterwards. Come then, call me first. I don't know when I'll be back.'

She went back to the dining room, her heart singing, trying to look nonchalant.

'Well, what was all that about?' Brid was all ears. All eyes were on Clare.

She smiled blithely at them. 'He just wanted to let me know St Brendan's are in the finals this week, and he didn't have *my* number, and he knew I'd be here.'

'Is it that important?' Brid looked sceptical, but fortunately Tommy began to praise Lorcan to Monica and they all joined in. There was little doubt of their fondness for him. He had been a stalwart throughout Tommy's illness, dropping in to the hospital twice a day, and over to Brid's several times this past week. Clare didn't speak, unable to think of anything to say that wouldn't reveal her feelings. She felt like a window was open to her soul. She sat quietly, enjoying their obvious warmth towards him.

'Well, Clare, you're not saying much for a change,' Monica joked. 'Are you not part of his fan club? I can't wait to meet him.'

'Sorry, I wasn't thinking. I'm a bit tired – I didn't sleep well.'

The chat changed to yarns about growing up, about Kathleen their mother, and about how the neighbourhood had changed. They were all in some way euphoric, glad this reprieve had been granted to them – this last supper. The atmosphere was heightened. The evening flew, and Clare finished her meal without tasting a bite. Peter insisted on taking Monica and Tommy home, and, grateful not to have to drive across town, Clare said her goodbyes and left in a taxi.

It was nearly midnight when she arrived home. She checked the machine at once. There was a message from Paula, and there'd been two hang-ups. She dialled one-four-seven-one – one had been from a callbox somewhere in west Belfast. She supposed, hoped it had been Lorcan. She got ready for bed, wondering whether to call Paula, who she hadn't talked to in a couple of days, or to keep the line free in the hope he'd call back. The phone rang, solving the problem – it was Lorcan.

'Is it too late?' He sounded anxious.

'No, not at all, I've only just got in. It all went on a bit longer – as you can guess.' She felt almost shy. There was a pause, then, 'I was hoping you'd call.'

'I meant, too late to come over?'

'No, but won't they wonder at you going out?'

'I'm in the hospital. I can be there in five minutes.'

'Come, then.'

He came straight to bed as soon as he arrived, undressing beforehand this time, letting her see him. She felt by doing this he was letting her know she could look, touch. Clare was, as before, overwhelmed by desire for him. She felt too, an awe of the man, a strong need to cherish him, and a longing to make love to him with her whole heart and soul. Even thinking these thoughts was intimidating for her; did they invalidate everything that had gone before?

They didn't say much – like a dumb show. It was all action, with no accompanying grunts. This pleased Clare. She had felt latterly, with Tim, that the sound effects were upstaging both

their performances, as if honest lovemaking had slipped beyond their grasp. She should have realised then that it was all
going bad, but she had wilfully ignored the signs, hoping that
somehow this turn in their mutual sexuality was a natural development, the next stage. Instead, as she now saw with hindsight, it had indicated a troubling need to distract from real
feelings and pursue the baser side of both their natures. Even
now, she felt cheapened thinking about it.

She pushed Tim from her mind and concentrated on the
present. Lorcan was a bit surer with her this time, checking
her eyes for affirmation that this touch and that was right. His
kisses were slower too, a lot slower, displaying a tenderness
that hadn't surfaced the first time. She was relaxed doubly by
the fact that she had also managed to find the time to put in her
diaphragm before he arrived, even though she hadn't been sure
this would happen. As Paula was fond of saying, 'It's always
easier without an audience, darling.' Then she would usually
proceed to lower the tone by recounting the many times hers
had skidded across the room and ended up covered in fluff.

Lorcan had told her when he arrived that he would spend
the night, assuring her that no one in the parish house kept a
record of their comings and goings. He lived with three other
priests, one of whom, Father Cahill, was old and feeble and
only said a daily Mass at six, and then seemed to sleep all day.
They didn't even have meals together – Sunday lunch sometimes, at the most. They were all on such different timetables,
he said. Father Lynch didn't interfere much, and the other
priest, Father Donegan, who Clare remembered as an odd sort,
kept to himself. Minnie Madden didn't come in until after
eight o'clock Mass. Then, according to Lorcan, she spent most
of the time pretending to clean and concocting some sort of
meal or other that could be left in the pot and heated as needed.
'I think she just changes the meat in it. It's a sort of ongoing
Irish stew. Awful really.' He laughed. 'You know, you've
never cooked that curry for me, what with all the fuss about

Tommy. You'll have to do that for me sometime.'

They made love twice, and then lay in each other's arms and talked all night. At some stage they must have dozed off, but it was well after dawn. Clare felt so happy, she didn't want to think of all the various ramifications. What did unsettle her somewhat was that despite his doubts about celibacy, he insisted that his vocation was still strong. He felt that he would always want to be a priest. He'd never doubted that once in the last eighteen years. Clare was unsure how that would affect them.

She hadn't believed in God for years, although perversely she held on to many of the superstitious trappings of her religion. But this wasn't the time to think about things like Lorcan's vocation. Intimate as they had just been, they barely knew one another. It was too early. She was living for the moment, as was he. There was a hunger about his desire for her which thrilled her, fired hers. The lovemaking went on for hours, as if stopping would somehow allow the passion too much time to reason with itself. They eventually fell asleep wrapped around each other, his skin adhering to hers. She felt sated, drowsy. She awoke to find him lying quietly, just gazing at her.

'How long have you been awake?' she asked.

'Oh, hours,' he smiled. 'Just enjoying lying beside you. I can't believe what I've been missing, but it's been worth the wait.'

'Was I snoring?'

'Yes, like a train.'

'Was I?'

'No, not at all. You breathe so softly, little sighs of pleasure. I kissed your shoulder and you smiled.'

Clare laughed. If any other person she knew was to come out with this stuff she'd tell them to wise up, but somehow his sweetness made it seem like the most wonderful compliment she'd ever heard. They made love again then, and this

time he took her more forcefully, startling her with the swift-
ness of her pleasure.

'God!' she said laughing when they had collapsed again.
'You learn fast.'

Breakfast was a leisurely affair. She couldn't get used to the
newness of having him there. They sat on the bed balancing a
tray. He was wearing her dressing gown and she a T-shirt, so
when the doorbell rang they were both flustered. But it was
the postman, a parcel too big to go through the letterbox.
She glanced at the writing on the label: it must be the script
from Paula, her new play – the play she was hoping Clare
would be able to do. Another time Clare would have torn it
open at once, but it could wait. She threw it on the sofa relieved; she wasn't sure what she had expected. The excitement
of almost being caught seemed to arouse Lorcan again and he
pulled her back into bed, making her hold her arms up and
taking her T-shirt off slowly, pulling her towards him, making
her a prisoner with her arms held back. She thrust her breasts
towards him and he took her nipples in his mouth, sucking
softly till she could bear it no longer. She turned around and
for the first time took him in her mouth. He was harder than
he had been yet. She arched herself up, holding him now in her
hand, and eased herself onto him. She was trying to wait for
him, feeling intensely aroused. Her body flushed, about to ex-
plode with pleasure. The phone rang. Their automatic response was to slow down. She listened, letting the machine
pick it up. First her own message, and then Maura Oliver's
friendly voice about to leave a message. Had it been anyone
else she would have ignored it but she leapt from the bed, and
lifted the receiver.

Maura Oliver was a warm open woman who somehow managed to be wholehearted and enthusiastic about life, without being gullible. She was someone whose opinion was sought after and valued by a wide circle of people. Clare had always admired and loved her, and enjoyed her company, so when Clare overheard the occasional bitchy remark about Maura, she would dismiss it simply for what it was – jealousy. Perhaps it was something to do with the Irish propensity for knocking success, but the Olivers were sometimes the subject of bitchy conversations – albeit half-hearted ones – because the couple had simply no obvious faults. Perhaps there was a certain little tincture of complacency, of self-righteousness, but it was more than offset by a healthy ability to laugh at themselves. It drove people mad, this lack of things to gripe about. Even their close friends made jokes about them being too bloody perfect.

Maura had phoned Clare and invited her for lunch in one of the new restaurants that had sprung up in Belfast over the past few years. It was packed, being popular with ladies who lunched as well as the professionals. Clare hadn't been to this one before. Too pricey. Maura asking Clare for lunch was not too unusual in itself; after all, they had promised to meet up when Clare had seen her at the play. But it would be hard to be her usual nonchalant self, having just slept with Maura's son. Clare felt her acting skills would be required in spades.

She realised, though, that by strengthening her ties with the parents, she would have more ammunition to hold Robert at bay. Surely he would balk at an involvement with someone nearer his parents' generation?

Maura was already seated at the table when Clare arrived. Clare had walked to the restaurant, wanting to be free to have a few drinks with their meal to steady her nerves. Maura Oliver had what Clare's mother had referred to as a 'good appearance'. She dressed well; her clothes were always fashionable without being ostentatiously so – expensive. She was of medium height, a bit shorter than Clare, with pale grey eyes – exactly like Robert's, Clare suddenly noticed. Dark brown hair, shown off by a good cut. She wore little makeup, and didn't look anything close to late forties, which she was. She was wearing a pale lemon-coloured linen suit, with a white shirt. Clare supposed it was this season's colour. It was elegant as well as casual. Clare had always found it hard to bridge that particular fashion gap. She cheated by wearing jeans a lot, and silk or linen shirts, relying on a slim body to help, and occasionally, as before her recent trip to London, buying a good jacket or something dressy to jazz up her casual look. She had been losing weight since she came back – hardly surprising really, given all the emotional turmoil. Maura, on the other hand, battled with a slight tendency to gain weight, which she blamed on her five pregnancies, but regardless of her shape she always looked well. There was a bottle of wine already chilling by the table, and a waiter came over and filled Clare's glass. Gratefully Clare took a few gulps.

They chatted at first about her father and how he was doing, then touched briefly on Tim and how Clare was coping, then chatted about the couple's annual barbecue which they held each July, and to which Clare was invited. But throughout the meal Clare was strained, poised for the real point of the meeting, which she sensed had yet to come.

And it did, right in the middle of the pudding – some confection of apple and cream with calvados, which Maura had insisted she try, and Clare due to nerves was having great difficulty in swallowing.

'There's something I want to ask you, Clare – about Robert. I know you two got close during the play.'

The remark almost knocked Clare sideways. She sat still. A pulse throbbed in her neck and her mouth was dry as Maura continued.

'I'm telling *you*, Clare, because I can't think of anyone else who would understand.' Maura's grey eyes looked at her perplexedly. 'I think Robert is involved with someone, possibly an older woman.'

Clare's head spun. She tried to speak, but couldn't articulate. 'How do you mean?' she finally managed.

'Well, we haven't really told anyone this, we felt it better not to, but Robert left Oxford last year under a bit of a cloud. A series of stupid things really. He had been infatuated with one of his tutors – a woman in her late thirties, and had begun to pester her. Then allegedly he started to stalk her, and eventually he got extremely drunk one night and she claims he attempted to rape her – although he says she had encouraged him. The truth is, that it was all a bit messy. We sorted it out by taking him away and getting him psychiatric help. John and I felt he would do better here in Belfast: we could keep an eye on him, especially now that things have calmed down a bit. So John bought him the house and we're fixing it up.'

Clare listened – transfixed.

'Well, to get to the point,' Maura went on, 'I had a call from Siobhan. They're very close those two, and she says he told her he's having an affair with an older woman, though he wouldn't say who it was. He told her he's in love again, and the woman was something to do with the acting world.

Siobhan normally wouldn't break her brother's confidence, but, in this case, she felt she ought to.'

Maura shrugged. She was playing with an expensive ring on her right hand, twisting it round. She was obviously ill at ease. 'I thought *you* might have an idea who it was. You know, perhaps it's this agent in London – isn't she a friend of yours? I mean, he was over there with her last week. I thought if I talked to you, you might know, or perhaps you could find out. I'm sick with worry. I haven't even told John – he's in the middle of a big case, and he took the whole thing last year very badly. He's been in much better form now that Robert appeared to have his act together. I haven't seen Robert, he hasn't been down since he got back from London, but I've spoken to him on the phone, and he's been odd, evasive, not himself.' She stopped. Her face had paled, as if the effort of unburdening had been too much.

Clare thought *she* was going to faint. Her head was spinning. Her mouth opened but the words locked. 'Maura, I don't know what to say,' she ventured. 'I know for sure it's not Diana – but maybe I can talk to Robert.' She trailed off. Shame made her feel like spilling everything out now, but she had to talk to Robert first. She felt fearful too. This fear was mixed with a desire to erase the last month of her life. God, the whole episode suddenly seemed tawdry.

Maura sighed and continued. 'I hope you don't mind me telling you all this, Clare, but you've no idea how bad things were last year. Robert's been so much better recently. At first they thought he had a mild form of schizophrenia, but it was apparently what is known as a psychotic episode. He doesn't require medication or anything, just lots of moral support and – gainful employment. You know, Clare, the acting seemed God-sent, and we couldn't believe his luck in getting the parts so easily.' She looked at Clare for a response.

'Well, it's a lot easier for young men, but I think he's got talent. So does Diana, or she wouldn't have taken him on.'

Reassured, Maura continued. 'We were so proud of him in *Sticks and Stones*. It was a great play. You were wonderful in it as well. It's been so long since we'd seen you on stage.' She smiled at Clare fondly. 'Robert adores you, he's always thought you were wonderful, and he's so grateful to you for getting him an agent.'

Clare could feel the blush and the chill creep over her simultaneously. 'Maura, I'll have a chat with him. I'm sure it's nothing important. I've said I'll go out for a drink with him some day this week, so I'll call him tonight, and don't worry, I'm sure it's nothing.'

The older woman took her hand, 'Oh, Clare, you're a pet. I'm sure I'm making a fuss over nothing. Let's have another glass of wine. Are you driving?'

Clare shook her head.

'Good, nor am I. I asked John to drop me. I felt like having a drink.'

They finished lunch, and Maura absolutely insisted on paying. She waved away Clare's attempt, saying, 'Don't be silly, Clare, this is my treat, and it's been such a relief to talk to someone.'

Clare felt her deceit was transparent, but she smiled and accepted graciously. They parted with a promise to get together again soon. Maura had some things to do in town. Clare was meeting Monica to go shopping.

She did her best to stay cheerful with Monica as they plodded through the shops, buying all the silly little things Monica felt necessary to lighten her exile: Bisto, Bird's custard, Tayto cheese-and-onion crisps, and, of course, Marks and Sparks knickers. They nattered away about things in general, but Clare's heart wasn't in it. She couldn't get her meeting with Maura out of her mind. Eventually, when Monica had had enough retail therapy, they went for a coffee.

Clare sat down and blurted the whole sorry saga of Robert to her sister. Monica was sympathetic, but she thought Clare needed to sort the affair out fairly quickly. 'Like yesterday, Clare love. I don't like the sound of him, a bit obsessive.'

'Monica, don't please! That's exactly what Paula said. He's beginning to really worry me now. He seemed OK before. With hindsight, I suppose it was a crazy thing to do, but I was feeling in need of a bit of sex or attention. I actually thought it would mean less to him than to me. I mean he's a kid, I thought they all liked to fly their kites a bit, as Daddy would say.'

'There's no point in recriminations now. It's done, you just need to sort it out before the whole thing spirals out of control. Why don't you meet him for a drink, and tell him the truth, blame it on the fact that you're not quite over Tim, and you just wanted a bit of a fling to feel better? Say you really did fancy him, but surely even he can see the whole thing is insane?'

'You're right. I'll call him when I get home.'

She felt wretched. Part of her wanted to tell Monica about Lorcan, have the balm of confession for that too. But she wasn't ready to tell anyone: it was too raw yet, and too frightening. Not that Clare thought Monica would find it shocking. Monica and Al were friends with a number of priests in their liberal Californian town – gay, straight, and even some married ones. They could cope with anything. She knew Monica didn't think priests should be celibate, an opinion she'd often expressed to Tommy (who naturally thought she'd been corrupted by living in the States). Tony, Brid, and Clare had had a lot of mileage out of the fact that the priest who married Al and Monica was gay – although they hadn't told their father this. He'd found it odd enough that the wedding had taken place on a beach – but he had been so relieved that his grandchildren were finally going to be legitimate – that he had kept his mouth shut.

By the time Clare got home it was after six, and she was in a bit of a state. She had been putting off the meeting with

Robert, she knew that, hoping it, he, would just go away. But it was time to get the whole business over and done with. She called his home. Much to her relief, he wasn't in, but she left a message suggesting they meet tomorrow for lunch in town. Now that she was fired up she didn't see the point in waiting. She hoped Lorcan would phone tonight. He had said he would.

She was in bits, she realised, and wanted to be relaxed when he called. She had a bottle of wine in the flat; she opened it and poured a glass. She didn't feel hungry enough to eat a meal again, so she had some cheese and crackers instead.

She and Lorcan hadn't seen one another since the phone call from Maura had interrupted their lovemaking. But they had spoken on the phone several times. She hadn't explained at the time, or indeed on the phone since, why the call had upset her so much, and he hadn't pressed her for details. She had appreciated that. She would tell him about it when it was all finally sorted out, tidied away.

Although only two days had passed, it seemed longer. When she didn't see him, the implications of their involvement seemed terrifying. She needed to see him for reassurance, and she knew he felt the same. She would suggest he came over tomorrow night: it would be something to look forward to after the ordeal of a lunch with Robert. She would need some consolation.

Clare had agreed to meet Robert in a bar in town. He had wanted to come to her flat, but she felt that neutral territory was called for, and insisted on the Kitchen Bar for a late lunch. It was packed, being noted for its home cooking. They ordered, keeping the chat light at first, the usual topics, lack of forthcoming jobs, her father's health, and whether or not Robert should move to London.

'Diana thinks it would be the best thing for me to do.'

'Well, it would, of course. You'd have a wider canvas there, more opportunity.'

'Maybe, but you obviously don't think it's great or you wouldn't be here.'

'Robert, you know perfectly well why I'm here – to get a break from my personal life, not my career.'

'You've done well here.'

'Yes, I've been lucky, up until now, but I did spend the first month out of work, and I've nothing lined up. There are no women's parts of consequence in any of the plays coming up.'

'Would you think of moving back to London?'

'No, I'm not ready to, not yet. I have another two months left in the flat, then I may buy somewhere here, or I might even move to Dublin. I'm not sure.'

'Would you consider moving back to London to live with me?'

Clare was dumbstruck. She tried to phrase her answer in her head before saying it. Her instincts told her this mattered. 'Robert, I'm really flattered that you would ask me this, but I'm simply not ready to begin another relationship. It's the wrong time for me. I want to be on my own for a while.'

He put his head down, saying nothing, and when he looked up at her, she saw to her horror that his eyes had filled with tears. He blinked and they streamed down his face. He seemed oblivious to the fact that any of the other customers could see, although lunchtime was drawing to a close, and the numbers in the bar had dwindled.

'Clare, I love you,' he said, fixing his grey eyes on her, beseechingly. 'I really think we could be good together. You could at least give it a try. Anyway, Diana thinks you should move back.'

'Diana has no right to discuss my personal life with another of her clients!' Clare retorted angrily, glad to have some reason to vent her emotion.

'Did our time together mean nothing to you then?'

'Oh, for God's sake Robert. Yes, yes. It did, of course it did. But it was fun, just fun. I thought it was an enjoyable interlude. I didn't think for a minute you would attach any more significance to it than that either, to be honest.'

'So I'm a real toyboy then.' He snarled the word at her. 'Something to play with, then discard. Is that it?'

'No, of course not. Don't be silly.'

'Well, what then? Should I have paid you?'

She flushed. He had raised his voice considerably, and a couple seated to their left were settling in with an expectant look on their faces.

She got up, went across to the bar and paid the bill. 'C'mon,' she said. 'Let's go for a walk, somewhere less public.'

He sat there mutinous. She thought he was going to refuse

to budge, to continue the scene, but abruptly he got up and followed her out.

Her car was parked near the BBC. They walked in that direction, not speaking.

'Shall we go for a walk along the towpath, and then I'll run you home,' she suggested.

'If you want.'

Clare felt impatient with him, his childish behaviour, and the whole wearisome business, but it had to be sorted out. This was a time for diplomacy, not to display her true feelings.

The River Lagan was central to the entire revitalisation of Belfast. The city was built round the river. European money had been put to good use for things like the cleansing of the Lagan, making it home once more to fish and various other forms of wildlife. The old towpath had been tidied up and it was possible to walk or cycle all the way to Lisburn, some ten miles from the city. The part they chose to walk along began at Stranmillis, near Clare's flat, and continued to Shaw's Bridge. It was a quiet, peaceful place during the week, with only the occasional jogger or cyclist passing. Every couple of hundred yards there was a bench. They stopped at one of these and sat down, watching a moorhen bob down the river, its red beak bright against the water. Neither spoke.

After a while, Clare said gently, 'Robert, do you not think you are being a teeny bit unreasonable about all this?'

'In what way?'

'Well, I'm sure every time you've been with someone before, you didn't automatically expect it would mean a relationship. Did you?'

'No, not at all. But you're different. I've always fancied you, I told you that.'

'But your parents, what about them? I mean, have you given them a thought?' She was being less than forthcoming, she realised, but somehow bluntly telling him that she wasn't remotely interested didn't seem a good tactic. 'What would *they* think?' she said.

'Well, if we lived in London, then we wouldn't need to tell anyone at first, and if we stayed together, eventually they'd get used to it. I mean it's only society that says men should be older than women. Surely you're not that conventional.'

'Oh, Robert. It's not just the age gap, although that does influence things – I mean, we're an entirely different generation. I'm twice your age. I was your babysitter, for God's sake!'

'That didn't seem to matter when you were screwing me.'

She took a deep breath. 'I know, and the sex was wonderful. I'm not trying to take away from that, but I've just finished a relationship, and it was painful. I'm not ready for another.'

He said nothing. He had picked a dandelion and was shredding it energetically. 'OK then,' he said quietly. 'Perhaps we can see each other occasionally, maybe once a week, for a drink or something.' There was a challenge in his tone.

She took his hand cautiously. 'No, honestly Robert, I don't think that would be a good idea. I think it would be best to leave things for a while.'

'Best for who? For you – is that what you mean?'

She ignored the jibe and continued. 'And if you want my opinion about what you should do regarding your career, I think if you seriously want to make it as an actor, take Diana's advice, move to London.'

He wrenched his hand away. 'I need to go now,' he said. 'If you don't mind, I'll walk home. Thanks for the advice.'

She sat on the bench and watched him walk down the path. Her head was in turmoil. She found it impossible to work out her own emotions. She knew in her heart that the days spent with Robert had been a foolish sop to her own vanity. A pathetic attempt to boost her confidence in her desirability, to purge all thoughts of Lorcan from her brain, and, ultimately, a crazy thing to do. Perhaps if Lorcan hadn't come on the scene so soon afterwards she would have toyed with Robert longer, for indeed toying was what it had been. After a while, she walked to the car park and drove home, feeling wretched.

As she pulled up to the door of the flat, she saw Lorcan sitting in his car outside. Her mood brightened at once. She parked and went up and tapped on the window.

He looked up, startled, then his face lit up.

'I was listening to a play,' he said. 'It's from here, you should be in it.'

'Phone the BBC at once and tell them that.' She laughed. 'Coffee? Did you want to see me? Or was this just a good place to pick up Radio Four?'

He followed her into the house, and she moved into the kitchen, picking up the kettle, suddenly feeling happy again.

He pulled her towards him and kissed her. 'God forgive me, Clare Murphy, but I have thought of you nonstop today. I had to see you.' He hugged her, lifting her off her feet.

'I'm glad,' she said simply. 'I wanted to see you too.'

They were sitting side by side, drinking coffee, when the door opened and Robert walked in.

He looked disconcerted to find Lorcan there. 'I didn't mean to barge in,' he said uncertainly, 'but the door was open.'

Clare and Lorcan stood up guiltily.

'Oh, Robert, this is Father Lorcan O'Carroll. He's just dropped by. Lorcan, I'm sure you remember Robert from the play.'

Robert looked at Lorcan and slowly held out his hand. 'Pleased to meet you, Father.'

Robert turned to Clare. She looked at him, unsure of her next move. He seemed to sense something. Clare could see his face change.

He looked at Lorcan, who had sat down again, and smiled insincerely. Then he turned to Clare, who had moved to another chair. 'I'm sorry for storming off on you, it was silly of me, and you're right. I will think about London.' His tone oozed intimacy. 'Aren't you going to offer me a cup of coffee?' he said, enjoying her discomfort.

Clare felt her blood run cold. Wordlessly, she filled another cup and handed it to him.

He looked at Lorcan appraisingly. 'Sorry, Father, this must be very boring for you – lovers' quarrels, and all that.' He looked meaningfully at Clare.

They sat uneasily for a minute, and then Lorcan, who had remained the most composed of the three, stood up. 'Well, you two obviously have things to talk over, and I should be getting back. Thanks for the coffee, Clare,' he said, and left.

It was all Clare could do not to run after him. She felt sick. Robert sat on the settee drinking his coffee, a triumphant smirk hovering around his mouth. She couldn't think of a thing to say to him.

Clare busied herself in the kitchen and tried to keep calm. The air around her felt thin, and her body felt as if it had parted company with her. What on earth had Lorcan thought? She felt he had been wrenched from her by Robert's unexpected arrival, that some intensely intimate moment-to-be had been snatched away forever and replaced by this hopeless uncertainty. What was Robert thinking? What had he sensed? She was unsure, and she had no wish to compound things by attempting an explanation. Her stomach churned; she needed to get out of the flat. She waited until Robert had finished his coffee, and then she said she was going for a swim. 'I need to clear my head.'

He didn't move. He put down his cup and melodramatically clasped his head in his hands. 'You fancy him don't you?' He sounded anguished. 'Why was he here?'

'He called to see me – for a chat. We became friends when Daddy was ill.'

'You fancy him,' he repeated. 'I can tell. Are you fucking him?'

'Robert, he's a priest.'

'He's a man! I *said*, are you fucking him?'

'Robert, I don't know what you're talking about. It is

possible to have friends that one is not sexually involved with.'

'One is not sexually involved with,' he mimicked.

'I'm going now,' she said, and took the empty cup from beside him. She walked out of the house, her bag slung over her shoulder, feeling grim. He came with her. They walked towards the pool in silence.

They parted at the park. She had a profound desire to tell him to go away and never come near her again, but instinctively she knew this would be a dangerous move, so she gritted her teeth and said goodbye. She looked after him as he walked off, his hands deep in his pockets, his head bent, an air of pain hanging over him like a canopy.

She went into the PE Centre. She would swim until she was calm. She needed the soothing feel of the water, buoying her up, holding the weight of her thoughts and worries for half an hour. Then she would have a long shower: she would wash herself clean, free of the whole sticky mess.

The swim helped – superficially at any rate. She left the PE Centre and stopped by the flat briefly to check the machine, then she drove straight up to see Frances, who, as always, was glad to see her. As usual Gerry was out improving himself. Clare busied herself helping Frances with all the bedtime and bathtime rituals. She read stories to the children. It was nearly ten o'clock before they had a chance to sit down at the kitchen table for a chat.

Clare gave Frances her account of the last twenty-four hours, spilling it out in a torrent, but somehow unable to tell Frances that she had made love to Lorcan. The secret wouldn't leave her; it stayed deep inside, refusing to be told, and therefore invalidating the true import of everything else. But even if she could have spilled it out, nothing could be served by telling Frances, Clare felt the weight of the deceit. It was the first time ever she'd held back anything so important from her friend. She returned from her thoughts to the story of Robert.

'I thought the worst was over when I managed to get him out of the Kitchen Bar without a scene. Jesus, I didn't realise what was coming.'

Although she was trying to sound flip, she knew her friend wasn't fooled. Frances put her glass down and shook her head. 'Clare, love, I don't like the sound of all this. I don't want you to think I'm preaching, but are you sure you know what you're doing?' She looked meaningfully at Clare. 'Just be careful, too, with Father O'Carroll. I know you probably think you can just be friends, but getting involved with a priest can only end in tears. I don't know *what* to say about Robert. If I were you I wouldn't bother telling anyone what happened with him. It sounds to me like he's just a bit weird. It was daft to get involved in the first place.'

'Frances, I know that now, but it's done. I just want him to go away.'

'Well, if you refuse to see him, he'll have no choice in the end, and ultimately it's his word against yours that anything happened.'

'That seems a bit mean.'

'Well, maybe it is, but you've tried the reasonable approach, and look where that got you.'

'I'm worried about his parents. Sometimes I think I should just ring Maura and tell her the truth.'

'No, that's crazy talk, Clare, it's the last thing you should do. She really wouldn't want to hear it. He's her son, after all. She'd only resent you.'

'Jesus, Frances, he's nearly twenty, he's not a child. I mean if I didn't know his parents, I wouldn't give a shit about it. It must happen all the time.'

Frances said nothing. Maybe things like this did happen all the time, but usually in the tabloids, not on her doorstep. It all seemed very removed from her life, and alarmed her far more than she was letting on to Clare.

'I'm going to ring Lorcan and explain everything to him.'

'No, Clare, please. It's not really any of his business – your private life, and if you do tell him, it's only going to increase the intimacy between you. I'd leave it, honestly. Sure, maybe he didn't think anything was up.'

'Oh God, Frances, you could have cut the atmosphere with a knife.'

They began to talk about other things then, Clare suddenly not wanting to give herself away any more. Frances took the cue and asked no more questions.

At about half eleven Clare drove home, despite Frances's exhortations that she should leave the car and get a taxi. She had drunk almost an entire bottle of wine, it seemed to her without effect. She was hoping frantically Lorcan had called in her absence, but there was only a message from Monica to confirm that she would see her in the morning, and a call from Paula wondering why she hadn't heard from her. Clare phoned her at once.

Paula listened spellbound as Clare gave her all the gory details about Robert. Again Lorcan featured only as a hapless witness. She was starting to believe this story herself, almost.

'Christ, darling, he sounds like a character from a Ruth Rendell book. If I worked night and day I couldn't come up with a better plot. What a run of bad luck!' But she was sympathetic and concerned for Clare, and didn't know where to begin to advise her. 'Darling! You poor thing, what a nightmare. For God's sake, don't tell Lorcan a thing about Robert; say he's just a lunatic with a crush on you. And don't get too close. I know he's a dish, but the priest bit rather complicates things, doesn't it? I mean – just think, my love,' she said in an effort to cheer Clare up, 'if you did get off with him, you'd have to start going to Mass again, and he'd insist on marriage and then he'd probably not allow you to use birth control and you'd end up with ten screaming kids or something. I mean, you'd be gaga in no time.'

In spite of herself Clare had to laugh. 'I'm gaga now – Jesus,

Paula, I mustn't be right in the head. I don't know how I got into all this.'

'Yes you do, you disobeyed me and went back to Belfast. So come back here at once, and leave the whole sorry mess.'

Clare talked to Paula for over an hour, anything to put off being left alone with her thoughts. She had almost convinced herself by the end of the call that the moments with Lorcan hadn't happened. The memory had such an unreal quality to it anyway. Her ear hurt by the time they'd hung up. Eventually she went to bed and spent a sleepless night, hoping for a call that never came. She debated whether to call the parish house first thing in the morning and went as far as getting the number, but she felt depleted by all the emotion and lack of sleep and decided to let things sit. After all, it had been less than twenty-four hours. He could call yet.

She had promised to meet Monica at an auction, of all places. Monica had decided that she could finance the trip home by purchasing some 'antiques' and reselling them on her return. Clare doubted it, but she supposed it was worth a try. She occupied herself, having decided to spare Monica the gory details of yesterday. Monica was absorbed in the antiques, and they were a distraction too for Clare. The sisters had an interesting morning. Clare wasn't in form for buying any-thing, but Monica seemed delighted with her chest of old Irish linen and bundles of old postcards. She had also acquired an ornate Victorian chamberpot, and was wondering if she could take it as hand luggage. They loaded them all into Clare's car and drove to Kinsale Street for lunch, where Monica promptly unloaded all her purchases to show her father.

'In the name of God!' Tommy exclaimed when Monica took out the chamberpot, 'What's that? A po? Sure, you don't know who's been sitting on that. Or what they've done in it. Holy God, it could have every germ of the day. I don't think you'll be allowed to bring that into the country. Is it not Livestock Regulations? I ask ye, what's the world coming to when people go spending good money on oul pos!'

Monica and Clare were convulsed at his reaction.

'Have yis no toilets there or what?'

'It's an investment, Daddy. It'll be worth money there. I'll probably be able to sell it for three times what I paid for it.'

'Well, honest to God, it's changed times that oul pos' – he spat the word out contemptuously – 'are worth money. People are daft, if you ask me.'

Tommy was slowly recovering his strength. Monica had been great for him: she wasn't as combative as Clare, and she was always in good humour. He would miss her when she went back. She had a week left, and although she had planned originally to spend it in Donegal with friends, she had changed her mind at the last minute.

'I don't want to leave him, I have a feeling I'll never see him again,' she had said to Clare earlier as they shopped for lunch. Clare didn't want to admit that Monica was probably right. She had disagreed strongly,

'Nonsense, Monica, he's well on the mend. He'll outlive us all.'

Clare had an audition for an ad in the afternoon, a beer commercial. Diana had fixed it up last week. Clare supposed she didn't stand a chance, but she was glad to have something to do. Auditioning for things like this meant suspending all feeling anyway. One's hopes were always there to be trammelled and thwarted by polite meaningless people mouthing platitudes. Their minds, a lot of the time, were very firmly made up already, but they dutifully trawled through lists of hopefuls because the game had to be played. Clare hated the whole process. It was so demeaning, and yet actors endured it stoically to pursue a career that they were hopelessly drawn to. Years of fruitless auditions could turn people from giving extroverts, full of hope, to bitter, warped people with every crumb of compassion knocked out of them. Ads were the worst. They paid so badly – in Northern Ireland anyway – and if you were lucky enough to get one, you could wear out your face very quickly, for virtually no money. It was a necessary evil though, because the quick fix of maybe a thousand pounds would tide people over while they waited for *the* part. Not for the first time, Clare wished that whatever compulsion had made her choose this career would evaporate. But she was also aware of the quick-turnaround theory: one good part could suddenly heal years of pain. Amazing, but true.

These auditions were held in a hotel in the university area, one of the many new hotels that had sprung up since the cease-fires. There were several people she knew waiting in the foyer of the hotel, including Aislin, who had been in *Sticks and Stones* with her.

'You've just missed Robert,' Aislin informed her, pausing in the middle of an affected double mwah mwah kiss.

Thank God, thought Clare, maybe my luck is improving after all.

She had driven past the parish house on her way over, and debated if she should leave a note, but in the end she hadn't. She would just have to hang on. Trust that he would eventually call her. After the audition – another cattle call – she debated whether to stay and have a drink with the gang, but she had to get home to phone watch. She would really have to suppress her dislike of the bloody things and get a mobile – everyone seemed to have one.

She had prepared herself for an evening of disappointment, but she was only home half an hour when he phoned.

She had run the expected conversation in her head a thousand times, but the sound of his voice drove her script clean out of her. She dried up, unable to think of a single thing to say. The blood pulsed in her ears. Her mouth was dry.

'I'd like to see you,' he said. 'Is it OK if I come over?'

'Of course. When? Tonight?'

'Yes. It'll maybe be after twelve though. I've some hospital calls to make.'

Clare had a bath, tidied the flat – anything to pass the time and keep busy until he got there. She was in a fever of anticipation, unsure what would transpire, and emotionally too drained to know how she felt. She had considered every possibility, from seducing him when he arrived and assuring him Robert was a lunatic, to confessing every detail of her sexuality from the age of fourteen, so that when he arrived she felt wounded, open. She longed for him to heal her, longed for him to tell her none of it mattered. Only now, this moment. Perhaps they could take back the stolen afternoon.

He arrived just after midnight. It didn't augur well that he was wearing his priest garb. He caught her look. His eyes soaked into hers.

'I've been in the hospital.'

She nodded. 'Yes, you said.'

'Clare, I'm not sure why I'm here. I have no right, but . . .'

'Yes!' she interrupted, frantic. 'You have. You have a right, there's nothing going on between Robert and me. There's nothing. I'm so sorry about the other day.'

'Clare, listen to me. I have no right to make demands of you. I'm a priest, I'm breaking my vows being with you. I can't expect you to come to me *pure*.' He said the word in a whisper. '*We* wouldn't have happened if you'd been like that.'

His words wounded her, tore at her deeply. She felt soiled, used. 'What are you saying?'

He hesitated. 'I know it was so sudden with us, and you're a grown woman. I'm not naïve enough to expect you to be a virgin. I'm sure you had unfinished business with others, perhaps Robert. I mean, I have no right to expect you to be free for me as soon as I felt ready to have you.' He looked at her, his eyes pained. 'I also know that sounds awkward. I was jealous yesterday, sexually jealous – I suppose. I've never experienced that before.' He blushed, but held her gaze.

'Robert has a thing about me,' she said. 'I've tried to discourage him, but he won't give up.' It was part of the truth, she thought, yet this man was hard to lie to. Was it his uniform that invited full confession? She wasn't sure.

He had a cup of tea, but didn't stay long and they didn't touch, just a quick peck as he was leaving. He promised to phone her the following morning and come for lunch. She felt raw when he left, partly assuaged, but fearful that he was changing his mind about her, seeing sense.

The phone rang shortly after he left. When she said hello, the caller hung up. She dialled one-four-seven-one, and heard 'The caller withheld their number,' but she knew in her heart it had been Robert.

When Lorcan phoned next day she suggested they meet elsewhere. She had a fear now that Robert might arrive again. She needed to be sure that she and Lorcan could be alone undisturbed, to spend a few healing hours together.

'How long do you have?' she asked him.

'All day if I want, though I met Monica today when I was in with Tommy, and she's asked me to come to your daddy's for my dinner this evening. Apparently Tommy has restarted his mission to save me from Minnie Madden's cooking.'

'Let's meet for lunch in Killyleagh. Do you know how to get there? There's a pub in the street that leads up to the castle. The Dufferin Arms. It's easy to find.'

The road to Killyleagh was winding. Clare drove fast, the small car bouncing along the grey road undulating before her, its suspension pushed to the limits. She drove on, cutting sharply through the bright green fields with their carefully trimmed hedgerows either side. County Down. 'Basket of eggs scenery'. Clare remembered this description from school Geography. One-hundred-foot-high hills of boulder clay.

What were they called, drumlins? And local folklore (at least in west Belfast) had it that this fertile land was given to the Protestants, and the Croppies (or Catholics) were driven up into the bogland of County Antrim where the land was only good for turf and grazing sheep. Another example of historically perceived injustice.

It had just rained heavily, and the sky glowered. The clouds hung low, like a roof over the countryside, black, and menacing, heavy with water. A magpie swooped across the road from tree to tree. Blast it! Now she couldn't blink until she saw another, but she was in luck. Its mate was directly behind, and she smiled her relief, aware that her superstitions – all handed down faithfully from her mother – were absurd.

She had been an emotional mess since the incident with Robert. Getting out of town was a good idea, and for some reason Killyleagh had appealed. It was within an hour's drive of Belfast, on Strangford Lough. Frances told her she had been to a really brilliant Van Morrison concert there a couple of years back. Apparently you could get a decent lunch in this pub, and, better still, she had never been there. It was worth a visit.

The air brightened and a dazzling shaft of sunlight hit her directly on the arm. The rain seemed to be over for now. A rainbow arched in front of her, a soaring arc of bright colour cutting through the gloom of the wet sky. Tim had often teased her about her superstitions, pointing out how laughable they were. On one occasion she had made him stand with her for ten minutes in the rain without blinking till she saw a second magpie. Admittedly that had been a bit over the top, but she'd just come out of an audition for a lead in a telly.

She didn't care if her feelings were laughable. The sight of the rainbow cheered her. She took it as a good omen. It affirmed that she was doing the right thing. They would find a way out of the miasma.

She arrived in Killyleagh on time. The castle walls were splendidly impressive as she drove up the sloping street to the pub and parked the car. Perhaps they could go for a walk in the castle grounds after lunch. She had been struck forcibly on her way through the town by the red-white-and-blue-painted pavements. For all of her childhood, these had been markers of where *not* to tread. Did the fact that she had chosen to come here signify that she was stepping off the right path – following the desire line?

She hoped not.

Lorcan's car was already parked in front of the pub. She took a deep breath and went in. He was sitting at a table near the door. He had an orange drink in front of him. She wanted to kiss him, but refrained.

'Did you have any trouble finding it?'

He shook his head.

'Are you here long?'

'No.' He held up his glass and indicated the level. 'I'm here about two sips.'

'I'll have one as well.'

He went to the bar and returned with a drink for her, and two menus. They looked at each other appraisingly.

'I feel like James Bond,' he said, placing the drink in front of her and gazing into her face.

She laughed. 'I think you've got the wrong spy! Surely you would just be making your entrance now, in your flash car, with a bevy of beauties on your arm.'

'Well, you know what I mean. All the subterfuge is a bit unsettling. Don't get me wrong, I wanted to come, I need to see you, and I think I can guess why you don't want to meet at your place for now, but this seems crazy.'

'Well, it's reasonably touristy at this time of year, and it's unlikely that we'd be known.'

He reached and pulled her to him, kissing her. 'I really want to be with you, Clare, you have to believe me. I know it will be difficult, but if it's meant to be, then we'll have to deal with that. I'd like to think we wouldn't always have to hide. That we can be together like this when we choose.'

It was their first afternoon as a couple. They walked in the castle grounds after lunch, then drove (in convoy) down to the lough shore and sat companionably holding hands, looking out at the changing sky, the wheeling sea birds, the grey Irish skies with clouds scuttering upon clouds. The day was drying out, the rain blown away, and it was warm. They sat on a rock at the water's edge, and talked, their words ebbing and flowing with the lap of the water. She loved the ease of conversing with him. He lifted her hand and almost absentmindedly kissed her fingertips. His sensuality was so overwhelming – how had he buried it all these years?

She asked him.

'I don't know really. I didn't let it surface. I kept busy. I pushed all thoughts away, you know? And,' he added with a chuckle, 'I stayed well away from occasions of sin like yourself . . . Now, are you going to tell me the real reason we're here, for example?'

She told him. She told him of her pain at losing Tim, and its aftermath, about Niall, and about Robert. She told him of her love for him and of her need to be with him. He was a good listener. He had learned to be.

'Do you still want me, now you know all about my wicked life of sin?'

Although her remark was tongue-in-cheek, he answered her seriously, and his reply satisfied her. 'Of course I want you, I think I've made that fairly obvious, but I'm frightened too by my feelings. They're so exclusively for you, that I know if you can't return them, I would confess and get on with my life and my vocation. I know it's wrong of me to lay that burden on you, but it's how I feel now.'

Clare's heart soared when she walked beside him. She loved the strong feel of his hand grasping hers, the softness of his fingers brushing her hair back, the easy warmth of his voice. Her feelings overwhelmed her, she was intoxicated. But inside, something held her back; her betrayal by Tim had taught her caution and self-doubt – this was a dangerous venture. She'd have to tread softly: the wound left by Tim's leaving had some way to go before it healed.

'Can we fool everyone if I come over tonight?' she asked.

'I hope so. You're an actress, aren't you? Pretend you're in a play and I'm the wheezy old parish priest with an alcohol problem, though God forgive us I'm sure Tommy couldn't live if he knew the truth.'

They left Killyleagh reluctantly late in the afternoon, and decided against going back to her flat for an hour before dinner though they were both half crazed with desire. They had nearly made love in a field but were interrupted by a man walking his dogs. She headed home, phoned Monica and got herself invited to the meal.

'You know him quite well anyhow, Clare, don't you? He seems lovely; he's popped his head round the door a few times, and he's as nice as everyone says. I mean we're used to Father Tom' – this was her friend in California – 'but all the priests I remember from here would put years on you, they were so dull and dreary. Daddy wants me to meet him properly and I'd like to thank him for being so good to Daddy. I'm sure he's enough on his plate in *this* parish.'

It looked like it was going to be an interesting evening. Tommy and Monica were both sharp as tacks. She'd really be putting things to the test. Something in her was driving her to test things out, take risks. She hoped she'd have the nous to carry it off.

For a man of his age, Tommy was adventurous about his food preferences and always ate with relish. He was wiping his plate with a round of pan loaf. It embarrassed Clare watching her father eat: he wolfed his food, a little trickle of curry ran from the side of his mouth, and he made smacking sounds of enjoyment, but no one else seemed to notice. Clare had arrived over at Tommy's unsure of what to expect – although nothing could have prevented her from being there. There was something thrilling about seeing her lover sitting at her father's table, relaxed and chatting. Clare had felt nervous at first, but after a few minutes of chat she relaxed and began to enjoy the conversation, which was wide-ranging, with everything from California to Minnie Madden's cooking on the agenda. Monica had cooked a Thai meal, a green curry; she had done it beautifully, and it was a great success.

'So he got a curry out of *you*, Monica,' Clare laughed, and looked at Lorcan. 'I've been promising him one for weeks!'

Monica mistook her, thinking she was referring to Tommy. 'Well, Daddy was telling me he misses your curries, Clare, so this is my attempt to match up. Thai food is all the rage at home.'

'Aren't you grand all the same Tommy – eating the Thai

food,' Lorcan remarked with affection. 'My own father now, he's a great man for the spuds and meat all right, not adventurous at all.'

Tommy was regaling them with stories about the district when he was growing up, and all the events of the last twenty-five years. He had a great yarn about being lifted by the army coming out of Mass one day, a HUMAN TEA-BREAK. It was well known in the district that the patrols would lift someone when they wanted a break to give themselves an excuse to go back to the barracks. In this case, of course, it was mistaken identity: they had thought he was one of the old IRA men from the district. Tommy joked that he had had so many free drinks on the back of this incident that he hung around outside the church in the hope it would happen again. 'Can you imagine a seventy-year-old terrorist?'

The yarn became more dramatic each time he told it, but this was Tommy back at last to his old self. In flying form. Every now and then, Monica and Clare would catch each other's eye and the unspoken relief of having him there and back to form would flit across their faces.

It had a strange quality about it, too, entertaining in Kinsale Street. The house had been so small while they were growing up and there were very few parties thrown. Not even for their birthdays. Just the odd get-together and certainly nothing ever resembling a dinner party. Family gatherings tended to be at their grandmother's house, and then just at Christmas. Kathleen and Tommy would never have presumed to ask any of the priests for dinner, thinking themselves not 'grand' enough, but things had changed. It was so much less formal these days. Mind you, there was still just about room for four round the little table, and as soon as they had finished eating and had a cup of tea, Tommy announced he was off down to the pub. He got restless sitting at a table for long, and hated it at Brid's when she had one of her 'fancy dinners'. That he would only put up with once a year, at Christmas.

Lorcan cried off the excursion to the pub. 'I go there tomorrow night with the drama group,' he said. 'I don't want them to think I'm getting too fond of the jar – you know how fast word travels round these doors.'

He got up to leave, thanking Monica profusely. Clare walked to the door with him. It all appeared relaxed, natural. As he was turning to go up the street he mouthed to Clare, 'I'll call you later.'

Clare went in to help with the dishes. Tommy went off to McAuley's. Neither of the women was in the mood for the smoky bar, glad to enjoy the chance of a chat together. Clare wanted the recipe for the curry and Monica wrote it out, delighted all the ingredients could be got in Belfast no problem.

'Ah sure, we're awful sophisticated got, what with the running water and all,' she joked.

The subject inevitably turned to Tommy. Monica was upset at the idea of leaving him again.

Clare was making all the right reassuring noises when, out of nowhere, Monica looked her in the eye and said, 'You're very taken with him, Clare, aren't you?' There was no need to ask whom she meant.

'Am I?'

'Well, I'm asking you. It looks like it to me, anyway.'

'Do you think Daddy noticed?'

'I doubt it, but *I* did. Nothing too obvious. Just a little frisson between you when it appeared no one was looking. Is there something going on?'

'No, Monnie, you're not far off the mark. Maybe I do like him too much, but I can't really talk about it. It's awkward really.'

'OK. Let's change the subject. Just be careful: you know what this town's like and you've enough on your plate. What about Robert? Did you sort that out?'

'Not really. It's all been a bit eggy. I could kick myself for ever being so deluded as to sleep with him in the first place. I feel so confused about things now, Monica, and I don't want to move unless I have a job. My life seems so complicated suddenly.'

'Sure, it wouldn't be you if it wasn't.' She looked at Clare. 'Mind you, you're looking wonderful. You have a glow about you. Maybe the excitement of it all agrees with you.' She paused, lifted the plates and began putting them away.

'Nothing will happen with Lorcan, Monica, if that's what you think. More than anything, we're just friends.'

Monica looked at her meaningfully. 'I'm not saying it will, all I'm saying is, be careful.'

Robert was waiting outside the flat when Clare arrived home. Her heart sank. She felt ready to scream but asked him in through clenched teeth. He followed her into the living room and sat down. Clare stood.

'Don't worry, I won't stay long,' he said. 'I've come to tell you I'm moving to London in a few weeks.'

Relief flooded her. 'That's great, Robert. I'm sure it's the right decision.'

'There's another thing. I thought that if your lease was up here, you might want to rent my place. It'd be cheap. I'm looking for a tenant.'

'Thanks, that's really good of you, but I've two months left here, and then I'm not sure. You know what it's like in this business. I'll go wherever there's work.'

'So you might move back to London?'

'Perhaps, eventually – I suppose. I had thought of Dublin for a while. There's a wider choice in theatre than here, and I could get up to see Daddy more often than from London.'

'Clare, I love you a lot, and if you change your mind about us, I want you to get in touch.'

She felt sorry for him, but also felt angry that he was being so insistent. 'Robert, please. I *meant* it when I said let's just be friends. There can't be anything between us. It was fun, but crazy, believe me, I wish you could forget it ever happened.'

She heard a car and, started, looking towards the window, inwardly panicked in case it was Lorcan.

He noticed, following her glance. 'Are you expecting someone?'

'No.' She shrugged. 'I thought it was maybe my sister Monica. She may drop over later.'

She didn't offer him anything, and after sitting for about ten minutes and getting no encouragement he stood up to leave.

'Are you coming to my parents' barbecue on Sunday?'

'Yes,' she replied quickly, 'I hope to. Will you be there?'

He made a face. 'Me? Oh yes of course, all the beautiful children lined up for show as ever. We match the beautiful house, you see, not to mention the perfect parents. We're essential accessories.'

'Robert, your mum and dad are absolutely great. You know that. I think you're being very unfair to them. It's usually a great day out, and they're so proud of you, they just want to have you there for that reason.'

'I don't know, maybe you're right, but I just don't feel I measure up these days. Dad has been great about the acting, but I am the only son, and I think he had his heart set on me following in his footsteps. Incidentally, he's been appointed to the High Court. They're both delighted about it. I think they'll be announcing it on Sunday.'

The phone rang, startling them, and she picked it up. Lorcan.

'Can you call back in five minutes?' she said.

'Oh,' Robert said with heavy sarcasm. 'So I've five minutes to get out?'

Clare sighed heavily. 'Robert, please. Give me a break will you!'

'I'm sorry, I can't help myself. I just want to be with you, I keep hoping you'll change your mind about us.'

'I don't think so. It doesn't feel right, and I'm sorry if I've hurt you. But I can't manufacture feelings I don't have.'

He walked to the door then, and she followed, proffering a peck on the cheek, and he responded by kissing her roughly on the side of her mouth, saying. 'See you Sunday then,' as he left.

She closed the door gratefully behind him, turned on the television and sat down to wait for Lorcan to ring.

She tried to relax, to think of anything other than the phone ringing again. The restrictions of the relationship with Lorcan were starting slowly to impinge, but it had, after all, only been a couple of weeks. She'd have to chill out, as Monica would say. He had proved very reliable up till now. Clare could feel herself more and more drawn to this sweet-natured man, although she still had deep qualms about his undoubted Catholicism. Hers was so far gone, apart from the emotional and superstitious side, that she realised this could become a barrier, but it was jumping the gun thinking this way. It had struck her before that he might find the real world hard to deal with. He had worked in a fairly tough parish, but always pro-tected by the cloth. But he was likeable and mixed easily, and perhaps these qualities would suffice him. She was sure of one thing, she needed him now, and she could feel he cared deeply too. That would have to suffice.

Eventually he called to say he was on his way. She was glad she wasn't working early these mornings: all these late nights with Lorcan were throwing her body clock out of kilter.

There was something different about his demeanour when he came in. He looked a bit guarded.

'What's up?' she said at once. 'Is something wrong?'

'No, no. Tell me, did Robert just leave?' he asked.

'He was here, about three quarters of an hour ago. He called to tell me he was moving to London, but he's gone almost half an hour. Why?'

'Because I am almost certain that he is waiting on the corner of the street.'

Clare groaned. 'Oh, for Christ's sake, Lorcan. He's going to do my head in. I mean he's a fucking lunatic.' She jumped up. 'I'm going out to him now to tell him to leave me alone.'

Lorcan took her arm, restraining her. 'No, please, Clare, don't. You'd be best to leave it. He'll eventually go away. Anyway, I can't stay long. I'm on early Mass and I have a very sick parishioner, so I'll just have a cup of tea and go.'

The night was balmy, and even this late in the evening, the sky was still light, a false night, brightened by a full moon, but Clare drew the curtains. The warm air made her feel open, restless and loose, a feeling she had not often experienced in Belfast. She was unable to translate it sexually because of the circumstances. Her nerves felt tightly strung: she was seething, unable to relax, cross at herself for losing this opportunity. Robert had spoiled the evening, ruined it for her. For the thousandth time she cursed herself for giving in to her baser instincts and sleeping with him.

When Lorcan left she felt emotionally adrift, incomplete. Her one consolation was that Lorcan had understood her anxiety about the situation and had been both supportive and understanding. He didn't dismiss it as insignificant.

Robert's behaviour had begun to frighten her. She asked Lorcan to phone her when he arrived at the hospital, and he did, reporting no sign of Robert as he left. But sleep didn't come easily, and though she had locked and bolted the door, she couldn't relax. When daybreak slid through the curtains, she was a wreck. At seven, bleary-eyed and with a metallic taste in her mouth, she forced herself to get up and go for an early swim.

The morning was still. She passed one other person, a young boy walking, or rather dragging, a little white dog. The park was wet, dewy, the air still heavy on the grass, the multicoloured flower beds waiting for the sun to raise the sap and ready them for the day.

Brid threw the fourth outfit on top of an ever-growing pile of clothes on her bed. It was hopeless. She just couldn't decide what to wear. She felt frazzled. She wished for the hundredth time that she had bought something new, but it was Sunday, and there was nothing she could do about it now. She and Peter were invited to the Olivers' for the afternoon bash, and it was outdoors and the style would be crushing. There wouldn't be a woman there who would be wearing less than six hundred pounds' worth of clothes. The Olivers, strictly speaking, were not part of Brid and Peter's circle, they were actually friends of Clare, but Peter had recently finished a long case with John Oliver, and they had been included in the guest list to the barbecue. Brid felt insecure about the whole thing. She never quite felt at ease with these people with their perfect life, perfect home, wonderful clothes, and flashy friends. It was all very well for Clare: she took in her stride parties like this, mingling with enviable ease. At any rate, they all regarded Clare as some kind of celebrity, just because she had appeared on the stage, and in a few TV films. The other annoying thing was that Clare looked good in anything. She was easily the best-looking of the Murphy girls. She never seemed to put on any weight. Of course she hadn't been through childbirth, which hadn't helped Brid. There was a Murphy tendency to gain weight. Clare used to joke that her aunts Susie and Sally, Tommy's two sisters, looked as if someone had sat on them. Brid felt sure that she was fighting a losing battle. Her fat genes had been laid down in childhood. Even Peter had a large appetite. It was probably something to do with the Famine. Something deep in the folk memory, Brid thought, all this emphasis on eating up.

Naturally slim, Clare appeared to have inherited the best of the genes. And at social gatherings she was like a magnet; people flocked to her. She was witty, confident, amusing, and, to Brid, intimidating. She supposed she should give Clare a ring and offer her a lift, but Clare would probably be staying to the end, and they would have to get back. Peter's parents were staying with them and looking after the boys, and his mother would be moaning if they were too long. Not because she minded, but because she liked to have something to get at Brid with. She had never really approved of Peter's choice of wife. They had hoped he'd do a bit better socially, and a wee girl from the Falls Road – even with the honours degree – hadn't really fitted the bill.

Peter to be fair, wasn't at all bothered by it all, he knew his own mind, and he loved her. Brid had married him because she thought this was about the best match she could have made under the circumstances. She had fancied him a lot at first, and then slowly realised that he was just a bit ordinary, but he was the first man who ever seemed really keen on her, and he was a law student. She knew she needed the safety net of a husband with a steady, dependable job. She had had enough of wanting during her childhood. She had watched her mother scrimp and save and do her best with the little she had. She knew enough to get out of it. All the girls in the family had. Of course there had been no way Clare was ever going to stay in west Belfast – or Ireland for that matter. Brid was convinced that if she hadn't hooked up with Tim she'd be in Hollywood by now. He had sapped a lot of her ambition.

Clare had always been the glamorous one, the one who turned heads. Even as a small child she had put Brid in the shade. She won medals for Irish dancing. She said poems for all her dad's cronies without batting an eyelid, and she attracted people like flies. As soon as any of Brid's friends met Clare, they lost interest in her. At least in Brid's head they did, so in a way it was a relief to Brid when Clare went to live in London.

Brid and Peter had married soon after that, and although it was not a passionate relationship, it was comfortable, and they had rubbed along nicely over the years. His mother was the only thing that ruffled the waters. Her awful snobbery was wearing. Naturally she was delighted to hear where they were off to today.

'Oh the Olivers. Isn't that lovely, I must tell Marge' – this was her golfing chum. 'I believe he's very highly regarded, and a Catholic for once.'

John Oliver was at the top in Northern Ireland law circles, respected. A big name, a big earner. Fidelma had always been impressed that Clare was close to the couple, and mentioned them frequently to Clare when she saw her. 'I wouldn't be surprised if he landed on the Bench soon.' Fidelma had said to Clare last time they had coincided at Brid's. Perversely, Fidelma loved Clare because she was 'famous' and confident, and because, with her bully's cunning, she sensed that Clare could take her or leave her. No doubt she would have had no objections to Clare as a daughter-in-law. She had been lukewarm about Brid from the beginning.

'At least she's a Catholic,' she had sniffed when Peter told her of his decision to marry Brid. Though it had to be said that in Fidelma Fitzpatrick's pecking order, Protestants with money were a bit above working-class Catholics. Mrs Fitzpatrick was a bigot too, only not one of the obvious ones. She was sorely lacking in charity and at the same time, to use a phrase of

Tommy Murphy's, 'always atin' the altar rails.'

She pretended to vote Alliance, it fitted in better with her mixed-religion bunch of golfing friends, made her seem fairer-minded. But Brid was sure that, like all the middle-class Catholics she knew, Fidelma actually voted SDLP.

'You'll have to let me know what the house is like,' she'd said. 'Have a good gander at it, I believe it's the last word.'

Peter had promised her a blow-by-blow account to shut her up.

Brid finally settled on a black dress and cream jacket with short sleeves. She didn't want to show the tops of her arms, they were too plump. This would have to do. She left the other clothes in a heap. She was too frazzled to put them away. If Fidelma was poking in their bedroom and found them, well she could get stuffed. Brid was in no mood to be houseproud.

Before they left, she relented and phoned Clare. The machine was on. Clare must have left. They hadn't talked about it anyway. They'd met briefly over at their father's house a few days ago, and Brid had forgotten to mention it. She started to leave her message anyway. She may as well get the credit for thinking of calling.

'Hello Clare, it's me. Peter and I are just leaving for Cultra, and wondered . . .' The phone was picked up.

'Hi, Brid. Look, I'm not going, I'm not feeling too good. I've already called Maura to explain.'

Brid was annoyed now. Much and all as she grumbled about Clare, her sister was good company, and knew everyone, even though she hadn't lived here for years. She also was someone for Brid to talk to when she felt awkward. Now she would have to hope that Peter wouldn't talk shop the whole time, and leave her to talk to another wife. The last law do she had accompanied him to, she had spent most of the time marooned on a settee with an absolute fright of a woman who had nothing to talk about but what model BMW she drove.

'I'm sorry you're not well, what is it? A hangover?'

Instantly, she regretted the remark. It sounded so bitchy.

But Clare took it at face value. 'No it's not. I have a mi-graine and I feel a bit low, Biddy.'

Clare's use of Brid's pet name touched her. 'Do you want me to come round?' she asked. 'I have really good painkillers.'

'No, don't bother, honestly I'll be fine. I told Maura if I felt OK later I'd come on down. Don't worry,' she added, 'you'll enjoy it, Biddy. You know you'll be fine when you get there.'

'I expect I will. I just couldn't find a thing suitable to wear.'

'Sure nobody notices what anyone wears at these things. They're all just interested in themselves.'

'Maybe that's what it's like in London, but this is Northern Ireland. They don't miss a trick here.'

'Go on, Brid, you'll be grand. You probably look great, you usually do.'

Mollified, Brid hung up. Maybe Clare would arrive later, and anyway she would always relax when she'd had a drink. And predictably, it was a lovely day. The Olivers could even control the weather.

There were lots of people already there when they arrived, quite a crowd in fact. Brid had noted the Special Branch detail at the gates on the way in. There would be quite a few top-notch guests. Other judges, maybe some people from the Northern Ireland Office. Their ability to mix freely with both unionists and nationalists had occasionally earned the Olivers the name of 'Castle Catholics'. But Brid wasn't worried about that sort of thing.

The Olivers' house nestled on the shores of Belfast Lough, and was reached by driving down a leafy lane off the main Bangor Road. The cars stretched several hundred yards up the lane. Mainly German and shiny, Brid noted. There were two young lads ushering the guests to parking spaces.

The house was a large double-fronted Victorian redbrick, with spacious lawns and a tennis court. Today, in the beautiful weather, the lough shimmered, and the industrial blemishes on the far shore were obscured by a summer haze. A few boats at sail completed the idyllic view. There was nowhere like Ireland when the weather obliged, thought Brid.

Maura Oliver was over to greet them as soon as they arrived. She looked stunning. She was wearing white slacks, and an expensive-looking navy and white top with a matching cardigan tied casually round her waist. Very chic – French no doubt. Brid immediately felt plain and overdressed.

'Brid, Peter! I'm so glad you could come.' Maura indicated over her shoulder. 'John is round the back supervising the barbecue – it's about the only time he ever cooks.'

Within seconds there was a waiter at their side with a tray of drinks. Brid took a glass of champagne. Peter asked for fizzy water and the man went off to get him one. It was all beautifully organised, caterers hired and the like, and Maura seemed so relaxed. When Brid entertained she would be sick with nerves for the entire time and rush around worrying if everyone had enough to drink and eat. Of course they never entertained on this scale. Few did.

'Did you talk to Clare? How is she?' Maura asked Brid. 'I felt so sorry for her when she phoned this morning to say she had a migraine. Poor thing, it's such a lovely day to be stuck in bed.'

Maura excused herself, and moved off towards another couple who'd just come in.

Peter had met someone he knew – a lawyer of course. He was a small, squat man, who looked uncomfortable in the heat. His glamorous wife was talking to someone else. Brid dutifully hovered, waiting for Peter to introduce her. She hated all this, and wished again that Clare had come. Peter seemed only to know all the bores, mainly earnest solicitors with no craic at all.

She had just reached for a second drink when the Oliver children, the older ones, began to move through the crowd inviting everyone to come and get some food. Brid would have recognised the children from their parents. They were attractive, confident children, obviously used to socialising. Robert she had met recently, the night they had gone to see Clare in the play. They had met him afterwards, a lovely boy. He had been very good in the play, though Peter thought he was daft to give up Law for a shaky career like acting. Still, he'd probably make it, he seemed the type. She passed him as they walked round to the tables at the back of the house. There were tables and chairs set out on the lawn, and a marquee erected in case of rain. John and Maura thought of everything. The sides were rolled up, and food was being served from there. People were waiting in line, attended to by waiters with trays of drink. There was a light-hearted buzz, and the chat nineteen to the dozen. Brid started to relax: the drink and the ambience were having the desired effect.

While they were waiting in line for food, Robert came up to the people in front of Brid and Peter to chat. Emboldened by her few glasses of champagne, Brid tapped him on the shoulder and smiled at him. 'Hello, Robert. It's Brid, Clare's sister. How're things?'

He looked at her coldly. 'Not the amazing Clare Murphy's sister?'

His tone unnerved Brid. It was so unexpectedly rude, but she pressed on, thinking perhaps she had imagined it, despite his stony face. 'Yes, we thought you were great in the play – with Clare. You both were. I mean we really enjoyed it.'

'Yes,' he said with emphasis. 'You're right, Clare was great in the play and great in bed too – a talented girl Clare Murphy.' He grabbed Brid's arm, hurting her, and pushed his face into hers. Quietly, menacingly, he asked her, 'Who is she fucking now that she's finished with me? Is it her friend the priest?'

He turned abruptly, and walked off down the garden. Then he stopped and turned to look back at Brid who was standing there, feeling humiliated and on the verge of tears, and he shouted at the top of his voice, 'Give Clare my love, won't you? Tell her it was the best FUCK I've had this year. No doubt about it! She's a brilliant FUCK.' This last word was hurled at Brid so loudly that several people turned in his direction.

He walked into the house. Brid thought she was going to faint, but Peter helped her to a chair and handed her a plate of food.

Almost immediately, Maura Oliver came over and joined them. She seemed distressed, and apologised profusely.

'Brid, I am so sorry. Robert is very ...' Maura hesitated. 'Emotional, and he hasn't been himself recently. Are you OK?'

'It was just such a shock,' Brid managed to stutter. Her mouth felt crooked and she wanted to cry. 'I have no idea what he's talking about. I thought he and Clare were good friends.'

'Brid, Robert has been having emotional problems. I'll call you tomorrow. It's just impossible to talk now. I have to get on with this business.' She nodded towards the milling guests, all of whom were affecting not to pay attention. Brid could practically hear the rustle of antennae.

'Don't worry, Maura,' said Peter. 'We know actors are a temperamental lot. He's probably going in for some Method acting – learning his next part.' It was the nearest Peter could come to a joke, and Maura accepted it as gracious absolution and moved off to see to the other guests.

Still shocked, Brid and Peter left as soon as they deemed it polite. Peter had been as shocked as she had at Robert's behaviour. 'He's just an indulged middle-class brat,' he told Brid. 'It's unfortunate that you were his victim, pet, just try to forget it. He was probably on some class of drug or other.'

But Brid couldn't forget. All the way home in the car, the words resounded in her head. 'Is she fucking the priest?'

They sounded vulgar, threatening and worst of all, frightening. Brid didn't even want to think about what it all meant until she had spoken to Clare, and hopefully get an explanation. But first of all Fidelma Fitzpatrick had to be faced. She was sitting awaiting their return. Revelling no doubt, in the expectation of a blow-by-blow account of the afternoon. Well, she would be disappointed.

She wasn't sure what Peter ended up telling his mother, but she excused herself pleading a headache, the truth really, and went upstairs to phone Clare. There was no answer. The machine dutifully trotted out its message. She waited.

'Clare, are you there? It's me Brid, could you pick up the phone? Call me if you wake up or when you get in. Please, it's important.'

Clare was in bed with Lorcan when the phone rang at seven o'clock. She froze at the sound of Brid's voice, then, at the words 'it's important', she leapt out of bed. Brid sounded upset. It was unlike her to leave such a message. Something must be up.

'Oh God! Lorcan, I'd better ring her. Something's happened to daddy.'

Oh, please no, not again. Why else would Brid be ringing? Surely to God she should still be at the Olivers'. Maybe the party had finished early.

'I'm sure he's fine, Clare,' Lorcan assured her. 'He was at Mass this morning looking fit. Call him first. It's probably nothing.'

Hand trembling, she dialled her father's number. Tommy answered at once.

'God, I'm getting very popular, all the same. Brid's just off the phone. She was looking for you.'

Clare chatted for a few minutes and, reassured, hung up. Lorcan had got out of bed and begun to dress, but was easily persuaded to get back in. Clare decided to call Brid tomorrow. It was probably some old gossip about the party, about Brid feeling inadequate with the County Down crowd. It could wait.

After making her apologies to Maura, Clare had phoned Lorcan and asked him over for lunch, knowing for once that

Robert would be fully occupied at his parents' party for the afternoon. Inevitably, she and Lorcan had ended up in bed for most of the afternoon. Lorcan was free until the next day. He had said he would spend the night – this was only the second time he had been able to stay. Partly due to the incident with Robert, she wasn't as relaxed as she would have liked, but she wanted him to stay. She wanted it to feel like a normal relationship. He was more confident about staying over than she was. She had questioned him endlessly about the parish house, if they would notice he was out or not.

He reassured her. 'Honestly, no one knows if I'm there or not. We all lead our own lives, and I've two days off. I've sort of hinted I might be going down to Tipperary soon – which I am, but if I'm missing they may assume that's where I've gone.'

It would have to do. As she had suggested, he had left his car parked in the next street. At least they could depend on feeling totally relaxed and unspied upon for the afternoon. She had felt bad about lying to Maura, but she couldn't have faced the party with Robert there anyway.

Clare was feeling happier than she could remember in recent months. It was bliss really, waking up beside Lorcan, feeling this enveloping closeness. A surfeit of happiness. The consuming passion of a new love affair. The sun was streaming through the window, catching the small hairs on the back of his neck. She loved his sweet smell, the soft pinkness behind his ears. She nestled her head against his, snuggling closer to him.

'You're a dreadful woman.' He groaned into the pillow. 'You're only making me want you again.'

'Good,' she said, turning in to him.

About ten o'clock they finally got out of bed, reluctantly. She couldn't get enough of him. She had dressed, and was pouring some orange juice when the doorbell rang. They froze. Clare motioned for Lorcan to go into the bedroom, and tentatively moved through the hall to the door.

'Yes, who is it?' she called, not opening it.

'Clare it's me!' It was Brid's voice, sounding somewhat fraught.

Clare undid the chain and let Brid in slowly, hoping she was leaving enough time.

'Is something up?'

'I suppose you could say that,' said Brid. She followed Clare into the living room, sat down, and began to tell her in a quiet, strained voice, full of emotion, what had happened at the Olivers' the day before. As Clare listened, a clammy, sick feeling spread through her. When Brid had finished, she looked at Clare beseechingly. Clare put her head down, unable to think of a thing to say.

She heard Brid's voice become squeaky, panicky. Seeking reassurance, sounding frightened, confused. 'He's got it wrong hasn't he? You're not involved with a priest, are you? I mean perhaps Father O'Carroll – maybe he thought that there was something. Y'know people make mistakes all the time.'

Clare looked her at her sister's wretched face, misery etched across it.

'It's not true, Clare, please. Tell me he's wrong.' Brid whispered the last word.

'Of course he's wrong.' Clare surprised herself with the calm denial.

Brid made a little noise somewhere in the back of her throat. A strangled sob, signifying relief in the midst of her pain.

Clare continued: 'Robert's a bit unstable, a crazy boy. He has a thing about me, I'm afraid. I'm really sorry it happened, Biddy. Weren't Maura and John about?'

'Yes, and they said as much, about Robert I mean. But they had so many guests I expect they couldn't deal with it. They said they would call this morning though, and they haven't.'

'Well it's only half ten, I'm sure they will.'

Clare felt weak even thinking about it all, and almost ready to pass out with the tension of having Lorcan in the next room. She was thankful that she'd only got as far as pouring one glass of juice, and was keenly aware that there were two coffee cups and two wineglasses from last night still on the table. Worst of all, Lorcan's coat was lying over the back of the chair. She had to get Brid out of the flat, and fast.

Brid had unwound a fraction, but her remembered shame

still engulfed her. 'Oh, Clare, it was a nightmare. Everyone was looking at me.'

'Brid, love, I'm sure they didn't hear half of it, you know. And if he made the remark about the priest directly into your ear, I'm sure no one else heard it.'

'Maybe not. Peter didn't hear that bit,' said Brid mollified. 'And of course I didn't tell him. He'd have been shocked beyond belief.'

Yes, thought Clare grimly, I'm sure he would. 'Let's go up the road for a cup of coffee,' she said, steering Brid towards the door. 'I need to go to the post office.'

And before Brid had time to protest, they were outside. As they walked up the street, Brid began another account of the day, who was there, and who was nearby when it had happened. It sounded frightful. Clare expected Maura would call her, wanting some light shed on it all. What had happened later? How much had he told them? His theories about Lorcan were pure speculation. He had no actual proof. She could deny that. She was glad now that some sixth sense had stopped her urge to confess to Frances, even to Paula, but she felt suffocated by it all, choked. Her mind flitted over all the possibilities, all the facesaving ways to counteract Robert's behaviour. How to halt the tide before they were all engulfed in it. She suddenly wasn't sure how she felt – numb if anything. She felt submerged in all the messiness, and longed to swim to the surface, to escape. She pushed all these feelings to the back of her mind and steered the subject to Monica's leaving, which was tomorrow. Glad at last to forget it all herself, Brid willingly allowed her. They went to a little place on the Stranmillis Road and had coffee and talked about Tommy and about Clare's job prospects, and Brid's forthcoming holiday, which she sounded like she needed. Clare didn't feel she could risk walking back to the flat with her, unsure if Lorcan would still be there. So, when they had finished, she left Brid to walk back to get her car, and made an excuse about calling over to the PE Centre to see if she'd left her card there on Friday, and said goodbye. They were going to see each other that evening anyway. Clare was bringing Monica over to Brid's later to have a farewell drink.

Lorcan had gone when she got back. He had made the bed, and there was a note on it, written on the back of an old electric bill envelope.

Hope you are OK, will call you later, I love you xx Lorcan.

The first words he had written to her. She folded it and put it in her pocket. She passed the rest of the day catching up on things round the house, phoning Diana to see if she'd managed to set anything up, listening to Schubert's Cello Quintet, reading. No one phoned. At about five she had a shower, got dressed, and went over to her father's.

'Well, you're over early!' Tommy looked up from his *Irish News*, pleased to see her. 'I'm just in myself, I was at a wee lunch and *musical afternoon*' – he made a face at the last two words – 'for the pensioners at St Brendan's Hall. Lovely grub. If you're looking the wee one, she's upstairs.'

Monica was sitting on the floor of the back bedroom packing. She had a large squishy sports bag open in front of her, and what looked like the contents of a grocer's shop spread out around her. In spite of everything, Clare had to laugh.

'Monnie, for God's sake! What are you up to? Surely to God you'll never get through that much custard. I mean you'd have to be eating sherry trifle till it comes out of your ears.'

'I know, it's demented isn't it? Never mind, I'll just have to get another bag. Brid said she had some old one she was throwing out. C'mon. I'll leave it for now and we'll have a cup of tea.' She looked at Clare closely. 'Are you OK? Has something happened?'

'You haven't talked to Brid?'

'No, I'll see her this evening. What's up?'

'Robert – he more or less told Brid about us – me and him I mean.'

A groan from Monica, then, 'Oh Clare, love, how? When?'

'Yesterday, in front of the entire County Down smart set, apparently – at the barbecue.'

'What?' Monica sat bolt upright. 'Christ. What did he . . .' She trailed off, seeing Clare was close to tears.

Haltingly, Clare outlined the whole incident as Brid had told it, making it real for herself with the telling of it, and scaring herself too. She told her the remark about 'fucking' the priest too, hearing Monica's gasp of shock. While Clare talked, her eyes travelled the room, marvelling at how small and poky it was. She had slept here for twenty-one years. Tony's pale peach paint hadn't managed at all to obscure its shabbiness. He had painted the old wicker chair pale green to clash gloriously with the walls. She could remember her mother standing on it, with a stool on top of it, to paint out the face of the wee fairy man Clare could see on the ceiling. Brid had been staying with a maiden aunt, and Tony was in the cot asleep. It had been a damp patch where a slate had come off, but when she wouldn't be pacified her mother hadn't dismissed her fears, merely said, 'Well, sure, we'll paint him away then.' She wished she could paint Robert away. She remembered being panic-stricken that her mother would fall off the wobbly stool. But her fear of the face had been stronger. She had been about six then. The ceiling had a white patch for years after that.

How had she come from being born in this room, within the sound of the church bells, to having an affair with a priest? What would her father, reading his newspaper obituaries downstairs, make of it all? She didn't want to find out.

'Jesus, Clare!' Monica said when she had finished. 'I hope you just denied it all to Brid. About Robert I mean. No one actually has any proof and Robert well, he sounds like a bit of a looper to me. People would take your word against his any day. I'm sure you're thanking your lucky stars now you haven't got involved with Lorcan,' she added.

Clare ignored this and answered the first query. 'Yes of course I did. I mean she would have found it hard to believe I had, but maybe he's told his parents. I really don't know what I should do now. Oh God, Monica.'

'Well, you could always come back with me and get away from them all.'

'Don't joke, I just might.'

'Well you know you're always welcome, though person-ally I think you'd go bats out there.'

She was right actually, she would. Clare had often puzzled about Monica's ability to blend so easily into her other life in the States, how had she curbed her natural Northern scep-ticism, the blunt Ulster way of dealing directly with life, and slotted so effortlessly into line with the ageing hippie commu-nity. She had married her lovely easygoing husband, who was the only person Clare had ever met who lost sleep worrying about global warming. On her visits to California she had ob-served them simply going on with things, living their lives of quiet achievement, no obvious excitement, bringing up the children. Al working at growing his organic vegetables, fixing things about the house: monotonous but satisfying chores. Monica no doubt found a comfort in it all, Clare realised that. Yet when she came home for visits, she slipped easily into the sarky tones of a born-and-bred Ulster girl and, as Tommy would say, she was out gallivanting to pubs with her mates most nights.

They talked about the situation as Clare drove to Brid's. Tommy had decided not to come.

Peter answered the door to Clare and Monica. 'Thank God you're here,' he said. 'I just called Tommy, and he told me you'd left. Brid is in a terrible state about Robert Oliver. You'd better go up to her.'

Monica and Clare looked at each other uncomprehendingly.

'She was fine this morning when I left her,' Clare said. 'Has she got herself worked up about it again?' Clare could feel the exasperation rise in her voice and she tried to take it out, even as the words left her lips. Brid could be trying when she got one of her hysterical fits.

'Well, we just heard it on the news about ten minutes ago.'

'Heard what?' Monica asked him.

'About Robert Oliver drowning this morning. It's terrible news. Only nineteen too, and the only son. I'm sure they're devastated.' Peter's voice cracked – a rare show of emotion for him. He was walking ahead of them up the stairs, assuming they were directly behind him. 'She's in the bedroom.'

Clare grasped the banister. She thought she was about to faint. The blood drained slowly from her face and her insides melted. There was a whoosh of air from the door as one of the boys ran in. She felt it was raining darkness. The grandfather clock in the hall ticked loudly. Accusingly. Then she remembered to breathe again and turned to Peter. 'Peter, what did you just say?'

She could barely articulate the words. Monica was silent, waiting, watching Peter too.

'God, I'm really sorry, I'm sorry. I thought you'd have heard. It's awful news. John and Maura's son Robert drowned this morning. They pulled him out of the lough, but they couldn't revive him. It was on the news. I thought you'd heard.' he repeated. 'Brid is in an awful state. I know she told you about the incident at the party yesterday.'

Monica grasped Clare tightly by the arm. 'Peter, we didn't know,' she said calmly. 'This is the first we've heard. I think we all need a drink. C'mon, Clare, let's sit down.' And she led Clare back down the stairs and into the living room and guided her onto the sofa.

Clare was dazed, stunned. She had no feelings yet. She saw the rows of questions flit across her vision but no words formed.

Monica appeared to be the only one in control. Peter

234

indicated the drinks cabinet and Clare watched her unscrew the cap of a bottle of Martell and pour a large measure into one of Brid's Waterford glasses. She fitted Clare's hand round the glass, closing her fingers like you would a child's. In a trance, Clare lifted it and knocked it back. Her nostrils pricked and the liquid burned in her throat.

'When did it happen?' Monica asked Peter.

'I'm not sure. It was on *Newsline*. They mentioned the fact that John had been made a judge and Robert had died in a tragic accident in Belfast Lough this morning. They mentioned him being in a TV play and his recent performance at Lagan. That was all. I'd better tell Brid you're here, she must have heard you anyway.' He sounded distracted. He left the room.

Clare's thoughts swam into focus. This morning, when she had been with Lorcan, waking up slowly. She had been so glad that Robert wouldn't be round to bother them. He had been dead when she had been thinking that. The half-remembered words of an Auden poem flashed through her brain. About suffering, how it takes place when someone was walking dully along. Something like that.

Grief assailed her, grief, or was it self-pity? She wasn't sure. She felt a wave of sorrow for Maura and John: what must they be feeling? This was coupled with an urgent need to know every detail. How could it have happened? Why? Robert was such a good swimmer. He was young, fit. It couldn't have been an accident. Oh God, Why? How? Why him? Could he really have been so unhappy? Was it all her fault?

Superimposed on these feelings was a sure knowledge that she had no right to this searing, giddy sorrow. No right at all.

Brid came in then, pale-faced. Her eyes red-rimmed.

Anger surged through Clare.

Jesus, Jesus not now! Not again. I can't stand it if this death suddenly becomes *her* property, like Mammy's death was. Becomes the vehicle for the untold grief in *her* life. She was the only bloody one allowed to grieve, to mourn, our mother. The rest of us forfeited that right.

I had left and deserted her. Monica had left and deserted her. Tony was a son, different. Brid had stayed till the end. Holding her hand when she drew her last breath, closing her eyes, folding her hands round her beads. This undid everything that had gone before. These actions conferred ownership, gave Brid the right to claim her as hers alone. Last rights.

My mammy My mammy My mammy, words rising like a litany. Clare could hear it now, five years later. Brid's cry, like a ripped wound tearing at all of them, as the first sod hit the grave with that awful hollow thump. We all grow up dreading the clumping sound of the first sod on our mother's grave, don't we?

Brid clad in black. Making Clare feel garish in her blue coat. They were standing unevenly in the muddy graveyard, the mountains luminous behind them as they balanced on two other newly dug graves. A sea of familiar faces, all tuned into the right expression. Brid being led sobbing away by Peter. Fidelma following him, dressed elegantly in black. Fidelma making sure to say hello to the friends made *after* university in case *anyone* would think she knew them when they were nothing.

Christ, why was all this in her head now? Robert's face burned on her brain. She wanted to scream.

I made love to him, I held him in my arms. He came inside me. A part of him is still in me. I did this to him, it's all my fault. I can still feel his skin, his dead skin. His lips. His dead lips. His hair falling over his face. The waves washing over him, pulling him under.

I am culpable – *mea culpa, mea culpa, mea maxima culpa!*

Someone was screaming loudly. Brid? Monica's face was pressed to hers, her grey eyes huge, troubled, concerned. Her soft hand was patting Clare's. Holding her against her breast, warm, soft.

'Clare, pet, you're OK, you're OK. C'mon, calm down.'

Brid was sitting there quietly, looking anxious. Not screaming at all.

But Clare had heard her scream. Where had the screams come from? Loud jagged wails tearing her open. Clare had heard them. She'd heard them, but they'd stopped now. She was tired. It was all so sad, so sad, and so awful. Awful. Her head was going to burst. There were too many things in it.

Clare adjusted her position for the umpteenth time and tried in vain to make herself comfortable. She had been awake for almost twenty-four hours, and knew that it would be a good five hours more before she could find a comfortable place to lay her head. The plane hit an air pocket, and she heard the captain say something about refastening seatbelts. Normally she was afraid to fly. Terrified, even on short hops from London to Belfast, imagining, like Yeats's airman, that she would meet her fate up in the clouds. But she knew it wouldn't happen this time.

Monica and Al were picking her up, taking her to the mountains. Taking her to their home outside the quaintly named Eureka. Monica had been insistent over the phone. She wanted her to come. It was the best thing. Frances had organised tickets. Brid had paid. She didn't want the money back. It was a gift. She wasn't to worry, just go, and unwind. Come back when she was ready. *Better,* they meant. Even Tommy, who seemed a bit confused about it all, was happy for her to go.

'Sure a change is as good as a rest, and don't be using me as an excuse. You needn't be worrying on my account. I'm well back to form, just the indigestion.' He had remarked to

Monica on the phone that Clare was in a bad way. 'I'm worried sick about her so I am. You couldn't see her behind a trammy ticket she's that thin. Must be because that English fellow's getting married.'

Tim was indeed getting married: Kezia was pregnant. Clare felt nothing about this when Paula told her, only a vague sadness. Her pain had been too focused on everything else.

She looked out of the aeroplane window. She was glad to have the side of the cabin to curl against. The plane was full: August was still the height of the season. She had tried to read her book, or sleep, but the daylight had defeated her, flying as they were into the sun. It had raced ahead of her to California and was waiting for her again. She pulled down the shade and closed her eyes, visions of the events of the past month floated unceasingly through her brain. The funeral Mass, the huge crowd spilling into the aisles. Hushed voices, a people used to violent death, confident in the rituals, sounding the responses to the priest, filing reverently past the coffin. Standing in long lines waiting patiently to receive communion. The quiet surge towards the church doors at the Mass's end to be greeted by John and Maura and the four girls. They stood silently, their faces grey with the grief of it all. The pain streamed out of them. Clare had watched them, shaking each hand. She watched as they bravely thanked people for coming. Their smiles flitted briefly and painfully as people struggled to come up with some crumb of comfort. What was there to say? Their only son, their adored brother, was dead. Dead. Dead.

She heard too in the churchyard the muted murmurs, the voices blending rumours and reasons: *'still drunk, been drinking all day . . . family hadn't missed him until the police came to the door . . . apparently, someone had seen him go in to the sea, and alerted the coastguard . . . a man and his girlfriend pulled him out, already dead . . . couldn't be resuscitated.'*

Then the voices lowered an octave, a hushed whisper. *Drugs involved*, and so on. But a lot of it was guesswork, speculation.

The official version, death by misadventure, was all the Olivers gave. The truth went to the grave with Robert.

She had gone to the funeral Mass with Brid and Peter. It had been on a Wednesday, and Monica had already left the country. Some of the cast of the play were there. Niall, surprisingly, had flown over from London. She was pleased to see him, but felt unable to join him for a drink that night. Diana had sent a large wreath. She had phoned Clare when she heard the news. 'Ghastly, darling, simply ghastly. What could have possessed him? His whole life in front of him, great prospects, such a waste.'

Clare hadn't gone to the graveyard. She couldn't have faced that part. She had gone back home with Brid and Peter. She had written to John and Maura, but her words had looked so meaningless, and sounded so hollow, that she doubted they would offer a crumb of comfort. She phoned a few days later. Maura had been so thankful to hear from her, telling her how sorry she was Clare hadn't come along to the house the evening of the funeral. She would have been so welcome. There'd been a great crowd. People had been so kind. She thanked Clare for the letter, and the pictures of Robert that she had sent. She had taken them at the dress rehearsal of *Sticks and Stones*. Maura's thanks were so effusive that Clare felt much worse. She had sent the pictures to have them away from her, and then to have Maura so grateful. To listen to his mother, her life ripped apart by his loss, crying over the phone, sobbing about the fact that Clare had known him as a little boy, was more than she could handle. But that, Clare knew, would be her penance. Never to have the luxury of confession and absolution, but to keep it darkly, corrosively within herself.

Paula and Frances had both tried to put Robert's death in perspective for her, had tried to reason with her. Part of life's rich pageant and so on, but nothing helped. She couldn't stop blaming herself. All she wanted to do was talk about it. Think about it. Rehash it all endlessly.

In the days immediately following the funeral, before that phone call to Maura, Clare had thought that she could cope. After all, Robert's death might have happened anyway. Robert had a history, however slight, if not of mental illness, then of being a troubled boy. But as the days bled into each other, she felt as if the wound within her was deepening, and swallowing her. She had caused it. It was her decision, taken so lightly one night, that had started the chain of events that led to his death. It had been her desire for some affirmation of her own sexual worth – her lust. And, worst of all, she felt it had been her selfishness. Her selfish need to feel wanted, loved, admired. She said as much to Frances.

'But, Clare love, if you follow that logic, then it's Tim's fault for finding someone else and leaving you vulnerable. I mean we could go on like this forever. It's sad, regrettable, tragic for John and Maura and his sisters, but try to get it in proportion.'

Paula was equally brusque. 'C'mon, Clare, my love, you've got to leave this, get on with your life. You said he'd had a crush on an older woman before, and he was obsessive. It was his destiny. Be realistic about it at least.'

Sensible as all this advice was, it didn't manage to make her feel any better. She tried to go about her daily tasks, to avoid drowning in the flood of remembrance, but for a start visits to the pool were out. There was no work in the offing, at least in Ireland, and she didn't have the heart for socialising.

She read a lot, poetry mainly. Escaping, and finding comfort in emotions distilled. Tommy didn't say much, but he recognised a change in her demeanour.

'You were fond of that wee lad, weren't you? It's an awful pity for the parents all the same. It's a heartbreaking thing to lose a child out of time. They'll never get over it, but I suppose they'll have to get on with their lives. For the other children at least. Ah, sure we all go the same route in the end.'

She was going over to see her father every day now, and

seeing more of Brid as well. Robert's death had forged some unusual bond between them. It had affected them all, the whole family. Monica had left the day before the funeral, hating to go more than usual in the circumstances. She had been worried about Clare, but Clare had reassured her,

'I'll be fine, it's just the shock.'

Monica had understood and said she would call her, and then had tried to persuade her to come over for a break.

Clare was glad to have the comfort of it. But she had no intentions of going at that stage.

Tony had been shocked by Robert's death too, having just finished working for him. 'Did he do drugs, do you think?' he asked. 'I used to see funny wee pipes and things lying about. I'm sure he didn't mean to drown himself. He was probably out of it.'

Nothing was ever mentioned again about the episode with Brid the day before Robert died, although it was undoubtedly a step on the road to whatever finally happened. Doubtless Brid and Peter rehashed it among themselves.

Clare still wasn't sleeping. She'd got some pills from her father's GP – she hadn't found a doctor of her own yet – and she took one every night, but they seemed only to hold her in sleep for a few hours. Then she would lie in the half-sleep, full of dreams and visions and anxieties, until finally she was fully awake and lashing herself with recriminations and stretching her pain to fill the hours.

It was Brid who finally decided she should go off for a break. She had come back from two weeks in Cork and been shocked at the shape Clare was in. She was, to put it in Tommy's words, 'failed away to nothing'. Brid had rung Frances and Paula. Neither of them had heard from Clare in over a week, despite repeated phone calls and messages. Brid stopped by the flat the day after she got back and told Clare of their plan.

'Looks like I have no say in this,' Clare said when she heard the proposal.

'Not a lot. Clare, we're worried about you. What do you weigh? You can't be even seven stone. Daddy's worried sick about you. Diana told Paula you'd turned down an audition at the National, and frankly, Clare, you can't go on like this. I don't care how close you were to Robert. Your mourning's out of all proportion.'

Clare had never fully told Brid that she had been sexually involved with Robert, but Brid acted as if she knew, and she seemed to have accepted it. Perhaps Frances or Paula had confirmed it to her. At any rate, she wasn't judging her for it, and if anything was to stand out in Clare's mind from this time, it was her big sister's support, which she was dimly beginning to remember again from childhood. Images of Brid holding her hand coming from school, Brid hitting big boys on her behalf: she had forgotten all that. When did that closeness float away? When Tony came? Or was it after Monica's arrival? She remembered being fixated by her little baby sister. Or was it when Clare's personality began to blossom and cast Brid in the shade?

The stay with Monica and Al would be a respite. In a way it was a cowardly move – she was escaping rather than facing the situation head-on – but her strength had gone, this was all she felt capable of doing. She agreed to stay for a month: she could work part-time as they had a friend who owned a vegetarian restaurant – what else. It seemed her only option. She was going crazy in Belfast.

Lorcan had been there throughout. Horrified by it all and, despite his own pain at being somehow a cog in the wheel of Robert's destruction, he had tried as best he could to comfort her. But it was useless. Nothing would take away her pain. Nothing lessened her guilt, which only seemed to increase as the days passed. Locked inside her, thrumming on her brain.

She hadn't seen Lorcan in the immediate aftermath, telling him she needed time to think, and he had been hurt, but he had left her alone for the few days as she requested. They had communicated by phone. He had listened patiently to her anguish, her claims of culpability, and had tried to reason with her, falling easily into his natural bent to counsel. Yet this too became a barrier. The more understanding he became, the more estranged from him she felt.

A week after the funeral, he had come to the flat to see her. It was late morning, and she was still undressed. She had been finding it difficult to get her act together in the mornings. She would awaken feeling wretched, from a restless night's sleep, and, in those first few minutes of consciousness unsure why. Then, like a slow flood, it would seep through her, and she would feel raw, scorched by it. Somehow her affair with Lorcan and the death of Robert had become locked together in her mind.

She didn't have the will or the energy to cope with all the ramifications of their being together. She felt overwhelmed by the thought of continuing. Up until now, it had been her desire for him, their mutual desire really, that had driven things. She had allowed herself to be carried along by the sheer force of the attraction. Now, it seemed, it had all to be thought out. Decisions had to be taken, people told. Moves made. Her brain teemed with the possible permutations.

What would his parents do? What would the parishioners think? Imagine the reactions of the drama group? Would it kill Tommy?

And, most alarming of all, if they decided to go for it, would they find that it was all a terrible mistake? What if he resented her for taking him away from his vocation – his life's work so far?

But all she said to Lorcan was. 'It's all my fault. Robert died because of me, and I've ruined your life. I led you astray. I'm not good enough for you.'

'Clare, pet, you can't blame yourself for this. You can't. Robert was a mixed-up boy. You've got to let it go, move on, and, with due respect, I have reached the use of reason. I was more than willing to be led astray.'

'How can you say that? If I hadn't slept with him, hadn't met you, he'd still be alive.'

'That's nonsense, you don't know that.'

'That's what I feel.'

He tried to hold her, touch her, kiss her. But she was frozen. Her lips stayed cold, and she just couldn't respond. It was heartbreaking for him and puzzling too, given her passion up until now. Lorcan simply didn't have the confidence or the experience with women to take charge, to shake her, jolt her out of it all.

'Why, Clare, why?'

But she knew she was punishing herself, not allowing herself the healing comfort of his love.

'When I was a little girl,' she told him, 'I read a story about the Snow Queen, who cast a spell on a brother and sister. I even remember their names, Kay and Gerda – the boy was called Kay. I used to think that was so odd. She froze his heart – the Snow Queen did. I think a splinter from a mirror pierced it. He couldn't love, couldn't feel. He didn't even know his own sister. I know it sounds melodramatic, but that's how I feel now. Frozen.'

'I know the story too,' he said. 'Hans Christian Andersen. So I'm not even allowed to attempt to thaw you out. Is that what you're trying to tell me?' He was calm, but he sounded hurt.

'Why would you want to?' she said, realising how childish she sounded. 'Anyway, I don't know if anyone could.'

'But you weren't in love with Robert.'

'I know that, and I *am* in love with you. At least I think I am, but look at the consequences. If this happened because of my sleeping with Robert, what will happen if I take you away from the priesthood?'

He said nothing.

'And how we can we live here? How can we let people know, like Daddy, or Brid? They'd hate me.'

'Clare, we have to be honest about this. We're adults. This is the rest of our lives we're talking about. If you do love me then we can face things together, and if we want this enough, then it will work out.'

'How can it work out now? Don't you see this has forced all the decisions on us too soon? Surely you can see that?'

'Yes, of course I can, but I do also know I love you and I want to be with you.'

'Lorcan, you're a priest. It's not possible as things stand for you to be with me.'

'I suppose I can apply for laicisation. We can get married, and go away. Or go away and get married. We can do it whatever way round you like.'

'I can't ask you to do that. To make that big a sacrifice for me, it's too much. I know how much it means to you, your vocation, your religion.'

'Not as much as you do. We can move in together. I want to marry you. I want to have a family. I am sure of this. Very sure.' He looked at her levelly. 'Clare, I've thought and prayed a lot about this. I think that my vocation was already weakening when I met you. If I examine my conscience, I was starting to feel disillusioned by it all. It's not like you set out to ensnare me. I let it happen. No, that's not true. I wanted it to happen.'

She said nothing, but she could tell he meant it.

'Please believe me, I will leave. We'll work it out. We have to.'

'I'm not sure. Daddy couldn't cope. It would kill him. He loves you. It would seem like the worst betrayal to him.'

'Then we'll wait.'

'You mean till he dies?'

'No, I mean until . . . I don't know what I mean. All I know is that I love you with all my heart, and I don't want to lose you. I think you're worth any fight.'

She feared that the stars in their courses augured against what she wanted. She wanted Lorcan. Only him, just to be with him. But what now if she were to pursue it? This need for Lorcan. Could she live with the consequences of her actions? If she decided to go with him, would her choice resonate and effect yet another death? Just at this moment it wasn't bearable.

He left dejected that day, and she cried for hours. The days passed and her doubts weren't assuaged by all his talk. She was making him miserable and it tore at her to behave like this. But she was locked into the spiral.

The day before she was due to go to America, Lorcan came over again to see her.

They had arranged to meet. As soon as he came through the door she sensed at once that there was something different in his demeanour. Her prepared farewell speech seemed somehow inappropriate. Mentally she shredded it.

She would stay in touch, she told him. All she needed was the space to think. Perhaps eventually they could work things out, but right now she needed some time to reassess her feelings, her motives.

When she had finished her speech — for despite her attempts not to make one — that's what it had started to sound like — he took her arm firmly. Wordlessly, he led her into the front room. There was a large mirror above the fireplace. The fire was a gas one, a coal-effect. It was unlit: she noticed that someone had thrown a sweet wrapper on it. She looked down, staring at it. Wondering what he was going to say. Feeling the righteousness of his pain.

'Look.' He turned her face to the mirror, pushing his face against hers. 'You and I, we need each other. This is real, Clare. It's right. I know it is — and you've got to be honest and face it.'

She said nothing. There were no words.

'All right then, go. Take as long as you need. I'll be here if you need me. Just come back when you're ready.'

And he left. She hoped fervently that he had meant it.

The plane shuddered, and for a brief moment, she thought they had landed, but she looked out at the clouds drifting by, and realised she was still up in the air.